PANICKING RALPH

Bill James

PANICKING RALPH

W. W. NORTON & COMPANY

New York • London

First published 1997 by Macmillan, an imprint of Macmillan Publishers Ltd
Copyright © 1997 by Bill James
First American edition 2001

Manufacturing by Quebecor Fairfield

A CIP catalogue record for this book is available
from the British Library.

ISBN 0-393-04762-8

W. W. Norton & Company, Inc., 500 Fifth Avenue, New York, N.Y. 10110
www.wwnorton.com

W. W. Norton & Company Ltd., Castle House, 75/76 Wells Street, London W1T 3QT

1 2 3 4 5 6 7 8 9 0

For Nan Holden, good friend of Ralph

1

'Peeping Toms, darling,' Christine said suddenly, giggling in that untroubled way of hers, which could be nice, and could be so damn simple-minded. 'Well, they're too late.'

'What?'

'Up behind the old concrete defence post. Binoculars. We're both covered up all right, aren't we?' She had her blouse off, but wore a high slip underneath.

'I don't see anyone.'

'Perhaps I'm wrong.'

'We ought to move,' Ralph Ember replied.

'Darling, they'll go,' she said. 'There's nothing to see. Wankers.'

'Dress,' Ember said.

'What's wrong? We'll have to walk past them to the cars. I'll feel – well, embarrassed.'

'No, we'll detour. Come to the cars from the other side.'

'Ralph, we'll be into the mud.'

'Hurry.'

'What – you know them? Who are they?'

'It will be all right, but hurry, Christine.' Wholly unscared she gazed up the beach, as if they were only pathetic. This was one drawback in knowing a woman with such a happy, Church background: Chris could never realize what slaughterous urban evil was around these days as the norm. *As the norm.* It was true nationwide, but especially here, in this, Ember's beloved home realm. Things were bad and would get worse. Britain was becoming Detroit. Naturally, Christine did know *something* of slaughter and of evil, but thought they were to do with Bosnia, Herod or the Holocaust – all the big and distant themes. These two lads were big enough, and close. Of course, he knew why they were here. Someone had heard he might enter the business scene. Someone had decided he should be stopped. Someone was not keen on competition.

As Ember and Christine prepared to run, she said: 'You all right, Ralph?'

'All right?'

'You seem – almost ill.'

Yes. 'Get a fucking move on, will you,' he replied. 'Darling. This way. Let's make some distance.'

2

It should have been utterly fine with her out here this after-noon, and always had been before today. In fact, time spent at the foreshore together had invariably been more than fine. It had been epic. When the sun was warm enough, they would come for their love-making to this unkempt strip of beach on the edge of the town. Although the area could certainly have been more beautiful, it was probably remote enough, or so Ember had always thought before this. Any intruder would be seen far off and in good time. The male might be hellishly exposed when conferring sexual pleasure.

The point was – a terrible, tragic point today – the point was, he never carried armament when out with Christine, even now, in these very tricky times of non-stop hazard and business jockeying since the death of Kenward Knapp. It would have seemed gross to wear a handgun: guns were to do with that other part of his being. And so a hellish blood-bathed irony – he had delicately wanted to protect her feel-ings, but could not protect her body, her life. Nor his own. Delicacy was often one of his failings. He knew that.

Obviously, to call this area a beach might be stretching things. The sea was there for sure, far out when they had arrived today, just visible, coughing mildly, still ebbing. And, thank God, some strips of recognizable sand always lay up towards the sea wall, not golden but cleanish. Otherwise, what sort of streaked mess would they have been in going home to their decent commitments after these meetings? Mostly, though, that slab of coast was the fat, black mud flats, broken by deep gullies widening towards the sea.

When they arrived today, the mud had looked glossy and rich under good late-autumn sun. A mild wind made scudding, haunting shapes from greenish factory effluent. Stuff washed up or dumped along this stretch deterred trippers, even in high summer, luckily: dead tyres, deader sheep, a one-sleeve khaki bumfreezer overcoat, two doorless fridges, the rusty skeletons of seven linked cinema seats, three thousand wave-sluiced nappy liners. The wind had hummed pleasantly through shattered bits of window glass in a big, dumped heap of builder's rubble. Over Christine's shoulder he could see for what must be a couple of miles, and behind him were two banks of pebbles which would shift and clatter a warning if anyone came near that way. Warmed by the fingers of sun and the nearness of Christine, Ember had been able to relax. Almost always she brought him such wholesome serenity. When with Chris, he often felt he could easily settle for what he had: herself, obviously; then his house, Low Pastures, and ownership of his club, The Monty; various business commitments; Margaret and his daughters; a growing civic status despite everything; plus the mature student degree in Politics, History and Religious Knowledge he would be landing soon. More than ever lately he had realized how much he needed Christine. She brought alive one whole fraction of him, if you could have whole fractions.

This afternoon Chris had flung her legs and feet up high

at the best moments of their passion, apparently to maximize good inner contact. This was a way of hers, and, though it might make her and him more obvious, he never objected: Ember believed you had to consider women's fierce needs, if and when possible. Also, as things went on, Ember had begun to claw hard at her shoulder blades in the style she liked when clearly on this last, breathless stretch to vivid climax. As ever, he could feel earlier scars and weals on the shoulders, and this would sometimes upset him, although she swore the marks came only from previous love sessions with Ember himself. He would have been damned offended to think her husband, Leslie, or others, did ecstasy skin-rips as well. Yet he knew he could not expect her to be his and only his. She lived with Leslie and she slept with Leslie. Christine never pretended otherwise. Simply, she felt her marriage had declined and declined, and, eventually, in despair, she had looked outside. Ember was not the first man she had turned to. That he accepted, also. In this kind of relationship, if you had any nobility you *did* graciously accept such conditions. All the same, it would have badly hurt him to think she acted as passionately with others as with him. He would never speak these thoughts to her, though. This, too, he saw as a noble quality: she was entitled to her privacies, just as he was, of course.

He had felt much easier when eventually she sighed with loving cheerfulness and lowered her legs. They had lain in peace for a while then, listening to the wonderfully busy cries of gulls and oystercatchers, sometimes eyes shut, sometimes gazing about, savouring their apartness.

3

But now came this hellish, murderous intrusion. These were people with a business commission: to take him out of contention before he and associates had even properly begun. The arrival of this pair brought a dark extension to an already dark pageant of local threat and violence. Clearly, Christine could never be told about all that. Oh, Jesus. He saw at once they must change their ground. It was a sweet site for a killing: no cover, no witnesses. 'Chris, quick, love. Please,' he called.

So, eventually, she stood and started to follow, though not as fast as he would have liked, and nowhere near as fast as he moved himself. Fleetness when it mattered was among his flairs. Without it he would not be where he was now in life. 'Good girl,' he said, as Christine struggled to keep up across the pebbles. And his voice stayed reasonably steady: in fact, considerate, almost selfless, not scared into a gasping squeak by fright, yet. Chris had on smart shoes, which slowed her, but she could definitely not be blamed for this, not justly, because, of course, when she left home she had to dress like shopping.

He glanced back up towards the defence post. Those two were coming down towards them, right out in the open, trotting, chatting together like folk on a gentle team jog. Ember would have been unsurprised to see guns in their hands, but no, not so far. Disgusting confidence glowed in people like these nowadays, and they ran loose and wild. Decency ... Decency? They'd never fucking heard of it. Or if by fluke they had, he thought they squashed it long ago. *Everything* was coming apart. Ember did not recognize the two men. They were white, one in a pale blue or grey suit that looked lightweight and scruffy: maybe someone had told him to take a seaside sunshine trip. He was around thirty, six feet and heavily made, with pig-tailed fair hair and perhaps a small fair moustache. He could have been a pinball arcade bum or university lecturer in social studies. The other was taller, thinner, younger – mid-twenties – and wore one of those long, belted trenchcoats that politicians' minders often used, plus a baseball cap, so casual and jolly. They would be hand-picked, but not for modishness.

4

'I feel a kind of, yes, I must say it, I feel a kind of outright joy. More than optimism. Outright joy.' Lane's wan features tried to get to grips with this excitement. Harpur had never known him so blazingly positive. At least, not since he became chief constable. Drive, authority, wiliness stoked his brown eyes. It was good to see Mark Lane happy. He deserved some healthy interludes of belief in himself, and in policing, and in the continuance of the human species.

Iles said: 'Harpur and I happened to be watching from this office window as you arrived this morning, sir, and, looking at your face then, I commented, "Something rather wonderful blooms. The chief will have a role for us, Colin. A designated and fruitful role." You recall that, Col?'

The assistant chief liked answers to his questions. 'I often feel I can pick up the whole daily mood of the city from that window,' Harpur replied.

'Opportunity,' Lane said. 'The theme word. *Opportunity*. Yes. We can wipe out the drugs game here entirely, post Oliphant Kenward Knapp.'

Iles struck the desk lightly with his fist to signal controlled ecstasy. 'This is surely what leadership – the highest leadership – is about, above all, sir. An ability to spot openings. A sort of divination. Wouldn't you say a kind of divination, Col?'

'In fact, sometimes when I gaze for a while from that window I feel the whole pageant of human life is there in capsule form,' Harpur said.

'Jesus,' Iles replied.

'To spot openings *and* to act, Desmond,' Lane answered.

Iles let his cropped grey head fall forward in apology. 'Forgive me. Of course, of course. What use to see chances if they are not brilliantly taken? But, as excuse for my omission, may I say, sir, that we are so accustomed to watching you identify ways forward and then follow them that one has almost come to take such gifted decisiveness for granted.'

The three of them were in Harpur's office. The chief liked informal conferences, far from his own suite. His predecessor, Barton, had been the same. It might be a trick they were taught on leadership courses. Lane sat in an armchair beneath the window from which, if it had been true, Harpur and Iles might have gazed down appreciatively on Lane's arrival this morning. The ACC had a perch on Harpur's desk. Harpur stood near a month-by-month breaking-and-entering wall-chart graph, which was rising.

The chief said: 'What I'm going to suggest might seem a simplistic reading of things to you boys, you so very much at the sharp end – assistant chief and detective chief superintendent – I appreciate that, believe me. And I hope you'll tell me if it strikes you as naive.'

Laughter crackled enormously from Iles. 'Naive, sir? That will be the day. I'd prefer to describe your particular genius as a skill at instantly isolating essentials. Col, is this how—?'

'Knapp's death has surely destabilized the whole drugs

trading business,' Lane replied. 'He was supreme in his evil and wealth. Why I say opportunity. Villains scrambling, scrabbling to inherit his filthy realm. At one another's throats. Preoccupied, off balance, hitched to unlikely, unreliable confeds. It's our time to hit them, Desmond, Colin. Squash these creatures before they even as it were start. Never allow them to become established, devilishly entrenched, as Kenward was himself. Of course, I don't wish you to read blame into that, Desmond, Colin.'

Of course not.

Iles cried: '*Destabilized*! Sir, this is exactly the word I—'

'Why I spoke of joy, you see, Desmond, Colin. Perhaps you thought it an extravagant term. But to end drugs commerce here – what would it mean?' His voice rose to between a holy chortle and a conqueror's anthem. 'It would show we can still win. Policing can win. Good can win. Evil is repulsed. New beginnings. Emblematic. It could be the start of who knows what, not just on our patch. Nationwide and, yes, beyond.'

The chief loved to think emblems, visualizing some action of his on this patch that might represent a revival of hope and virtue for the world, like the resurrection. Probably he did not presume to see himself as Christ, but at least as the one who rolled away the stone.

Iles crooned: 'This, sir, is so—'

'I gather people have fallen out of the race, anyway: the figure they called Bandy, for instance. Silver? And Misto not too thriving, I hear,' the chief replied. These were would-be potential inheritors of the Kenward fief, weren't they?'

'Probably, sir,' Harpur replied.

'Bandy, Silver, Misto – each would have been heading up a syndicate, I take it. Well, remove the boss, and that syndicate is nowhere. There's no substitute for leadership.' Lane paused, perhaps waiting for someone to comment, but neither Iles nor Harpur spoke, though Iles shook his head slowly for a time, as if made speechless by great truths. 'Who's left in the legacy race?' the chief asked.

Harpur said: 'We think Ember might be trying to put something in place. There's a word around.'

'Panicking Ralphy?' Lane asked. 'Into large scale pushing? This is new for him, surely.'

'It would be, yes. But he's a mixture, as you'll know, sir. Ember oscillates between cold sweats and fierce ambition and even guts. Perhaps he'll team up with old mates – say Foster and Gerry Reid.'

'Ralphy?' Lane asked.

'Part of this very destabilization, sir,' Iles replied. 'It brings changes of scale.'

Lane said: 'And didn't I hear Ember had gone honest, even civic? Doing a university degree? I've seen letters from him in the Press on worthwhile topics.'

Harpur said: 'Ralph has experience.'

Lane said: 'Experience? General criminal experience, yes – armed robbery and so on. No trafficking, I think. Does anyone imagine Panicking could organize a business?'

'Well, the thing about Ember ... somehow he keeps going, keeps getting bigger, sir,' Harpur replied. 'Country house, one daughter at a finishing school in Europe.'

Lane said: 'We find out about that "somehow", Harpur. And if it stinks, we hit him.'

'We've often tried, sir,' Harpur replied.

Lane spoke with a tremor now, like a seer nailing the sublime: 'I want them all – all taken out of the reckoning, Colin. I want our manor free of drugs trading and its contempt for decent living, free of its degradation and violence, its gangs and corrupt alliances. We will not become filthy London or filthy Manchester.'

Perhaps the chief scented sainthood. *This is a crack-free zone.* There might be a gong, too, though, oddly, he would despise that.

Iles said: 'It's a wholesome idea, sir.'

'It must be more than that, Desmond.'

Iles said: 'The eternal problem we have to decide is whether to leave overall pushing control here in the hands of locals, whom we can more or less chart and manage, knowing them and their foibles, or—'

'You ignore the point, Desmond. As you've ignored it at other times.' Lane was staring up angrily at Iles from deep in the armchair, like a cornered animal from its hole. 'But now I insist: no drugs business here at all. Erase.'

'Or, we annihilate them as you interestingly propose, sir,' the ACC replied, 'and so make a nice space, into which pile the big-time filthy London and filthy Manchester barons you spoke of, sure of starved, ready customers. We'd be the classic seller's market. This could mean we get *inter alia* a load of Yardies. No fun. There's still a lot to be said for leaving the trade with somebody almost civilized and basically feeble like Panicking, or the boys in a rival syndicate. Mansel Shale's a gent of sorts.'

'This "gent" used child pushers, one of whom was shot dead, Desmond.'

'Mansel deplored that, didn't he, Harpur?' Iles asked. 'He didn't know children were employed.'

'Mansel's dormant,' Harpur replied. 'He thought he should be undisputed top banana and withdrew when there was opposition. Plus the death of the child runner might genuinely have shaken him.'

Lane said: 'Then we have Keith Vine and Stan Stanfield teaming, don't we, Colin?'

'Probably, sir.'

Definitely: in fact, not long ago Vine had even suggested Harpur might like a clandestine post with their firm. That was Vine's sort of cheek.

'Beau Derek in on it, too?' Iles asked.

'Maybe not,' Harpur said.

'He's going to be pissed off with his former pal, Stan, if discarded. That could be useful,' Iles replied.

'But you are taking no account of what I—You speak as if a drugs trade were inevitable, Desmond, endemic,' Lane said.

'Yes, that's how I speak, sir.' Iles answered. 'The habits are there and have to be fed. Not just here. City life.'

Now, Lane began to yell. A skinny, noduled red line of rage lit up for a moment on one of his doughy cheeks, like a fifty-pence rocket in a dull sky. 'But this is a kind of despair. We do not tolerate it, cannot, Desmond. Not by local firms, not by intruders. We deal with it.' The chief suddenly seemed to smell the double meaning in that and put a hand to his lips. 'When I say "deal with", I mean expunge.'

'We follow, sir,' Iles replied.

'We cleanse,' the chief said.

Harpur saw that the old worries, the old terrifying doubts, had their brutal half nelson on Lane again. His breathing became jumpy. In his solitariness, the chief would be wondering whether Iles had a kickback share or even something bigger in one of these local confederations, and maybe Harpur himself, too. Was this why the ACC did not want the scene disturbed, by either police or invaders?

The chief, still pretty new in his job, had failed to get himself accepted, poor sod, and was excluded from so much, kept ignorant. Harpur had known Lane when he was a magnificent, hard detective on the neighbouring patch, but promotion dragged him down. Today, he wore civilian clothes: one of those suits Iles reckoned were made by convicts in Zaire from rejected mailbag cloth. Anger traces had gone from the chief's cheek, and his sallow face still kept a little of its previous radiance and hope. But any long discussion with the ACC could almost always put marks of fear into Lane's eyes, displace for a time their normal geniality, their 'fatal humaneness', as Iles called it. Nervous hate now alarmingly tightened the skin of the chief's neck and jaw. He had been off with some kind of serious breakdown lately. It would have started in part from his anxieties over what he saw as the speedy spread of unstoppable cosmic evil. And in part – the bigger part – from his eternal, pointless struggle to cope with Iles. Harpur sympathized. He longed for Lane to retire or get promoted to the inspectorate, not slip one day into helpless disintegration here.

Standing now, Lane said: 'What I want, you see, Desmond, Colin, is a sense of mission.' He gave a nice little apologetic chuckle. 'Am I laying on the rhetoric a bit today – "joy", "mission"? But nonetheless, yes, mission. A high duty. I will tolerate no obstacles. None, Desmond.'

'We are here only to transform your vision into fact, sir,' Iles replied, standing, too – an encouragement to Lane to go. 'Buoyed always by the inspiration you offer.'

The chief left, shuffling across Harpur's rooms in navy socks. Often he went about the building without shoes, also for informality, and perhaps to be quaintly lovable. It worked with some, though not always with Iles.

5

At home late in the evening Ember put some of his oldest clothes into the car boot, plus wellingtons and two large flashlights. It was well after dusk. He had carefully placed his Rover behind a couple of high laurel bushes on the drive at Low Pastures, so Margaret would not see from the house what he was doing. Should he take armament? Of course, now – tragically after the damage had been done. He pocketed his Walther, then drove out towards the foreshore again, thinking that Christine might conceivably be alive, though probably not. He would go, anyway. His hands on the wheel felt magnificently steady and strong. This was one of those times when Ember could almost truly believe people were wrong to call him 'Panicking Ralph', occasionally even to his face. Christ, look how composed he was, despite everything. But, of course, he could suffer moments and more than moments when he feared his disgusting nickname might be accurate. Immediately after running from that mess-up this afternoon he had gone through one of these spasms. And it was guilt that forced him now to come out to put things right, half right.

He did not know whether he would find her still there, nor whether he wanted to. If he did, it must be only because she was dead. Well, of course she was dead, and of course she would be there. The tide could not have crawled back that far yet, and nothing else was going to move her. Undoubtedly, he had to blame himself, for taking her to that place so regularly, for imagining it was safe, for not noticing the tails. And then, much more and more again, he had to blame himself for how he broke down: that greasy speed he could get into his sprinting, even over tricky ground, and even when he was supposed to be looking after someone else. Since he began trying to float his little trade syndicate, Ember had been more or less continuously nervous, and almost always ready to slide into fear. And so, these resurgences of his Panicking Ralph mode. Yes, when he fell into such self-loathing spells, Ember might mutter the two words to himself, as accusation. He would even stick the *y* on to make it feebler still: Panicking Ralphy, like a pants-wetting kid.

On his way, he stopped at a post box. Always for troubled occasions like this he carried with him a padded self-addressed envelope containing keys of the bank deposit boxes in Britain and his code tag for an account in Switzerland. He sealed the envelope and dropped it in. It was a long time since he needed this drill. So far, he had always been back home next day to open the envelope and recover the items. If ever he failed to return, Margaret would know what to do. She had a sheet of paper locked away which identified the keys and gave the other half of the Zurich code and that bank's address. And he had told her about the fat extra stores in the club loft and so on. She would be laughing.

But, Christ, *if ever he failed to return*. He hated thinking that phrase, but always did when posting one of these envelopes. *Failed to return* sounded hellishly like a soldier shot to pieces. This pillar box ritual usually upset him pretty badly, and it was even worse tonight, after months of lay-off. He sat for a moment in the car, stationary, trying to recover. Then, suddenly, he began an all-over sweat, and his shoulders ached: first symptoms of a panic. Hyperventilation and dizziness might come next. Worse could follow. Two or three times in the depths of a crisis he had actually had a vision of those gross words, *Panicking Ralph*, hurtling fast towards his forehead through the air, had seen them with terrifying clarity, red and flaming and reversed, as if to brand him, like Cain. It had happened this afternoon when she was hit. And the letters glinted again on the windscreen for a second tonight, alongside the pillar box. They faded quickly, though, thank God. Why, why was he so sensitive? Why so ruthlessly adept at self-knowledge?

As he drove on he wondered whether the mission made sense. If she was dead on the mud, and he was miserably sure of that, wasn't he – wasn't he? – what profit in coming back? Did it amount to a daft, guilt-coloured impulse only, a hopelessly late need to prove courage? That type of imperative was always with him. Certainly, he might drag the body up to the sea wall, clear of the tide. That was, if he could manage her. The mud banks were soft and damned engulfing, and he could think of quite a few acquaintances who would get a prize laugh if they heard he had been stifled that way: Ralphy flailing about, black muck blocking his mouth and nostrils, lumpily blurring the famed Charlton Heston resemblance. It might be difficult to budge out there when struggling with a load.

Panicking Ralph

Tonight, he did not park too near the spot where they had gone down together from the sea wall. That might be under watch by all sorts: by police, possibly, if the body had been found, or by the people who had killed her and who knew by now they had missed the real target. But then, God, God, what if she were not dead, only badly hurt, still alive out there somehow? Her injuries were in the body, not the head, and he didn't know where exactly. Because the shots had been meant for him, they would have caught her accidentally, not necessarily in lethal spots. From the way she had jack-knifed and twisted under the impacts, he thought she was hit twice and possibly three times, all above the waist, though, of course, he had not waited to look closely.

Sitting for a moment in the car, he realized that, if she had survived, he would certainly need to move her, or when the tide came she would drown. Or she would die of exposure first. He could not let that happen to dear Christine. He had to ask – ask as he had already asked himself so often – should he have left her at all, even for as long as this, even for those agonizing minutes earlier today? As the doubts and recriminations got at him, he felt symptoms of another panic come very fast: the sickening shoulder ache, sweat, a feeling that the famous, ancient scar along his jaw line had opened up and was exuding something warm and very surplus down his neck. His hands slipped on the steering wheel.

But was it really necessary to recover her himself? If Christine were alive – and, obviously, pray God she was, yes, yes, yes – if she were alive he could do an anonymous telephone call to the police and ambulance, couldn't he?

They would recover her. Their damn job. Perhaps she had been spotted already, and he would run into a rescue operation out here now. Jesus, he must have no face-to-face with police in this setting. If they were rescuing her, though, there would be lights and vehicles, all very evident. He could just keep driving, as if on his way elsewhere. This would certainly not be like passing by on the other side, because he would know she was being looked after by experts. Wouldn't it be outright crazy for him to run into risk for its own sake? Weren't there enough stresses dragging at him already?

6

He left the car among a few trees near the sea wall and climbed the slope of packed soil to do a survey. There were no lights and no vehicles. Suddenly, for a moment then, he felt a kind of almost mythic grandeur and a lonely, raw dignity as he stood gazing out over this sombre stretch of ground and murky water. He was fine again, to be reckoned with. It was as if he had found his setting and exactly fitted this hard elemental background. Hadn't there been a Viking chief called Ralph? The sea sounded nearer than this afternoon, but still a reasonable way off. He went back down, and near the boot of the car he stripped to his underclothes, then dressed in the old suit and raincoat and put on his wellingtons. Thigh-high fishing waders might have been useful, but he was no fisherman.

He longed for some moon, just to give him a general reminder of the layout here. Heavy low cloud clogged the sky, though. He would have to trust his memory and the flashlights. He put these on a strong cord to hang around his neck, so his hands would be free. Swiftly he climbed again, then walked for a couple of hundred yards along the broad earth wall towards the spot where they had gone down to the beach. The heap of builder's rubble and that string of one-time seats would be markers now. He had a flashlight on, but hooded by his hand, pointed right down, and part obscured by his trouser leg. From this height, even a gleam would be visible for miles, and he could do without the curious. This was a rendezvous for just two: his self and his strong self.

Then, before reaching either of his landmarks, he abruptly turned around and went even more swiftly back. He had forgotten to transfer the Walther to these clothes. He suspected he would not need it, but it would bring him confidence. It would bring him identity – that other identity, which was necessary now: lover, yes, obviously, but warrior, too. He had to be both.

And, then, of course, something in the wide, Panicking Ralph regions of him thought that maybe when he reached the car again he could just slide in even now and quit. He had come here – had selflessly forced himself to come here – and, having come, saw the uselessness of it. No more could be asked of him, surely. Surely. Get out immediately and change back into his proper clothes and orderliness at The Monty. This whole trip was idiotic, wasn't it? Yes, idiotic to assume there would be lights and vehicles if the body had been found. Police were not stupid. They would lie low, to see who turned up. Harpur himself, or even Assistant Chief Desmond Iles, could be around.

At the Rover again, Ember pocketed his Walther, then briefly stood undecided, listening once more to the sea and thinking about exit. He felt suddenly relieved not to be displayed any longer on the sea wall. God, all that Viking shit! Dismal recognition of his own weaknesses would often bring Ember to despair. What was he? Unalloyed rubbish?

Or had he at last edged through and up to real dignity and weight?

He closed and locked the boot, keeping the keys in his left hand, with one of the flashlights. He could still be into the driving seat and away in a couple of seconds. The right hand he wanted ready for the Walther. He fought with himself, searching for courage and an impulse towards duty, struggling to quell the yearning for another smart withdrawal. For a moment, he let the torch hang on its cord and put the keys into his left pocket. He turned his back on the car but did not move. Did not move *yet*. He *would* move up the sea wall in a few seconds, wouldn't he? Wouldn't he? Swiftly, he shoved his left hand into his pocket to check the car keys were safe. He was slipping further into dread. There'd been a lot of dread lately, ever since the savage death of Oliphant Kenward Knapp – Kenward, who for years had controlled all drugs business in, say, a twelve miles square area: say *conservatively* a twelve miles square area. His reign had brought a kind of stability: the Knapp kind. Then, one cataclysmic night, quite a while ago now, Kenward was slaughtered by envious gunfire right outside his own home. Oh, God, the effects of that! You could still see them, feel them, suffer because of them, die because of them: die for them in remote, drab terrain, like this wasteland.

After a while, he climbed back up the sea wall and began to walk again. Suddenly, the sea sounded appreciably nearer. This time he did not put the light on. Shrouded, it gave negligible help and was capable only of betraying him. He stared out towards the mud, in case her skin or some of her clothing might make a minor break to the blackness, but he saw nothing so far. Stupid to expect it: everything of her would be soiled. As he walked, he turned to look behind him pretty often. The people who shot Christine might suspect Ember would come back to find her. They would know, would know as a certainty, wouldn't they, that there was something strong, fine, resolute and, yes, heroic inside the Ralph Ember package, regardless of what was said about him by gossips and fools?

Nobody was caught for Kenward's murder, and probably nobody ever would be, because in this trade information somehow got turned in upon itself. And so, a vacuum. Ember saw the aftermath of that death as very like Yugoslavia or Russia: Tito goes, chaos comes; the KGB goes, the Mafia comes. Vacuums are unnatural and perilous. Always they produce a wild rush to fill them. After Kenward there had developed a ferocious, prolonged scramble to inherit arguably the most beautifully established wholesale cocaine, crack, Ecstasy and grass operation in Britain – possibly in the whole European Union, not excluding Holland. Ember was part of the scramble. Or at least he was *planning* to be part of the scramble. That is, until today. Were the dangers and agonies worth it? Stress had dogged him since the moment he had very confidentially mooted here and there his new trade ambitions. Very confidentially, but not confidentially enough: that was plain now. He felt lonely and hounded. Today, tonight, was the worst stress of all.

Soon he was able to distinguish the rubble heap, and he

stopped to do a real, systematic, sector-by-sector eye search of the mud flats right in front of it, once more trying to spot some trace of where she lay. Still nothing, though. He gazed behind him again, felt for the Walther in his raincoat pocket, gripped it confidingly for a few moments like a rosary, as just now he had fondled the keys. It was a long time since he had used a pistol – at least as long as his last pillar box routine – but he would be able to make a show, if pushed, probably.

7

He walked on, told himself he still had it in him somewhere to be noble and humane, to be big, to be fully Ember. Even through he might be searching for the body of one of his mistresses, Ember was able to find additional moral strength and resolve by itemizing in his head now all the boons brought by family. He had to admit Margaret, Venetia and Fay were true parts of his fine status. For heaven's sake, look at his daughters' gymkhana gear and ponies, as well as their private schools, Venetia's, the older girl's, a boarding place in deepest rural France, and *très, très snob*, in their lingo. Panic and/or absence of drive paid for all that? Don't make him laugh. He was the well established, even famed, Ralph Ember – and quite often these days Ralph W. Ember, a signature he used for occasional sound letters to the local Press, mostly on environmental and hygiene matters. If only she had been able to know of it, a girl like Christine would feel damn proud to be devotedly looked for on mud by a man of this standing.

Ember skipped down the sea wall in his wellingtons towards the slime plateau: if Christine were here he would reclaim her, by God. Whatever her state, she belonged to him, not to the sea, this creeping, sly invader. He located her very quickly. For a couple of seconds he allowed himself to think that the figure he spotted might be another of those shifting effluent shapes. Briefly he waited, in case what looked at the moment like the outline of a body should disintegrate and change in the breeze, then re-form as – as anything at all, but please God not a body. The figure stayed, though. In fact, a couple of tumbling tufts of effluent from elsewhere were blown across it, touched it, lingered for half a second alongside each other, still stuck to the figure like plants on a rockery, then cavorted off as a pair of Samoyed puppies. They had made the body seem even more solid and more certainly a body. Ember stared, looking for movement and for anything that said life. The torch beam would not reach her from here. It seemed to him that she lay face-up on a mud bank, but her nose and mouth possibly clogged in that way he had visualized for himself and the rich amusement of cronies. How could she be alive? No, no.

Once again then his mood abruptly backtracked, and he considered chucking this mad expedition. He owed that much to Margaret and his daughters. Why didn't he just chuck it all – including any perilous attempt to set up a dealership? Couldn't he learn from this afternoon and this evening, for God's sake? Ember had been expecting hellish trouble, though never at this cherished spot.

Yet, in his relentlessly up and down way, he still struggled not to succumb, fought himself, craved guts, tried to force courage on himself. He began to walk towards Chris, at first on dirty sand and shingle. She must have moved from where she had fallen. All right, the running this afternoon had been frantic, and his recollection of where exactly they were when she was hit might be adrift, but she seemed to him yards from where he would have expected, and much too far into the mud. They had been close to it, possibly – a slippery mix of mud and some sand underfoot. But now Christine lay on the slope of one of the black, soft, deep gullies, where it would have been impossible to walk, let alone run. She must have changed position after she was shot. Perhaps she had dragged herself, or crawled. It might be possible to move across the yielding mound like that without going under. But why would she crawl towards the sea and the gullies, rather than up towards the beach and the sea wall, where she might have been seen and given help? Possibly, she was too badly injured to know what she was doing, where she was going. Possibly her eyes had given up. Or possibly she feared those two were still about near the sea wall, and she had tried to hide and escape. But only Ember had managed to hide and escape, an age-old knack of his.

'Forgive me, Chris!' He yelled it into the scruffy seascape, half sick with shame, and the other half aware he would most likely do it all over again if he met the same perils. Possibly, too, in her disorientation she thought she was crawling after Ember for help, perhaps trying to call to him. But by then he might have been back at the car and exiting at full throttle, also in that way of his.

'Forgive me, Chris!' he repeated, at top voice, tears clouding his vision. He did not care who heard. In any case, the wind blew his cry out on to the dark mud desert, and he was pretty sure by now that nobody lurked here, waiting for him, waiting to correct their little error. The sand and shingle mix was ending, and his feet had begun to sink a bit as he walked, giving that wet suck-back sound every time he pulled his foot out for the next step. Christine lay stretched on the side of a black valley, her head towards the bottom of it, where the tide was starting to lap in gently now. Perhaps she had crawled over the edge and then slid, but not quite all the way. He could make out sledge-like tracks behind her. Chris's face was turned towards him, eyes open, he thought, though it was hard to be sure because the sockets were half full of mud. All her features were heavily smeared; her hair looked discoloured by the black filth and was stuck in stiff tails to her cheeks and ears.

He managed three more laborious steps forward, and knew on the third that this was as far as he could go upright. The mud was above his knees. Christ, but wellingtons had been a mistake. They filled and turned his feet and legs into a pair of dragging weights. It was as if his legs had simply become part of the cold acres and limitless tonnage of pressurizing, all-round muck, nothing to do with movement any longer. He leaned forward, getting on to his chest and stomach. His chin dipped in and he jammed his lips shut. It was very dark, but the flashlights were only a nuisance out here, and he took both from where they hung by the cord around his neck and pushed them deep under the mud. He wanted nothing left that could tell tales.

Ember began trying to get his legs out of the wellingtons, so that they could be legs again not just part of this rolling, sludge prairie. It took a while. Then, as he struggled, he felt himself slide forward a few inches and knew this must mean his feet and legs had begun to come free. He rested, his face turned to the side, his left cheek on the mud, pretty much the way Christine lay, except that her legs and feet were not buried. She had probably been incapable of walking and had crawled or slid the whole distance. Her feet were about five yards from his outstretched hands. She still had her fashionable shoes on. Chris's soaking skirt looked primly in place, stuck close to the full length of her legs. Lying there, Ember recalled a Cary Grant film where the star played someone wanting to lose weight and kept muttering, 'Think thin.' Ember tried to think himself light, buoyant on mud.

He decided it would be impossible to drag her back up the slope. Just striving to bring his feet and legs out had taken most of his strength. He doubted if he could climb up even alone. It would be better to go down into the bottom of the gully and pull her after him. Let the incline do the work. Then he might be able to edge his way with her along the flat channel at the gully's base and back towards where it narrowed and grew shallower and less engorging near the beach. Eventually he would be able to risk standing, and tug her clear of the softness and on to firm land. From the sea end of the gully water was entering much faster now, just below Christine's head. But there might be time. The water could even be an advantage. Soon it would be deep enough to take the weight of her body and give him help. After all, it would not matter if her face went under, as long as his was clear. On his hands and knees down there, or on his stomach, he could draw her along towards the land like a lifeboat with a wreck. That picture excited Ember, and brought him worthwhileness. Worthwhileness he craved.

Panicking Ralph

In a minute, he had worked his legs so far out that he was able to straighten them, and they broke through and were stiff on the surface behind him, the wellingtons left behind. He brought his arms back and folded them at his side like wings or snowshoes, then dug in the elbows and used them to propel him down the slope. He passed Christine, took a handful of her hair as he went, and felt her start to shift. She began to slide with him. His progess quickened suddenly, and he went into the base of the gully head first and much faster than he wanted, out of control, his legs up the slope. The icy water, about eighteen inches of it now, closed around his face, his own weight thrusting him down. He let go of Christine's hair as he struggled to lift his head, and clawed in a panic at the flabby sides of the gully for support. She continued to slide, though, and as he managed to raise his head and breathe for a second, her hardening body landed on him. It felt like being hit with a plank, and she forced his face back down into the tide and held it there. Frantically, he fought to push her off and to the side. He longed to scream, but his mouth and nose were still under the surface. There was a fierce pain in the top of his ear, and he realized it must be the big diamond stone of her engagement ring cutting him. He had already been aware of himself sinking into the mud again when he hit the bottom, and now, with her weight suddenly on his back, his arms went in to well above the elbows. Christ, why had he come out here? What use collecting a body? What use collecting a body if the sodding body was going to drown him?

8

At the bottom of the gully, acrid water already in his throat and lungs, near death himself, and with mud up to his armpits as Chris bore down on his back, he let his left shoulder sink in too, so that his body went on to the slant and she rolled over to that side, half or a quarter off him. Or less than a quarter, but it meant that by a frenzied jerk back of his head he could get his nose and mouth out and breathe. And breathe and breathe and gasp and gasp, part covered by her still, but sucking air and cough-spewing sea. Some part of her – perhaps her head, or an elbow, something hard and merciless – actually seemed to try to push him back under, but her full weight was not behind it now, and he was able to work his face to the edge of her. Oh, the brilliant stink of those mud walls and the poisoned water. Life. This was the true Ember. He might be liable to bad tangles of all kinds – bullets, doubt, abundant mud, the awkward crushing corpse of a beloved – yes, all of them, but he remained Ember, with the eternal pretty skill of pulling through.

In a minute, he drew himself a few more inches away from her to the left, and she slipped off him completely and fell with her face down into the tide. Very gradually he tried to right himself, bring himself on to his stomach and chest again, get that wider spread of weight. Crawling would be no good here because his knees and arms sank deep. He could just about get his hands and arms clear and put them out in a V to his sides once more, that vital extension.

Again he waited for a while to recover strength and try to dredge–purge his lungs. Then he realized he had been right, and the water was getting deep enough to be useful. He could feel it lift him a little occasionally. It froze his knees and balls and now and then welled over him and touched his arsehole like hot ice. Despite the cold, though, he would delay longer, until they were both virtually floating. He leaned across and affectionately gripped a good handful of Christine's soiled hair again, to make certain she was not carried back and seawards towards the mouth of the gully. She was his beloved prize. The breakers stayed small, but they were close now and had grown noisy. It was frightening, yet he forced himself to hang on. Oh, sure, he could hang on tonight, when she was dead, but not this afternoon, when . . . But he could not have saved her. Probably they would both have been killed. More than probably. Much more. So often Ember had needed to make the best of history. This was another of his flairs.

In fifteen minutes he was able to half swim, half flounder very slowly towards the beach, drawing Christine after him. Twice he had to stop for major vomits. He was glad of the darkness, so he could not dwell on the colour of these returns, but they now had a good, cleansing copiousness, not like the earlier poor retching. After another twenty minutes the tide was no longer reaching them, but by then he did not need its help because they were back on to a sand-and-mud mixture, and he could crawl and drag her without any fear of sinking in.

When they were clear and had reached all sand, he sat for a time with Christine, shivering and coughing again, and wanting to talk. Lovingly, he cleared her face a little with a nappy liner, especially around her eyes. Rigor was well under way despite the cold, but the exposure had not begun to change her yet, and he still saw beauty in her face. 'So, who says Panicking Ralph, Chris? I came, didn't I? Well, some panic yes, but constructive panic back there. Would I have had the strength without frenzied panic? It's my adrenalin substitute. They don't consider that, the positive side.'

He brought her to the base of the sea wall, carrying her now, hugging her to him not dragging, although she felt so stiff. There he rested again. When he was ready, he took her by the ankles and pulled her to the top, well away from the sea. His watch had not coped with the mud, but he thought it must be about 10 p.m. Would some bastard finding her take the big diamond? He could not bring himself to remove it. That had been part of her other, inoffensive life with Les. Her skirt had ridden up and he pulled it back down.

As fast as he could without shoes, he walked back to the car and stripped. For five minutes he rolled about naked in some tall wet grass, trying to get the worst of the mud off and temper the stench. He dressed in his decent clothes and put the others into the boot. The Monty would be busy, but he might be able to slip in through the trade entrance without meeting anyone and get a shower in the staff room. He would put the old clothes into his incinerator. Driving back, he went over everything he had done out there tonight and this afternoon. Nothing could lead to him. The wellingtons were not going to reappear any more than the flashlights. It would be reasonably safe to do an anonymous call to the police about her beloved body. The only hazard was that someone might have seen the car parked while he was retrieving her. It was tucked away, but a lot of people came here for vehicle sex at night and picked the most secluded spots. This would be a hazard, though, whether or not he made a call: Chris was certain to be found during the day and the police would then trawl for any unusual sights or incidents around the area. The most unusual – him battling with Christine's corpse in the Valley of the Shadow of Filth – they would not hear about, luckily, because it had been dark and they were hidden from the shore. However, he would need to work up a bit of an alibi or tale, in case some nosy sod had seen the car and turned responsible. Most people who came here late did not want to advertise, but they could make anon calls, too. He pulled in at a payphone and gave the message. Chris had lain about unattended enough. Also, there was Leslie to think of. It would be terrible, inexplicable news for him, his wife out there, bullet-ridden and streaked, but at least he would not be mystified any longer by her absence. From what he had heard, Leslie was quite a tolerable lad and deserved this posthumous consideration.

9

Under a shower at The Monty he held up his face to the warm spray and wept in full. He enjoyed the notion of his tears being carried away by these jets and disappearing down the hole with grimy traces of that terrible, noble time on the mud. In this flow the signs of grief and bravery joined. He felt genuine. The din from the water tank drowned all sound of his crying. Through the high open window a bitter smell of smoke from the club incinerator reached his nose and eyes as the soiled clothes torched, but it was not smoke that caused his tears. He sobbed to think of Christine out there still, probably, while police and ambulance people searched for the right bit of sea wall. Dirt-coated except her face, liable to discovery by dogs, tramps and foxes, bearing no identification since her bag had gone, dead in place of him, and, so to speak, utterly innocent, she would lie waiting in the dark. It hurt Ember, but also relieved him, that when police did find out who she was, her husband, Leslie, would be called to confirm, as if only *their* relationship rated.

Police might be baffled to note how the mud had been carefully wiped from her features. Perhaps they would deduce this was a loving act by someone, someone who revered her looks and could walk away from that big diamond, regardless, supposing she still had it when they reached her. Ember longed for the police to think all this, confer gallantry without actually putting his name to it. Gallantry was an adornment he really sought, even if anonymous.

Ember remained under those comforting jets for many minutes after all the dirt had gone and the water ran clear from him. He found that through sorrow and rage he had unconsciously, fiercely, clenched his hands tight on two tablets of Imperial Leather soap. His fingers cut into them and beigeish furls and slivers of the stuff forced their way between and clung to his knuckles, as sea spray clings to a cliff. A vengeance duty stuck to him like that now. Unthinkable to let people get away with slaughtering a girl he had just made fine love to, and whom he genuinely thought so much of, anyway. All right, her death was not deliberate, but did that matter? They had destroyed her, more or less in his presence. Of fucking course in his presence. True, he had been getting away. Well, they had both been trying to get away: not just a poltroon solo by him. No, no. He had definitely still been in the vicinity. Definitely. Hadn't they been firing at him? They would expect Ember to react to this now, retaliate, and, if he did not, it would confirm the slanders: all that alleged Ralphy yellowness, the rich flair for panic and little else.

Ember smeared fragments of the wrecked bars of soap about his body for their extra cleansing and scent, and when the pieces got washed off he toe-mashed them down the grating, as if disposing of evidence. Feeling spruce, he did not fancy re-dressing in the clothes he had worn to and from the foreshore. His grass bath had shifted much of the body mud, but it was not a perfect job, and his garments were stained and they reeked. Luckily, he always kept a tuxedo suit and dress shirt at the club for formal celebrations, like christening parties or the return of a member from really major jail. Ember put on this outfit and a pair of gleaming black patent shoes, then sat in his private office upstairs for a while, thinking. Although Christine's husband might be called to identify, Ember was unquestionably the one and only one designated to do vengeance: not the stupidity of vendetta, just a proper repayment. It was impossible to dodge the role in the way some might claim he had dodged this afternoon. He felt privileged and aggrieved. How could anyone expect her husband to avenge her death? Ember had never met him, obviously, but vengeance killings would be outside his range. Tranter, apparently very fat, ran a thin career designing and selling plastic, timed food-portion dispensers for cats and dogs whose owners were away. Chris said he had also patented a special flea powder for animals. So he had bonny talents, but not as an avenger. Tranter was your mild, gross small-businessman, and God knew how he could ever have afforded a diamond like that legit. Besides, Leslie must not learn how Chris died, and would have no notion of where to look for the chieftain who sent that volley team.

It could be any of four or five people running their own trade outfits, striving to occupy that post-Kenward vacuum, exclusively and for ever. There were Mansel Shale and Alfie Ivis; there was a bullshitting young slob, Keith Vine, and a bullshitting older slob, Stan Stanfield; there was Charles

Misto; there had been Bandy and Silver, but perhaps they had given up. And, then ... yes, what about ACC Iles? Harpur? Both? The rumours persisted that these two had a protective interest in one of the big syndicates. A disgusting suggestion, definitely: police – very senior police – aiding a drugs conglom. But, alas, that's how things might be. Everywhere, Ember saw a sad withering of public and professional responsibility. The French phrase, *fin de siècle*, might cover this slide.

Ember downed a couple of Kressmann Armagnacs. Soon he would descend and face folk in the bar. He had taken a quick look on the surveillance monitors and seen that, as a matter of fact, Keith Vine and Stanfield were in the club tonight, talking away together like the UN. This pair ran what was certainly one of the most up-and-coming trade syndicates. And they might have decided Ember was a threat. But both were Monty members and couldn't be kept out. He thought a shoulder holster under this neat jacket might be obvious, and put the Walther into a trouser pocket.

That attempt on him today showed Ember headed someone's list – Stanfield and Vine's list? Charles Misto's list? Alfie Ivis and Mansel Shale's list? Iles's list? Harpur's list? No knowing which, yet. Well, if he was on a list, he expected to head it. His natural status. Plus he now had this locked-on obligation to look for revenge, which meant more hazard. The thought nearly crushed him. But there was a toughness in Ember, too, somewhere. Had to be. Just as that pulped soap had pushed its way between his clasped fingers, outcrops of stubbornness would often force their way up through his general dreads and panics. So, although he might frequently suffer crippling fright – would never deny that – Ember also knew that others could be scared of *him*.

He glanced at the monitors again. When people like those two executioners failed, they would need to put it right very fast, to soothe their masters. Desperate, they might even try something here, in Ember's own fortress, when he was surrounded by friends ... well, more or less friends. The three monitors covered every part of the bar, and after five minutes' close inspection he felt satisfied they were not present. He saw only faces that were familiar to him: not necessarily people he felt fond of, but familiar.

Ember took a further decent helping of armagnac, touched the Walther in his pocket, and went downstairs. There were whistles at his get-up and he did a pirouette and a bow. He tried to keep The Monty a cheery place, despite occasional blood-soaked affrays and harsh tragedies. It was a prestige spot, still with traces of an earlier sedate life as a meeting place for authentic businessmen and professional people. Ember had insisted all the mahogany and brass stayed. But, God, he thought, running his hand over some wonderful panelling, this was a bit different from stomach-skating on mud. He, Ralph W. Ember, did not belong out there, yet he had gone for her, almost without quibble, like a fine gun dog after a dropped duck.

He checked with the bar manager. The evening so far sounded fine, no strangers. Ember smiled out at some parties of regulars. Vine and Stanfield continued their board meeting, heads so matey and conjoint. Occasional bits of paper passed, with note-taking. Ember gave them a wave. Vine waved back and Stanfield nodded in that stately way the bugger put on. Yes, changes under way there. Stanfield always used to work with a lad called Beau Derek, first-class on safes and accounts, but Stan had certainly shifted into something else. He and Vine probably had their let-us-be-Kenward operation well in place. Perhaps they were here to see if Ember was still alive. Well, let the sods look. It was only months since Vine added up to nothing but a scratch-around kid. Now, he had turned weighty. Ember watched their faces but neither broke with shock at finding him undead.

Although he would remain alert, Ember considered it possible that those thugs on the beach today had made their one ploy and would be too afraid to return and try again. He could sympathize with people who feared him. They might speak the standard slanders about his panics, but at the same time sense this was nothing like the whole tale. They recognized that Ralph Ember could be a deftly dangerous opponent. Why those two at the foreshore had been sent stalking. Their bosses wanted to remove *him* before he had a chance to smash *them*. The duo had shot so badly, so wantonly, through trembling dread. They had seemed relaxed as they ran down to the beach, but no. That pair had had deep, hidden awe of Ralph Ember. It was so natural, hired fucking nothings from nowhere. He had a name that reached out in reputation, and it was not Panicking. From now on they would discover what they had opened up today. And this was more than an avenging fury at the death of Chris, though God knew that existed: she had been an unmatchable lover, and, to some degree, wife. Oh, yes, to some degree.

Abruptly now, propped by armagnac, reassured by the peacefulness of the club, anger high over what happened earlier, Ember told himself he would after all stick with his business project. There had been moments on the beach when he almost promised himself that if he survived the shooting – with or without Christine – yes, if he survived he would forget about building a syndicate. The risk had looked ludicrous – and too damn real. Now, though, he cancelled that surrender. He could bring something positive from the blacknesses of today. Wasn't he famed for turning bad moments to profit? Gathered from various little, lucky, rough enterprises over the past few years, Ember still held in deposit boxes and The Monty loft about £70,000, cash. He understood that around £40,000 was needed to capitalize a good-sized syndicate, and set it up with the first stock. After that it was a matter of finding a sifted battalion of street runners and their established client access. A doddle, possibly. Comforted and resolute, he decided, yes, yes, it *could* still happen.

'Ralph!' Keith Vine suddenly called. 'Finery! What's the big occasion?'

'You and your directors' conference.'

'Ha! Of course. Well, we're due a refreshment break.'

Ember picked up a bottle of the Kressmann and walked out from behind the bar to their table.

'All OK, Ralph?' Stanfield asked.

'Brilliant.' He poured drinks and sat down.

'Branching out at all?' Stanfield said.

'Some irons in the fire. You've got to look for the opportunities or go under. Diversify.'

'Great.'

'How about you boys?' Ember replied. 'Hear anything of business openings in the widest sense, I wonder?'

'Lovely potentialities,' Vine replied, 'but only for very big contenders. Look at how poor old Bandy went under, and even Tim Silver chickened out. Misto? Very shaky, I hear.' You could almost see the sod swell because he had not chickened out and felt unshaky. He was obviously carrying something. Always, lately, this crazy bulge in his combat jacket pocket. Keithy Vine really thought he was a star now, and the gun shouted status, even if the naff jacket and his all-chin face shouted something else. Stanfield would probably be equipped, too, but you got no tell-tales from him, not in his features nor his clothes. Anyway, his bloody great, dimwit moustache gave him something to hide behind, and he had been around so long nothing could shake the arrogant sod. A yarn Stan probably launched himself said he was descended from Clarkson Stanfield, a famed sea and boat artist last century who knew Charles Dickens. It brought Stanley real snob poise. Women went for that. He was a casual, shag-around eminence: never any decent, settled relationship, just crude appetite.

'How's Beau, Stan?' Ember asked. 'Don't notice him with you these days. Not away? I see no trial reports.'

'Beau's sort of grown reclusive,' Vine said. He was mid-twenties, maybe, hardly any track record beyond very bitty burglaries, and possibly a sub-postmaster dead in a small-change raid. Nothing Olympic. This was what made the new bond with Stanfield such a puzzle. But all kinds of groupings would happen now the pushing scene had opened up. Vine was a novice, should have been readable, yet Ember still observed no flicker of surprise in his eyes at seeing him intact. Of course, he and Stan might have heard already that Ember slipped away whole this afternoon, in his indomitable style. Vine was just the kind to talk threats, but it would be Stanfield who did things, sent people. 'And the family, Ralph?'

'Great.'

'Those daughters – really grand schools, I hear,' Vine replied. 'Even abroad. France?'

'And you and yours, Keith?' Ember asked.

'Babe very much on the way.'

'Great.'

'The family gives a wondrous focus, doesn't it, Ralph?' Vine said. 'Regardless of all these other factors. I'm always telling Stan, but he stays solo.'

'If I could match the quality of Ralph's marriage, maybe I'd try it,' Stanfield replied.

'I'd be so lost without,' Ember said.

He left them and returned with the Kressmann bottle to behind the bar for a while. Usually, he came to the club in the early evening, then went home for a while to get on with some study, returning to see the place closed around 2 a.m. There had been special factors today, though, and his timetable was adrift. He went back up to the office and from there into the loft with a long-flex inspection light. He reached under some old carpets insulating water pipes, and brought out a couple of good, rubber-banded stacks of twenties. They looked about equal, but he sat on a trunk and counted them. One made £4,600, the other £5,200. He levelled them up. Important that. It was a thing you learned early when dealing with children, or with also-rans like the two lads he might use as team-mates in his new syndicate, Harry Foster, Gerry Reid. Foster liked to think of himself as hard, and Reid had a sort of charm and could drive to getaway standard. Ember took the bundles back down to the flat and put them in a duffel bag.

He dialled Foster. Harry lived off Ferdinand Drive, an unkempt area, and not too far from where DCS Harpur himself was, in Arthur Street. After a while Harry's bleak, cagey voice answered. He sounded fit enough. 'Harry, things are moving,' Ember said.

'This is . . .?'

'Right.'

'Moving?'

'I thought a get-together,' Ember said.

'When?'

'Tonight. I could come over. I've got something really useful for you.'

'Come over here? No. Not on.' Harry had always objected

to visitors, thought they drew attention: as if the way the bugger looked and dressed didn't already.

'Where you like,' Ember replied. 'Can you get contact with the other lad? Obviously, there's similar for him. These would be sort of inauguration tokens. I've been thinking about it for a while. Perhaps you're in need. Both.'

'We're all right.'

'Lads like you, you should be more than all right.'

'Well, I don't know. I don't know what he'll say either.' He talked doubtful, but the tone of caginess had gone. Harry smelled loot. He was good at that.

'This would be just for a discussion and general survey. I won't keep you up all night.'

'Survey?'

'The prospects,' Ember replied. He started some pressure. 'Listen, it's no trouble at all, me calling at your place. I'm looking super-respectable in a dress suit, so it's going to appear absolutely all right.'

'Dress suit? Christ, in this street?'

'Ah, you could be right. Pick somewhere else then.'

Foster chose an all-night services on the motorway – the sort of deadbeat thinking to expect from someone like Harry. Half the Free World's most sensitive business initiatives were planned in services car parks, and police did routine tours to check on new alliances. But do it their way. After three or four triple armagnacs, Ember took the driving out there carefully. He recalled that Harry had been reasonably domestic with a girl called Deloraine, glossy and loud, but full of friendship. Ember had often thought she might be worth a private approach. He would like her to get a sight of him in the dinner suit and handing out nearly £10,000 cash with a promise of more. But most likely she would not turn up tonight, even suppose Harry and Reid did.

10

'Don't worry, Col, I'm not seeking a last minute briefing for my lecture, well qualified in the topic though you may be.' Iles, vivid in full dress uniform, was on his way to talk to recruits on ethics and law. He sat down on a straight chair in front of Harpur's desk, looking as though he might not stay long. Harpur felt grateful.

'I hear we have an ID for the dead on the sea wall,' the ACC said.

'Wife of a lad who designs and sells timed machines for feeding cats and dogs, and his own brand flea powder.'

Iles let his mind fiddle with this for half a minute. 'Christine Tranter? Husband Leslie?'

'Yes. You know something about this death, then, sir?'

The ACC grinned and his voice grew soft and deeply amicable: 'Fuck off, Harpur,' he remarked. 'Sometimes I think you've acquired a diseased idea or two about me from dear Mark Lane.'

'I—'.

'Pathetic, Harpur.'

'Sir, I—'

'Where do I look for loyalty, then, Col?'

'How come you'd heard of Mrs Tranter, sir?' Harpur replied.

'Ralphy Ember's been seeing her for years, hasn't he, for

God's sake? Used to screw Christine on winter Tuesday nights in Leslie's old caravanette at the Swain Street multi-storey, two-hour ticket? I've probably got a note on it somewhere. One likes to keep an eye on Ralphy.' Always the deep blueness of the formal uniform and its rich quality seemed to bring a special, agonized malice to the ACC's face. He was still doing his hair *en brosse*, after seeing a late-night Jean Gabin film several times. Overall the impression was of a trusty prisoner in one of those lavishly financed Scandinavian jails. 'What happened to her?' Iles asked.

'Three bullets. Two Sokolovsky .45 automatics. That's at least £7,500 worth of guns.'

'Where?'

'Her back.'

'Running?'

'It's possible.'

'Stopping them on Ralphy's behalf?' Iles asked.

'We've nothing to say he was there.'

'Car?'

'There are so many hidden places, sir.'

'Yes. You get down there yourself off and as it were on, Col? And how *is* the girl student? But you're single now, a widower. We all miss dear Megan. Why should you have to bother with car sex when you can take your young bluestocking to the marital bed? She has scruples? How can that be – I mean, when she's—?'

'Mrs Tranter was mud-stained, though not the face. The tide has been up overnight, so we get no foot marks or anything like that on the flats. She still wore an engagement ring worth four or five thousand.

'Their warm-weather woo ground? Sweet. Ralphy did a loving tidy-up on her? There's so much delicacy in him! He'd never filch from a girlfriend. He was tailed?'

'Possibly.'

'Easy if it's their love routine. Ralphy likes regularity. This could be business competition after him?'

'Yes.'

'So Ember really does still crave a slice of Kenward?'

'Or the opposition fear he does.'

'But which opposition?'

'That's right, sir.'

Iles did some kind of calculations with his fingers. 'This sort of business potential, Kenward's domain – it's irresistible. For them. I understand the pull. Don't you, Harpur?'

'Ember might still be sitting on enough funds to launch a syndicate. He's harvested a lot of loot in his time.'

'He'd be keen to make proper use of that. Ralph will have the parable of the talents in mind, now he's doing Religious Knowledge for his degree.' Iles gave himself a bit of a brushing with the back of one hand and then stared for a time at his reflection in the window. This was where loyalty could be found. The ACC fondly yanked a whisker from his left nostril and put this on Harpur's notepad. It lay shiny and curved like a scimitar in Lilliput. Harpur said, 'I was going to mention it to the chief at our last session, but—'

'Wise silence, Col. One of your strongest facets. Lane's a towering sweetheart, someone I look up to as to a small god or InterCity engine driver, but we don't want to shove the poor, bladder-weak whelp back into depression, do we? I adored the flavour of him at our meeting. Mission! That fine old three-ply hulk, his wife, gave him this rallying call, Harpur, no question. I don't know if you've ever done anything with Mrs Lane, Col – I mean, in view of your quaint and ungovernable tastes, plus a certain generosity to the unpresentable – but I certainly would never say there's a total absence of sexuality in her. I'd guess, in fact, her teeth are undoubtedly her own. I don't care to hear of rubbish shooting at old Ralphy, even if they missed. He's part of the civic texture. Expensive weaponry. London's here already?'

'Would people like that hit the wrong target, sir?'

'Fair point, Harpur. But you've got to remember how very, very clever Ralphy is, especially when he's scared and into evasion mode. Metropolitan hacks will have come across nothing in his class.' Iles stood. 'Duty, Col. I'm off to tell these lads and girls that order, morality and good governance are in our keeping, and leave them to discover that in fact there is only strong-arm, chaos and fluke.'

'Well, you look the part, sir,' Harpur replied.

'Which?'

'Which what, sir?' Harpur asked.

'Order, morality and so on, or strong-arm, et cetera?' Iles said.

'Ember certainly has the drive and ability to create a firm,' Harpur replied.

11

Ember invited Harry Foster and Reid to Low Pastures. This was big. Ember hoped the buggers realized it. They would. They must see the difference between the pits they lived in and such a property, meaning not just the house but grounds in accord, with the paddock and stables.

'I've done a bit of research,' he said, 'and listed nineteen worthwhile street operatives we could supply exclusively within a five mile radius of the city centre. I'll let you see a map giving proposed drop points and defining territory exactly, meaning no border disputes, so damn profitless. Five miles is about right for keeping things manageable – I mean, distribution, collecting, persuading payment if and when, protection for our dealers, also if and when. These nineteen are lads, oh, and a couple of girls, indeed, yes, people with a regular, hooked, steady-paying clientèle that they really know, so there's wholesome confidence going both ways. Access to such established customer cohorts is certainly worth our purchase by a dab in the hand and favourable early terms. "The labourer is worthy of his hire," the Bible says, as you know. You'll probably recognize some of the names.' He read: 'P. W. Blake, Untidy Graham, Alan and Ginny Campbell, Eleri ap Vaughan, Hector Mills-Mills, Sid Quint, and so on. This was a while back, and there might have been small changes. For example, talking of the Bible,

Panicking Ralph

I believe Untidy went full born-again for a while after drifting pissed into a marquee gospel campaign.'

'I heard him preach the Word outside C&A's', Foster said, 'a banner and yelling he had been chief of sinners.'

'Untidy always grandiosized,' Ember replied. 'But he's back in trade now, experting in crack.' He held up the list, in its way a banner, too. 'Basically, this is still a sound, working schedule.'

Obviously, Ember had never done this before, allowed dangerous makeweights such as Foster and Gerry Reid in to his home. This was public relations. They still needed persuading towards full commitment. Out at the services the other night they had naturally taken the signing-on fee happily enough. But he could tell they were scared: 'hard man' Foster as scared as Gerry. They knew the routine hazards in big-time, big-money drugs. People got killed. A young girl runner had been shot. Claud Beynton, a businessman crammed with dazzling repute, had apparently committed suicide by gun in the mouth: suicide *only* apparently, though dead definitely. Not long after, disgusting street battles cost one dealer an eye, and another was wheelchaired for ever. And then most recently, and maybe conclusively, came the death of Christine. Naturally, these two would not know Ember had been involved in that, but they would guess a gang aspect: price of the weapons said it. Terrified by all this, Foster and Reid might chicken out, might even hand the golden-hello money back. Fear could do that to men.

Ember had therefore set up this little discussion at Low

Pastures to hearten them, build their morale. He considered it a one-off, inevitable sacrifice. On disk he had a full, properly worked-out business plan, and would not mind if Foster and Reid heard part of it. This list of possible pavement-level pushers was one aspect. Potential partners deserved a bit of basic information.

'Maybe what we got to consider, Ralph, many of them could have been bought up already,' Reid said. 'I mean, it's months since Kenward deceased and the trade went up for grabs. The business has to go on. Habits are habits. They've all kept selling.'

'Sporadic,' Ember replied. 'No organization. Anyone who has arrangements elsewhere we seek to buy back. At this stage, we don't want harshness. Be generous. I can assure you, we're well capitalized.' He had another grand for each of them today but would hold on to it until the end, to keep their attention. Of course, it would all revert to him out of profits eventually, under a standard-term Founder's Preference arrangement.

'Buy them back?' Reid said. 'Could be life-threatening, Ralph? Whoever's got them won't like us poaching.'

Well, Ember did not say anything or even make a gesture. He just looked around his drawing room slowly, the size and distinction of it, with the genuine furniture, some no-question Regency. These two would understand. He was telling them without any words or purple that someone who picked up a place like this and had the money to run it did not back off when a bit of opposition showed. This was exactly how he saw leadership: you took a couple of bottom-grade hangers-on who'd wear training shoes to such a home regardless, and built them into something combative, by money and inspiration. He loved *Daily Telegraph* obituaries of frequently decorated service officers, where you saw how prole subordinates had been transformed into gallant units on the North West Frontier by gritty and yet often flamboyant example from above: charismatic commanders combined both qualities. Always in life there would be an officer class and then the rest. The officer class had inescapable obligations. Himself, he would certainly never try to dodge these.

He said: 'We give our franchise holders a prime discount rate when they buy supplies from us, at least at first – till we've finished off the opposition, one way or the other.' He did not explain, because these two probably would not grasp it, but this was basic private enterprise: lay out plenty to capture the market and you could recoup and more once you smashed competitors. Core economics. 'We can give the good ones five hundred, even up to a thousand, as signing-on fee. I mean, when they agree to take their stuff from us, only us, for retailing. Oh, they'll come, fear not. They've heard of Ralph Ember. Well, heard of you two lads, as well, obviously.' He nodded hard to show he really meant this last bit. Then he said: 'I've got three good bulk suppliers lined up, entirely reliable people. They bring it in in quantity, unload to us wholesale, and we sell on to our cosy, contented network. In that fussy fashion of mine I've checked them out, toothcombed their backgrounds. It's routine.'

Bill James

'*You* picked them, solo?' Foster replied. 'How come we're not consulted, being parts of the firm?'

'I wanted to be able to show you something ready to go,' Ember said. 'Hack work. I thought, Get it out of the way quick, so we can go right away for expansion. As they say in government, Harry, I acted executively, in this instance.'

'That seems reasonable,' Reid said.

'But this is Harry for you, Gerry – always,' Ember replied in an easy tone. 'He's got to examine things all through. I don't mind. In fact, it's good, it's challenging. Down my college they call this "intellectual rigour". They heard of it from Cambridge.' He kept his voice light right through and slipped the wet joke in. No need for tempest. Get Gerry with him to begin, and slowly Harry would come, too. Gerry could be a true spiel king, unstoppable wordage, often with ramshackle grammar, and there was all that bloody denim. But he also had decency and passable sense not quite swamped. You could see he was offended by Harry's aggression. Best keep things mild with Foster, though, persuade him towards acceptance. Gerry's getaway driving was undoubtedly a fine art, but Harry, with his savagery and size, would probably be the Most Man in the syndicate after Ember himself. And, on top of that, Harry gave a neat route to Deloraine, though no need for him to know this, obviously.

Ember said: 'Standard to have two or three bulk suppliers on our books, in case one or more goes under. Two are London, one's South Coast, Hampshire. Perhaps I'll take a drive down to see that one soon. We want some geography

56

between them so a police squeeze in one locale can't starve us. These are dangerous regions, both. A man can lose friends there. But all right if you go gently.'

Harry helped himself to more vodka and orange, which was fair enough, although Ember did not like the way he banged the bottles back down on the rosewood. Then Harry banged himself down on the chesterfield, all to show he could not be impressed, which he was, silly git. If he sat down like that in his own den the furniture would revert to bits of cardboard. You'd think by twenty-five he'd have found some grace, or mere aplomb. Anyone looking at his behaviour today would understand why Ember normally tried to keep a long distance between the rough sectors of his life and this fine, family setting: just as he had tried to conceal these unpleasant aspects from dear Christine.

'What I want to know is, have we got people from those regions you mentioned here already – London and so on?' Foster blurted

'How do you mean?' Ember replied.

Reid said: 'This woman killed out on the foreshore. I got to say, Ralph, that give me a worry, too, when I heard.'

'I read this is the wife of some devoted friend to our four-legged friends, that's all,' Ember replied. 'A tragedy, but does that touch us, for God's sake?' Now, he kept his voice damn steady, nicely above it all, no mud on his breath. 'Domestic, probably. Suicide?'

'Three bullets from two guns? In the back? And this is Sokolovsky automatics,' Foster said.

'What we grapevined, Ralph. And the media.'

'I've no information to that effect,' Ember replied. He had no information at all on those haywire marksmen. He must find some. His life now was not just about getting a business scheme under way, though this had to be important. He must find the pair who destroyed Christine and put them out of the further reckoning. And find who sent them, if he could.

'Know the cost of those pistols, Ralph?' Foster asked.

'They're prestige guns, that's a fact,' he replied. Unsuitable, unsuitable, unsuitable to be holding this kind of conversation in Low Pastures. God, normally he would not use even The Monty for talking trade with people like Harry and Reid, let alone his residence. He had a business side and then a *business* side, and, as much as was possible, he wanted The Monty to stay on the business side. It must remain a place of prestige and good traditions. Ember saw himself as two very separable identities, one not quite as lousy as the other. Plus there were always eyes at The Monty, and to have close conversation there with Foster and Reid in the bar or his office could have been a pointer – the way Vine and Stanfield's sessions were pointers. Gossip would roll. The tale could reach Harpur and, if Harpur wanted, might even reach Iles. Those two, and Iles above all, would disrupt, either for their own interests, or for fun. This was what business savvy meant: knowing how to keep that rampant, grey, kid-fucker Iles well out of your portfolio.

'These foreshore weapons don't come from any local armourer – not Leyton Harbinger and Amy,' Foster said.

'The husband probably travels all over, catering for

nationwide pets,' Ember replied. 'He could have bought them anywhere.'

'A flea powder guru comes down the foreshore with a Sokolovsky in each hand, like Wyatt Earp?' Foster asked. 'This is what, £4,000 to £5,000 *each*, without ammo.'

'But I'm told he was big in his business, designing, not just selling,' Ember replied. 'People spend on their animals even when hard up, Harry. He might have treated himself to a pair of something fine from profits. Instead of a Porsche.'

'I ask myself, Why the foreshore?' Foster said. 'I mean, what's she doing?'

'But isn't this a famed spot for lovers?' Ember replied. 'There are tales about Harpur, for instance. Possibly the husband went after his wife and companion. Even a steady chap could turn vindictive finding his wife there.'

'The husband's still around,' Foster said. 'A case like that, some amateur with Sokolovskys, Harpur would have him same day.'

Oh, yes, this kind of talk – the violence, the seedy sex – seemed so very wrong to Ember for his lovely drawing room. But it was not always possible to keep the two aspects of himself separate. Foster and Reid had to be impressed and flattered and clinched for the syndicate, and it could not be done at The Monty. So, here they were in Ember's home now, mid-afternoon, with drinks, both wearing those loutish trainers and gazing at genuine old beams and so on, or out from the drawing room windows over the paddock and fields to the purifying sea. Ember watched from the windows, too, but for safety's sake, not the view. The foreshore shooting party could be about, still looking to put things right. He kept the vigilance discreet: alarm this pair and the special invitation was wasted. All right, the initial cash had already begun to make them feel bigger: nearly five grand each unprovoked, plus another instalment Ember told them would follow. But that night at the services they had stayed obviously nervy and hesitant even so, and, at the end of discussions, their garments gross with twenties, he still was not sure they would do what they had said a dozen times they would and come in with him. And who else was there, available fast enough? When they were breaking up then, he asked, 'What about another conference, lads?' obviously meaning to them another nought-heavy handout. 'Forget the services or laybys or supermarket car parks and come out to Low Pastures, my home', he had said, adding that fink-slinking about in no man's land rendezvous was not Ralph W. Ember's style. It had worked. The pair had been clearly overwhelmed by his offer, although they tried to act indifferent, as you'd expect, and Foster in particular.

Now, Reid said: 'What worries Harry, Ralph, and, yes, self, also – what is of concern about that foreshore incident is this old defence post, the blockhouse.'

'Which?' Ember replied.

'The body was not far from that, we're told, Ralph,' Reid explained gently.

'That blockhouse – used for deals, business convocations. Used for all sorts,' Foster said. 'Prime centre of commerce.'

Ember arranged a chuckle and poured himself a vodka and orange, then filled up Reid and Foster. Ember took the bottles and put them on the sideboard, a folded newspaper underneath. 'You're telling me this ordinary wife of a stalwart businessman was into the trade?'

Foster said: 'I'm telling you she was killed by very pricey metropolitan bullets, Ralphy.'

He'd let it go today, the Ralphy. It could be a slip, brought on by nearly a rhyme: 'pricey', 'Ralphy.' He said: 'One bullet's as bad as another, if it hits you in the right place, wrong place.'

'What the fuck are we walking into?' Foster asked.

'It's the scale of who we could be confronting, to be frank, Ralph,' Reid said.

Their fear was like another person in the discussion, present and uncontrollable. It had been the same the other night. Altogether that services meeting was quite a giggle, really. At the beginning, he had nearly laughed aloud, as the three sat there prim with lemon tea. Well, God, *they* were jumpy and shattered, yet *he* was the one who had secretly been out unaided on infinite mud a few hours before, freighting the dear body of a beloved, and yet was still able to behave towards them with poise. Ember's mother used to say, 'You're twice the man with a ten pound note in your pocket.' That night these sods had £4,900 each in theirs, but they did not look twice as solid to Ember. Twice nothing was nothing. Foster did not bring Deloraine to the services, and she was not with him this afternoon, either. Never mind, develop that later. Obviously, Ember said nothing to Foster and Reid today about the value of Low Pastures or the authenticity of bare stone in the walls, or about the acreage. That would have been crude. Let them just read what they saw for themselves. He had picked this time. It was sports afternoon at the university, and he would miss no lectures. And there was nobody else in the house. He did not want his family bumping in to these two scrag-ends. Margaret was shopping and Fay at school. Margaret would pick her up to come home. Since the shooting he worried about his daughter travelling alone. He even worried about Venetia at her school in France. Some of these people did not respect childhood or family.

Foster swigged more vodka and orange. 'Why's she shot in the back?' he said. 'She's trying to get away because she knows them, knows they've come for her. This lady's an obstruction.'

'And then from other reports around, she's been right out on the mud, Ralph. Well, perhaps fleeing in her terror, all-over soiled, but her face cleaned up, just her face.'

'This to confirm identity, evidently,' Foster said. 'Shoot first, check after. These were very seasoned people. They must have gone on the flats to bring her back, real RIP thoroughness. OBEs if they were in the ambulance service. They leave a fat diamond ring on her because that's not part of the assignment. This is specialization. They would be home on the motorway before she was even found, thinking of the next outing. Nice, tidy work. We start showing we're moving into the same area, where are we, Ralphy?'

'The fucking name's Ralph, Foster.' Ember got his jaw out, stretching the scar. That could be like a banner, too, sometimes: a battle banner. 'Where are we? We're standing on our own ground, that's where. We're not some woman, alone.' He was sitting on a straight dining chair, to give the idea they should not settle down and stay long. Reid had remained on his feet. 'Would we be showing them our backs, for Christ's sake? We know about resistance, I expect. We don't cave in because we spot Sokolovskys.'

'Ah, but you've seen a lot, Ralph,' Reid said. 'So much combat. Undoubtedly, you'd understand how to handle these situations. Us, we're—'

'You'd be first-rate, Gerry,' Ember replied. 'Haven't I heard from all sorts you're prime when there's stress?'

Foster said: 'Or we have to think it could have been Iles down the beach, or even Harpur. Not doing it themselves, maybe. But Iles would be in touch with suitable folk, no question. If she was in the way, somehow.'

'How?' Reid asked. 'How in the way? An ordinary woman.'

'Women, they hear things, spy things,' Foster replied. 'I've seen pictures of her. She looked good. Tits. Women like that get told secrets, get invited into big people's confidence. Iles would think it was class and a laugh to commission boys with deluxe pieces like those pistols. Style.'

Ember hated to hear him speak of Christine, would have hated it even if Foster had discussed her decently. Foster was from that other dirty realm where Ember went, but where Christine never did. He felt like sitting on this bastard's thousand for a couple of centuries. See if Foster's incisive mind could keep him and Deloraine in serviettes for a fortnight. But the afternoon was going, and Margaret would be here soon with Fay. Ember wanted no fights. He must get constructive. For good leadership, you acted like you already had agreement, took it as inevitable. That made the followers feel the plan was so sound nobody with sense could fail to see it. 'What I thought, you two lads talk to these nineteen, see how they're placed, tell them what's available, the discount and goodwill payment on joining. That's going to vary, obviously. Some of these people have bigger customer lists than others, and they'll deserve extra. Eleri ap Vaughan's created a real quality operation, for instance. She's got numbers, and they're reliable: a lot of salaried and private-means folk, upper-middle and middle class, who can appreciate first-quality provision and expect to pay for it. Not your back-street kids, mugging or tarting for their habit, and snorting at a rate to ravage nose and mind. They're bound to come and go, fail on payments. Yes, Eleri's on a premium, clearly a careful, long-sighted girl.'

Ember paused and smiled in apology. 'But I don't have to tell you. Your strength is you know this scene right through. You're familiar with these street pushers, respected by them. I admit, that side might be where Ralph Ember would not excel. Oh, they know of me, and, I hope, have some regard, but that's the point, isn't it, I'm a distant, premier-league figure to them? Not to sound arrogant, obviously, but this is their perception, and in business what people perceive is as crucial as what is. This kind of status, the Ralph Ember reputation, comes with time and a certain amount of quiet achievement, that's all. You boys are young, but you'll get there, too. At this juncture it's a true boon you're not in that

64

position, though. You can talk to these street folk as equals, and they're comfortable with you.'

He pointed at the list. 'There are problematical names here, too, of course. Well, Untidy Graham for one, obviously. What I mean is, even before he turned to Christ, he was all over the place, that Stipend Road shit heap he lives in and his clothes, the Zulu War waistcoats. Why he's Untidy. But now, on top, this other, extra-terrestrial factor. We're in a spot if he backslides to conversion and starts shouting his trespasses again in the middle of the town, because we'd be in the trespasses with him. It's going to be important you really talk to him, assess these leanings and see if he's definitely given God as much time as he's going to and won't be lapsing. Gerry, you'd be good at making that sort of judgement – sensitive and subtle. Then again, I've got Rufus Maitland on the list, too, but – I can be corrected on this – he's very new and a tiny stable so far, grass only, a minor prospect. We would not be buying him in dear, naturally, if at all.'

'Some traffickers could tell us to fuck off, they're already fixed up for supplies,' Foster said.

Gerry had asked about that earlier, all dealt with, but this was Harry, still turning on the flintiness to show he was Harry and analytical and undozey. Ember loved it, the attitude. It showed Foster was half, even three-quarters, in, and had started thinking out real problems that might show. He had swallowed the project, and Ember decided now he would give him the thousand after all. They needed encouraging. In the *Telegraph* obituaries, there was one sentence that often came up in different forms: 'He was devoted to his men and they to him.' Ember longed for it to be like that, though he did not expect ever to get a *Telegraph* obituary, not unless he really developed. Harry would learn this devotion to Ember. Foster had lumpy shoulders and a chest, and big, thick, fighting hands. At a low level of work they could be a plus, obviously. It might be necessary to do some unpleasantness eventually. Well, almost certainly. Foster wore his slabby, dark, young-Kray-brothers hair erected in a quiff, entirely non-Debrett. He had a long, oldish face, reddened up now with the vodka and aggro, and slitty blue eyes that wanted to tell you they had seen it all before, but which just came over uncharitable and edgy. Ember hated all narrowness. Harry was the sort who wore a ginger overcoat with the trainers. Maybe Deloraine went for all that, the brutal shape of him and the flashiness. Fine with Ember. Obviously, she was not a girl he would want to get long-term lumbered with. He would hardly be asking her to leave Harry and elope, would he? Deloraine was for a good and mutually rewarding but temporary experience or two.

'Should we meet resistance from pushers, we move on, try the rest. At this stage,' Ember replied. 'They'll come round, once they see our operation under way. Think of it like taking over a company, Harry. You buy up shares quietly and then when you've got enough to be a force the people who might have resisted you from inside will change, because they *have* to change: you've got the power.'

'It does sound very workable,' Reid remarked. 'I got to tell you I had my doubts, Ralph—'

'But of course you did, Gerry. What use confeds who can be browbeaten into any old scheme?'

'There's substance to it,' Reid replied. 'The way you've got it all laid out, Ralph.' Reid was also around twenty-five, skinny, nimble, unrelaxed inside the bit of blue jacket, the washed-out blue shirt and his jeans. If you could get denim teeth he'd have them. He kept his good red hair brushed very flat, like a thin wallet. His voice almost seemed to be looking for friendship, reminding of a weak kid, but he knew how to stay calm and, although he fancied oration now and then and lost track of the words, he had some clarity. Obviously, he appreciated what a strength for them Ember was. Foster appreciated this, too, but would never show it. That did not matter, as long as the recognition was there.

'We're circulating the street traders, getting ourselves spotted and marked, while you do what, Ralph?' Foster asked.

'Well, Ralph fixes contacts with the importers, yes, Ralph? All the main dealing and what-you-call it – logistics.'

'Seek terms with them. Set up the whole timetable of delivery,' Ember replied. 'This might sound easy but—'

'This is crux work,' Reid said. 'This is going on to dicey ground and talking big numbers. It's executive flair.' Foster's rough questions embarrassed Gerry, anyone could see, and he went out to what he called the toilet, whereas those with background said lavatory, especially in a place with history, like Low Pastures.

When Reid came back Ember brought the two packets of notes from the sideboard. It was time for them to leave, and he offered no more drinks. He threw one of the packets to each. 'For further business expenses,' he said. Reid, who was standing near the windows now, caught his and flicked the ends playfully like a dealer with cards. Foster was still in his chair and let the bundle lie on his lap, as though he had hardly noticed. Oh, so blasé. Ember said: 'I hear Misto and maybe Silver have fund problems. And Mansel Shale's not like he was, since the death of that kid runner. It's Vine and Stanfield we have to watch. But I can tell you we've got decent reserves, lads. Forty grand gets starter supplies and then, say, twelve for recruiting our pushers. I'd think Eleri's worth at least a grand for sweetener. Rufus a couple of hundred at most. But you lads will decide which of them is worth what. I've no hesitation in delegating that aspect to you, none at all.'

'Gee,' Foster replied.

12

When you tapped from outside on the windows of love cars at night near the foreshore seawall you could rely on pretty much the same response each time, and Harpur grew used to speaking into a vehicle through a gap of about two inches where the glass had been lowered, usually to people on the back seat, of course, and generally mixed couples. It was as if the occupants feared to dilute the momentary cabin magic by bringing their thin barrier down any further to externals. This was how Harpur liked to think of it, anyway, and now and then he had been warmly, darkly capsuled here with a woman himself. Who needed visitors?

Also, many of these people would be nervous and scared to open up more than this quarter turn on the window handle, in terror of identification, or of attack by another partner of the partner or by hirelings, or by sex-haven muggers – such rich pickings here. Harpur never received any response at all to his first tapping, but kept at it with the fifty pence piece. He knew how effective this could be: sometimes when Keith Vine called confidentially at Harpur's house with information, he announced himself with a coin on the kitchen window.

'Police,' Harpur would say, when the car window moved and there was a grunted question or curses from inside. 'I'm trying to trace all vehicles that were in this locality on 18 October, a warm, sunny autumn day.'

'Who says I – we – was here 18 October?'

'Were you?'

'Who's bloody asking?'

'I did mention. Police?'

'You some dirty voyeur or something?'

'Can you recall any particular car?' If Iles was right, and he might be, the particular car could have been Ember's Rover. But you did not prompt.

'Do you think I'm – we're – here every night, for God's sake?'

'It's only the eighteenth that interests me. Afternoon, more likely.'

'So, who are you? Exactly.'

'I'm talking to everyone down here. A little tour. Could you open the window a little more? Or a door? I'll back off, if you'd prefer.'

'What's that supposed to mean, "back off"? Are you saying there's something here you didn't ought to see? Know what I think? You're some perv peeping Tom. I'm coming out after you, you perv.'

'Oh, it's not worth dressing just for me.'

Usually, the window closed altogether then and, although Harpur would wait, nobody ever came out. In a while there would be the sound and half glimpse of swift movement inside the car, and it would pull away, driving more or less blind for a while behind the fond steaming.

These enquiries were unavoidable. If Iles was right and

Ember had been here and was the real target, this could be something more than the killing of a possibly straying wife. And so, Harpur's moves might have a bearing on the chief's loud wish for a cleansing of the patch and the Western World. Harpur, knowing this hope senile, or almost, still yearned to help. The next car drove away without the window being opened at all.

Harpur had all the registration numbers, naturally, but this added up to a poor haul for a night's work, and would not further the chief's gorgeous dream. Another vehicle.

'Police.'

'You what?'

'I need to know all cars in this area on 18 October, day or night. A car that might be standing a while unoccupied.'

'Unoccupied? Here?'

'Did you see anything like that?' To stand against these vehicles with his lips and ear in turn pressed to the glass and metal reminded Harpur of something he used to do as a small boy. There was a cemetery near his home containing big vaults, and, on some of these, subsidence had shifted the main top stone, making a thin gap between it and the upright walls of the tomb. Harpur and other lads would get their mouths to this slit and ask how things were inside and whether the situation could be recommended, or if there were snags. Then they would pretend to listen for an answer. In that graveyard, and here, now, with the cosy cars, it seemed important when you spoke to get your mouth to the same long, letter box shape as the opening, so you could place your message, reach out with clarity to those who

71

lacked all wish to hear. But he had to insist. 'Did you see anything like that?' he asked again.

'I'd love to help, really.'

'Yes, we would, really. We can tell it must be serious. Well, murder of a woman, isn't it? We saw the papers. And we know you have to do this, although embarrassing for you, we appreciate that.'

'And for us! But we're both over eighteen, mind.'

'And consenting.'

'Oh, yes!'

'Even if we hadn't read about it, we could tell how serious, because of using a team. But as we told the other one—'

'Which other one? Team?'

'Well, your colleague, must have been. Also visiting many cars the other night.'

'Oh? What was he like?'

'He's just a voice to us, isn't he, the way you're just a voice to us, and we're just voices to you. Let's hope!'

'What sort of voice?'

'An enquiring voice, a determined voice, like you.'

'But what did you tell him?'

'That we'd love to help, but— Well, the same as now. What else? We don't notice much outside.'

'Did he have anything from other cars?'

'Well, he said he was going to go on asking. Who knows? And then this rather amazing question. I mean, really amazing, wasn't it?'

'Oh, yes, *amazing.*'

'Had we seen a naked man rolling around in the grass on

that date you mentioned? I mean, this is some question for past 1 a.m., isn't it? Yes, he wanted to know that, as well as about the car.'

'Apparently, naked and on his own, just rolling, sort of frantic, in the middle of the night. That's what he had heard from one car, he said.'

'Well, regrettably, we had a giggle, I must say, hearing that. I didn't want to mock him, anything like that, but it sounded so, well, untypical? For this spot.'

'And had you?'

'What? Seen someone unpartnered messing about in the grass? I ask you! Obviously, whatever turns you on, if it does nobody else harm. And it's very safe sex, clearly, so probably even commendable. But comical, all the same.'

'Well, then he went. He said he had to identify a car. Absolutely had to. I think he might have been heavy. I'm not being pert or anything – not *a* heavy. Large. Well, police often are, I know. But maybe even fat. You boys are really very determined and thorough, whatever people say about police. I'd like to say I feel – I feel *really* protected.'

'I hope so,' Harpur said.

Another voice here asking questions? Another voice with more information than Harpur had discovered – if a nude man flinging himself about in the grass was information. Did any of it contribute to the chief's fine purpose? Harpur still wanted to contribute. Lane's longings came from his once grand soul, now shrivelled by responsibility: Harpur could not let someone who had been a great detective and was still a good man simply drop into break-up because of promotion and Iles. Lane, at his rank, was paid to have these broad-sweep, wholesome projects. Harpur, at his rank, was paid to crouch over shadowy, happy cars and infiltrate queries that might squeeze out something on Christine Tranter's death. Well, no, not really at Harpur's rank. This was detective constable work. But it could be sensitive in all kinds of ways, and he felt he should handle it himself, especially knowing the ground so well. This quaint trawl might lead towards some fraction of that brilliant regeneration Lane yearned for. If Harpur had luck, a tiny, short-lived reversal of evil, a fragile advance of good could come from these night-only parking spots. Such minuscule achievements were the height of what real policing aimed for. Lane envisaged so much more. Inspiring and poignant, really.

13

Ember longed to get on with developing the new business, especially its supply end where things could be large-scale perilous, requiring not just heavy cash but finesse and time. This was the kind of work only he in this firm could manage, the kind his big career had fashioned him for. Jesus, imagine Harry or Mouth-Mouth Reid going to London or the South Coast to negotiate with major importers! What image of the syndicate would fine established shippers get from those two oafish kids, Harry maybe in his fucking ginger overcoat? Responsibility for all that aspect had to be Ember's. But he found there were other responsibilities. His vengeance duties never left him alone, niggling for priority, pushing every other consideration back. Although he told himself that she had been married, and that there had been at least one other adulterous affair, he felt the obligation to set things right was on him, only on him. Stature meant responsibility.

The easiest way to get a line on the killers would be to check if anybody had seen their car. When you had a registration number you could ask someone to ask someone who knew someone who knew someone on the police computer to give you the ownership. Obviously, when you asked someone to ask someone, you had to pay the someone you asked, and give him more for the someone he asked and the someone he asked and for the someone on the police computer. Outgoings. But a duty was a duty.

The first thing, though, was to find a number. This was death in the afternoon, so he decided to leave questioning of night love cars near the seawall till later. First, he must talk to the scatter of house-owners and farmers on the hinterland. The police might be at that, too. He would need to go delicately. Better Harpur and Iles did not know he had elected himself avenger. Obviously, he did not want them connecting him with the death in any way, wondering why a hit team should come after Ember and his girl – that is, of course, if the buggers had not sent the hit team themselves.

He bought an Ordnance Survey map of the foreshore area and studied it at home, trying to work out where might be the best place to park a car in daylight, somewhere near that defence post. Ember did not much believe in elaborate planning for a job, because so many appallingly unplannable events could make all preparation seem crazy. But he did like knowing the geography, getting the sense of somewhere, either by a reconnaissance trip, or this way. It was a worrying bit of country: flat, boggy, criss-crossed by long, deep, water-filled ditches knowns as reens, very sparsely populated. People living out there were a mixed and often secret, hostile lot. They would include some bit-part villains, probably, though he was out of touch with that level these days and could think of no names or faces. He made good notes in his Filofax, planned himself a route from likely house to likely farm to likely house to gypsy camp to caravan site. Thoroughness he lived by.

Panicking Ralph

Margaret and Fay came in to the drawing room, back from the school run, and switched on the afternoon television news. He quickly folded up his map and notebook and put them into the briefcase. It had been Christine's funeral this morning, and he watched the screen, though trying to seem casual. The occasion made these grim vengeance obligations bear down even harder, the way her body had borne down on him in the gully, as if with a kind of terrible, fond blame. He could not have attended, of course, although he craved to. Yes, craved. After all, she belonged to him and had already belonged to him years before he reclaimed her body from the mud and sea, and made this solemn ritual possible. Yet he had known it would be lunacy even to spectate the funeral from a street corner. Harpur and possibly Iles would be at the service. Detectives granted that much to murder victims. Roster mourning would not stop them spying around, noticing faces, inventorying all non-family grief.

Margaret had slipped into the kitchen to make tea. Ember loved it when he could be at home for this wholesome together time. 'Mummy, come!' Fay called.

'What?'

'The mud lady.'

Instead of going to the service, Ember had done the usual thing for this kind of tricky grief situation and sent flowers under a false name, 'Penelope D.': Penelope in full, not Penny, probably from the classics, and with a nice refined tone. It seemed wiser to be female. He block-capitalized the name and his inscription, because you never knew who would be holding the cards up to the light: FOR CHRIS, IN ETERNAL FRIENDSHIP, which said some of it. Her husband might be puzzled by the tribute, but there were much bigger items than that to preoccupy Tranter at present, and Christine could have had women friends unknown to him. The surname initial only should suggest a true familiarity: no need to spell out. Margaret came in while the kettle boiled. Ember had in mind Devereux or De la Tour: the class touch again, plus interesting foreign hints. Had he been a woman he would not have minded being called Penelope Devereux.

No fancy wreath, like a dead hood's vulgar display in South London, just a tasteful spray of roses. This anonymity and the remoteness from her now did upset Ember, yet he consoled himself as he watched with his wife and daughter that he and Christine had had many unmatchably close moments, even on the day of her killing, and then afterwards, out in the muck. They had been so inseparably joined that she had almost drowned him, had nearly incorporated Ember into her death. Few could have experienced that level of familiarity.

'So sad, sad, sad, Mummy,' Fay muttered.

Even before the funeral Christine's murder had featured on network and regional television and in all the Press – film and pictures of the foreshore area, and portraits of her as she had been. They showed some of these stills of her again now just before film of the hearse. He felt those lovely hazel eyes hold him, as they always could. Thank heaven he had taken the trouble that night to liberate them from masking filth. Her pretty mouth looked as if about to talk to him, about to tell him she had died in his place and he must put that right. Those lips which had comforted him so sweetly so often had a holy right to instruct him now. Yes, all the different likenesses of her on the screen or in newspapers seemed to radiate this plea and command.

Margaret said: 'Such a beautiful girl. How could it happen to her? What is she doing alone at a spot like that? Well, if she *was* alone, I suppose.'

'Sanctuary,' Ember replied. 'It's just mud to us but important to birds. Watchers go there looking for sheldrakes and so on, often solo, to be unnoticeable. Then – oh, just gun-mad people about.' The kettle screamed its happy domestic message.

'What do you mean, Mummy, "at a spot like that"?' Fay asked.

'So deserted,' Ember answered.

'Yes, deserted,' Margaret said. She went out to the kitchen and brought the tea tray back. Ember thought what a comfortable, united family group they looked: a lovely blue Victorian teapot, real china cups, obviously, and the silver-trim biscuit barrel. Feverishly, he searched the screen for his roses and scanned all faces outside the church and in the cemetery, seeking those two killers. But they were not present. Why should they be? They would know Ember could not attend. If they still wanted him, and, obviously, they *did*, they would try to corner him elsewhere, anywhere and any time. He stared at the richly buff oak veneer of the coffin as it was borne up the churchyard path, and attempted to visualize Christine inside, wholly cleaned now in her burial gown. Yet he found that the images which shoved themselves forward in his mind were not of her but of those two emerging from behind the defence post and jogging down towards them, apparently relaxed, blessedly incapable and lethal. Oh, God, he had to nail them. It was business, but so much deeper than that, too. Manhood. Stature, again. Ember could be ruthless with himself, exorbitant with himself.

Despite his attempt to seem uninvolved, he must have dropped into a bit of a sorrow trance, staring at the television, because Fay said: 'Did you know her, Dad? She came to the club?'

'What? Oh, no, no.'

'She's not the kind for the club, Fay,' Margaret replied. 'That's what I mean – how could such a girl get implicated in this hellishness?'

She was saying in her downright hurtful way that you could believe anything of the Monty clientèle, including ending up shot three times in the back on a shit-heap. Ember noticed 'implicated', such a tainting word if applied to Christine, but let it go. He sipped his tea. 'Yes, just what Mummy said, Fay, dear – the mystery of it, the tragedy.'

The commentator spoke of the mud on the body and a theory that she had been moved after death. 'Police are mystified but believe the use of expensive Sokolovsky pistols might indicate a professional execution squad, possibly from London. They fear a gang connection. Police do not yet know why Mrs Tranter should have been chosen, an apparently ordinary local housewife. One suggestion is that she was shot in error, mistaken for someone else, or that she intercepted bullets meant for another person so far unidenti- fied. He or she might have moved the body. None of this would explain why Mrs Tranter was at this lonely spot at all, though.'

Fay said: 'Dad, if it's to do with gang war, will someone have to seek revenge? A terrible, undodgeable duty. You know, like that Hamlet, Prince of Denmark, on video in school.'

'Her husband is a cat and dog caterer, no prince,' Margaret replied. 'He won't be dwelling on revenge, only on his grief.'

'Right,' Ember said. He was not Prince Hamlet either, but, yes, the burden lay on him, and, yes, as definitely as when her body squashed him into the rivulet. Of course, some part of his mind yelled, Keep out of it, keep out of it! Wasn't he beyond all this kind of messy involvement now? Christ, for a long while he had felt entitled to think of himself as one of the '400'. This was Scotland Yard's target term for the select, dominant figures nationwide whose businesses had grown so successful they no longer took part in street oper- ations, but organized and profited from behind the cover of their prestige properties and a legitimate enterprise, like The Monty. At his place, The Pines, Oliphant Kenward Knapp had certainly been of the 400. Yet now, here was Ember, with at least an equivalent status moving suddenly back to very hands-on work. And a double amount of it: vengeance, plus building from ground level their commercial network. Inappropriate? Mad?

'Did she have children, Dad?' Fay asked.

'I believe the papers said so.'

'Oh, dear. I'm glad they're not at the funeral. They're not, are they?

'Somebody will be looking after them, love,' he replied.

'Whoever shot her – do they think of things like that, how upset the children would be?' Fay asked. 'Cruel.'

Yes, Chris had children, but, even if not, the revenge duty would have been just as unavoidable. He hoped he could briskly accomplish this bloody repayment, then get the firm's trading station quickly and efficiently established. As soon as it was secure, he would withdraw from day-to-day trafficking, would function only as company chairman or president, exercising a good, distant influence, and, of course, taking a founder's share of the returns. It pleased him to feel he was needed and that, even at his age, he could still give something out there: Ralph Ember had a street rating, not just the obvious boardroom mastery.

The film camera spent time on Tranter entering the church and, later, standing by Christine's grave. 'That's her husband?' Margaret cried. 'Such a blob.'

Even if Ember had not known it before, he could see Leslie would be nowhere as a man hunter. Despite all that arduous travel with the inventions, he had let himself get gross and lumbering. The seat of his morning suit trousers was a farcical acreage. An arse like that had no place above any girl, but especially not above Chris. Simply, Leslie had not deserved her. Obnoxious to think he might have put some of those scratch scars on her shoulder blades while monstrously . . . marital. Tranter had a porky face, too: plump nose with oblong nostrils. Fondness for animals meant he had to look like one? His appearance was unhelped by small-frame wire spectacles that made him seem nervy, and Ember guessed this would have been so always, not just in the stress of today.

The cameras did not enter the church, but tracked the arrival of hearse and coffin, and afterwards lurked near the interment. Behind Tranter at the grave were what must be relatives, and behind them Harpur and Iles, Iles getting what you could have believed was true regret into his thumbscrew face, unless you knew him. He had his blue Charge of the Light Brigade uniform on with staff-rank cap, and stood profiling for the camera like Prince Philip.

Ember picked up his briefcase and left to drive to the foreshore. He was armed again: people might guess Ralph Ember would come looking, determined. Before setting out, he opened his Filofax on the passenger seat to set his itinerary. He drove fast, wanting to talk to as many possible witnesses as he could before it grew late. All of his life had become a gallop, and, on the way out there now, he decided suddenly that he must arrange a year's suspension of his university course. 'Urgent personal reasons' would be enough to explain this to Big Vera, his History of Politics professor. If they knew his situation, the literature teachers there might recall the play about Prince Hamlet that Fay had mentioned, and understand the power of revenge compulsion. Had Chuck Heston ever played Hamlet? He dreaded a poor degree through lack of study. That sod Iles would never stop laughing.

He found out nothing at the farms or the houses or at the gypsy camp or the permanent caravan site. People were scared. They knew there had been a killing very close, and some of them lived in remote, unprotected spots. Their neighbours were bad enough, but now this horror, from outside. They feared any connection with what had happened, and especially a connection through someone who refused to identify himself. A mistake to wear a suit? They might take him for police or a debt collector. But what clothes could be right for a wild slab of no man's land like this? Continually he heard, 'Who wants to know?' when he asked about possible sightings of a car on 18 October. He had expected that, and did not answer, just kept on digging. The secrecy might be useless: there were a lot of folk who would recognize The Monty's proprietor.

At first he felt an enraged frustration. Christ, this was Ralph W. Ember being given the hand-off by a load of shady derelicts. But then, slowly, a kind of wondrous relief took hold: that tireless, polished instinct in him for self-preservation. Although he had done everything feasible in the search for vengeance, he could not progress. Perhaps the role was impossible. These enquiries had been thorough, relentless. He kept on until evening darkness, absolutely no skimping. And the thought sidled into his mind that maybe now he had discharged as much as he could of that grim duty. After all, there was only himself to satisfy. He had willingly, almost eagerly, imposed the burden. That meant he had the right when circumstances changed like this to offload. He could decide the task was impossible – though, obviously, if those two came after him again, he would wipe them out, not just for Christine's sake, but to make himself and the new firm secure.

He left the gypsy camp, last call in his notes. He had covered all the likely ground, collected a sheaf of rejections. Ember took the abuse and curses and threats and occasional near-violence passively, with a smile. Keep things quiet. There was nobody here with blood worth spilling. He would go back now to see the club was all right. Perhaps it had been a foolish, pointless outing, part of that more general foolish, pointless impulse towards vengeance. A distraction. He would concentrate again on the business, set it soundly on its way, then revert to his earned place among the 400 elite, and go back to his suspended place at the university. That 400 figure he loved: a joky echo of the famous 400 top socialite families in the USA. Marilyn Monroe in *Some Like It Hot* pretended to be a society girl, and so bored by always meeting 'the same 400'.

He was driving from the gypsy camp along a narrow road bordered on both sides by reens when a vehicle showing main beam lights came head-on towards him, moving fast. Impossible to get round it on this single-track, so he braked and felt at once for the Walther in his shoulder holster. The other car stopped a few inches from the Rover, its lights still blazing and blinding him. He pressed central locking for all doors. But, Christ, what use, what use? He was acting like a scared woman broken down on the hard shoulder. These were people with Sokolovskys. Did he imagine a door or window would stop them? Oh, God, God, it had been so crazy to come here. How could he have thought of himself as a cleansing avenger? Now it amazed him that he should have trekked around this blank landscape for hours, putting himself on display. He felt all the savage symptoms of panic grab him: that disabling ache across his shoulders, the sweat, the conviction that his jaw scar had opened up and any moment would shed its murky discharge over his collar and suit.

He became aware of what registered with him at first as a blissfully reassuring, domestic noise. Then, suddenly, he realized he had begun to screech in his terror, and the sound almost matched that boiling kettle's happy solo this afternoon. How far, far off that was now, its friendly call. Why couldn't he have stayed home? Why had he put himself on offer again? He gripped the Walther and waved it through 180 degrees and back, from side window to side window, staring for the buggers, but able to make out nothing. He stopped screaming and yelled, tried to yell, 'I'm armed. Keep back, you hear? Keep back.' His voice lacked meat, was all plea, no menace. From behind those lights they would see well enough that he was armed. They would see he was terrified, too. They would see that when he swung the gun one way they could quickly get to the other side and fill the Rover with .45 shells. Trapped behind the steering wheel, he was a spotlighted, unmissable target, unmissable even by these two, all chest and head.

And then he noticed the beams shift up fractionally on

his face. It must mean the two of them had left the other car and, without their weight, it had risen slightly on the suspension. He tried to stare out against the glare, forward through the windscreen, left, right. He put his own lights on to main beam. It was still nearly impossible to see anything ahead, but he thought the other car was a big Ford – a Granada or Scorpio – and he thought, thought what he had already known, that the front seats were empty.

When he had a panic, Ember would sometimes lose all strength in his legs for a while, and even in his hands and arms, but he could generally drag his brain out from under the weight of dread after a few seconds and get a crumb of sense from it. What his brain told him to do might not be possible, because of paralysis of the body, but at least he saw the options. Now, he thought, foot down and reverse away. Although the road was narrow, he could see all right through the back. And they were out of their vehicle and would not be able to chase at once, except running. He might be able to leave them. He had not switched off the engine. His hands were fairly steady, good enough to hold the Walther and able to release the handbrake and move the gear lever. His legs, feet – shit, oh, shit, he could not get them to the pedals, that terrible numbness. This was for the moment, only for the moment, he knew. It would go, but not soon enough.

Suddenly, he was aware of a face at the driver's window. He had the pistol already pointing there. This was where his brain told him to expect them. They would want to stop him driving, backwards or ahead – ahead to shove their car out of the way. He raised the Walther to the face and knew he had to fire at once, because they would not wait, not when they had him so available on a deserted road and there was a bad error to correct. Astonished, he saw the face break into outright terror, as if it had never looked down the neck of a gun before and did not know what to do. He had not hung about memorizing the features of those two gunmen, but he knew this was neither of them. Replacements after the others' mistake?

No. No. He recognized the piggy features and the wire glasses, the gross neck. Leslie Tranter threw up an arm to protect his head and Ember saw a swirl of blacker blackness against the blackness of the night. It was Tranter's sleeve. Funeral gear still. In his fright, Tranter pulled away violently from the window, that face receding into the dark, like a pause in a child's nightmare. Ember lost him. Again, the blackness on the blackness. Above the noise of his engine and through the closed window he thought he heard a cry and then another sound, an impact of some sort, and then another cry, but shorter, maybe stifled. He waited, but Tranter did not come back.

Ember sat unmoving, the gun still unfired in his hand, resting on his lap now. Crazily, he felt ashamed of it. To point an automatic at someone like Leslie seemed all wrong, crude, brutal. Tranter was from a different life. More than just pointing. The trigger had been half back. God, what would Chris have thought if he had killed Tranter, if she could have thought at all now? You take someone's wife, get her murdered instead of yourself, and then almost shoot the grieving widower! Ember, sitting in that glare, imagined himself on display as something eternally base. He had to escape this light. His legs and feet were answering. He could have backed away from the Ford. He could have banged forward and at least knocked the bugger's headlights out, possibly pushed the car from the road and exited.

Instead, he switched off, doused his own lights and left the Rover, to see what had happened to Tranter. Before moving, he replaced the Walther in its holster. For half a second on the road he supported himself against the car with one hand, still not completely sure his legs could do the job. The Ford's engine was running, but above this he heard distressed sounds from the water-filled reen, and stepped carefully towards it. Put off balance by his fright, Tranter must have slipped in. Soaked and weed-covered, he was trying to drag himself out now like some wounded walrus, crawling, grunting and coughing water. Ember knew this experience and bent down and offered a hand. With Tranter, at least, he could be a lifeline, not with Chris. Tranter lifted his head laboriously to see where the hand came from. He still had his wire glasses on and when his eyes found Ember he groaned and slid a few inches back down the slippery bank. The last time he saw Ember's hand it had been aiming the Walther.

'It's all right, sir,' Ember said.

Tranter, lying in the mud, thought about it. His legs were still submerged up to the thighs, green water lapping at the interminable seat of his striped trousers. Then he slowly lifted his arm and took Ember's hand. Ember felt the great, sodden weight drag at him. One or other of this fucking family might drown him. He widened his legs for better purchase and pulled. Tranter was doing what he could to help himself as well, pawing at the bank with his other fingers and trying for toe holes to push against. He began to move up and away from the water. Ember experienced a great rush of joy. Here was someone he could save. He was not disgusting, not selfish or forever ready to run. After a few moments, Tranter was able to stand. They both brushed some of the greenery and dirt from him. 'You're wet through,' Ember said. 'You should get into the car and turn your heater up.'

'Yes. *My* car. We mustn't mess up yours.' They climbed into the Granada estate, Tranter behind the wheel. He switched off the lights but kept his engine going, for the heater. There were what looked like half a dozen plastic food dispensers for animals on the back seat. 'Excuse me, but who are you?' Tranter asked. His voice was hard, although he stammered a little from the cold. He smelled dank. The car grew fiercely hot. Soon, he would steam.

'This was a weird situation – the two cars, head-on like that,' Ember replied.

'I knew your car. I've trailed it, you. Then got ahead.'

'Oh?'

'I had heard of your car from – heard of your car, well, from probably lovers in vehicles up near the sea wall. This car was seen there on 18 October in the night. Together with a man rolling naked in the long grass, alone, frantically. This strangeness made them take the number.'

Panicking Ralph

'This car?'

Tranter said: 'And then I come down here today and spot the same car seeming to tour around. Well, I had to speak. So, the confrontation.'

'That's certainly what it was,' Ember replied.

'But a gun.'

'Gun?'

'I saw a gun,' Tranter said.

'Where?'

'You, in the car.'

'This is altogether some tale,' Ember replied, wagging his head, mystified.

Tranter turned his crazy bulk towards him and said: 'Is it?' The face looked formidable suddenly, not piggy and comical, the neck as wide as Tyson's.

Ember said: 'Oh, through the steamed-up window, my hand, raised to you in a greeting, might appear like a gun. A handgun? Shotgun?'

'Look, why the hell are you here?' Tranter replied. He was shouting.

'I don't object to your aggressive tone, sir. You're clearly upset about something. I had some business calls this way.'

'But with a gun?'

'Was that what frightened you, imagining a gun? Made you lose your footing? Oh, dear.' Ember wanted to be off this road and gone. Yet he felt he owed Tranter some politeness, and not just for Christine's sake.

'My wife died near here. Was killed, murdered. No mercy.

But I'm telling you something you know, yes? Oh, yes, I think so.'

'My God. Yes, of course, I've read of this. Terrible. This would be a Mrs Tranter?'

'I came straight from the funeral.'

'Yes. On TV. A stain on the town. Well, condolences, obviously.'

'This was a wonderful, lovely woman.'

'I've seen pictures. But why come here? Perhaps to visit the very spot? I do understand.'

'I want to know what happened. I want to find whoever did it. Where else do I look?'

'Yet this is something for the police, surely, Mr Tranter. So distressing for you.'

'And your car here on that date. Rolling in the grass, you see. Then, a gun. Who are you?' He thumped the steering wheel with his fat fist. 'Shall I tell you who you are, you evil sod? I think you're fucking Penelope D.'

Ember said: 'You're very upset, Mr Tranter. That's inevitable. I don't know any Penelope, let alone *D*, to fuck or otherwise.'

'That would be like you, I know it, know it, some hatched name of that sort. And the *D* supposed to be for fullness, authenticity. People of your sort, expert in deceit.' He pushed the big, wet, stinking body at Ember again, and Tranter's hands came up as if about to grab him at the neck. Ember wanted to go for the Walther, but that could not be. It did not exist. Christ, though, for Ralph W. Ember to be manhandled, maybe hurt or worse, by some Bunter dog and cat man.

'I really would leave it all to the police,' Ember said.

'Police. Who trusts them? Do they care?'

'Some strange rumours about, I must say.'

'Rumours, nothing. Your damn car at the seawall.'

'I don't think so. A joker who knows I make calls around here told you that.'

'Rolling in the grass.'

'What's that supposed to be about?' Ember asked. 'And naked? Well!'

'You tell me.'

'More jokes. It's heartless of them, in the circumstances.'

'My wife was shot. When I see a gun—'

'The police say a team from outside, don't they?'

Tranter grabbed at Ember's shoulders with both huge hands. 'You were having my wife, my Christine? Some quarrel between you, bastard? Who are you? You think you've got a right to send pseudonym roses?'

'Let go!' Ember replied. It outraged him to hear Tranter speak of her as *his* Christine. 'You're overwrought. But you must get control. Didn't I save you from the reen, you fat prat?'

'Tell me, tell me,' Tranter yelled. 'All of it.' The grip strengthened.

Ember bent low inside those heavy arms and cracked down mildly twice on Tranter's nose with his forehead. Tranter yelled, let go and clutched at his face. Ember switched off the Ford's engine, pulled the keys from the ignition and opened the passenger door. 'It bleeds but isn' broken, Mr Tranter,' he said. 'Get home and have a hot bath

93

He backed his Rover to the first turning space and drove away. In the town, he looked out for a taxi rank, parked some distance off, then walked to it. The Rover's number was a liability. He gave good directions and a tenner to one of the drivers, and sent him with the keys to Tranter. Then he continued to The Monty and made sure his staff had had no problems tonight.

14

Harpur wrote:

Dear ACC,

This letter should never reach you. If it does, it will be because I am in bad trouble, or worse. Please act on my behalf in your gifted fashion, sir. A lifeline, if that is still appropriate.

I send the letter via a dear undergraduate girl called Denise, whom kindly keep your fucking eyes, hands and everything else off, regardless of what condition I am in by now, and whether or not I am ever going to see her again. She deserves a contented, decent and successful future, which clearly means you don't figure. She is a messenger only, and may well be weak with grief if this message has to be delivered. BUT DO NOT COMFORT HER, IN YOUR GROSS FASHION, SIR. I hope by the time you've read this far she has, in fact, gone, leaving no address or contact number. Those are her instructions, given verbally by me. I hope she has not read this material, but you being you will doubt this, and you could be right, she being she.

Two (2) pages of script follow, making three (3) in total.

At first, Harpur had thought he would write to the chief. Then he thought, no, for God's sake, he would not write at all. To write was more than unprofessional – dangerous, juvenile. Then he thought he would write to Iles. But Iles might be in on it, in on what Harpur wanted to write about.

Any point opening up to him? Desmond Iles looked after Desmond Iles. Whatever interfered with this prime, supremely caring relationship Iles destroyed. Christ, he had destroyed *people* on that account, let alone a letter.

By contrast, the chief was honest, wholesome, reliable, and had an inspiring, unselfish wish for general good. This last was another powerful reason for sending the letter to him, not Iles. What Harpur intended to do, and what he intended outlining in the letter, arose from a wish to aid the chief's wide mission: that purifying of their patch, and perhaps infinitely beyond. Harpur could be certain that Lane would instantly understand his motives for taking such risks, and sympathize.

And so Harpur had decided to write to Iles. Wholesomeness, understanding, sympathy were lightweight. He needed someone capable. He would not ask capable of what. There had to be a 60–40 possibility Iles was not crooked. Oh, no, no, better than that, much better. Say 62–38. And, if he was not crooked – i.e., confidential security consultant to a drugs syndicate at partner level – there must be at least a 50–50 hope he would do what was right with the letter. The mathematics came out, then, at 50 per cent of 62 per cent: 31 per cent, which in police work was a very fair chance.

Harpur had worried about how to address him. Although he had worked with Iles for years, he found he could not call him Desmond in writing. He also baulked at 'Mr'. But 'Dear Iles' would sound insubordinate, and he did not want to alienate him from the first words. His intervention might be crucial. Iles was easily alienated. Iles was more or less universally and chronically alienated.

Harpur glanced around Denise's flat in the student block at Jonson Court. 'Would you have somewhere reasonably safe, love?' he asked.

'Like?'

'If I wanted you to keep something for me.'

'Like?'

Possibly there were more shambolic rooms in the block, but this was the only one he occasionally slept in, so far. She was proud of the place, and always referred to it as 'Jonson Court, without an *h*.' Apparently, every fool knew that in literature there was this Jonson and another one with. Sometimes, when he felt like being a full red-neck cop, he told her she was an encyclopedia, as well as a fine fuck. 'This would be a letter,' he said.

She sat up in the bed, her face wide open, and scared, like a child's. 'What do you mean? Is this some "If I should die" thing?'

'Not a letter to you, love.' He tried to draw her back down into the bed, but she resisted.

'I know that,' she said. 'This is a To Whom It May Concern job, in case you go under.'

'Absurd. It's a letter to Iles, to cover me.'

'Cover you with what? A pall?' She looked tearful. 'Who leaves letters? Why else? How do you address someone like Iles, anyway?'

She was often unbelievably intuitive, spotted problems or chances without having been given even a hint. Harpur had wondered about 'Dear Assistant Chief', spelled full out, from respect. But this would alienate him, also. The word 'assistant' was filthy hell to Iles. People wishing to rack him deliberately emphasized those arse-crawling *S*'s in 'assistant'. He knew he should have been a chief years ago, and believed only some topmost corrupt conspiracy stopped him. Barton, Lane's predecessor, had occasionally allowed Iles to act as deputy and call himself that. Lane would never have it, even though the actual deputy, Missay-Noaks, was still seconded to the Third World, advising somewhere on perfecting a police force. 'Assistant?' Iles would occasionally scream. 'What am I, Marky Lane's gentleman in waiting?' Yes, he was waiting. Well, 'Dear ACC' would have to do.

'Where would you keep the letter, Denise?' he asked. 'I don't want some cleaning lady accidentally unearthing it. But perhaps she's on a long sabbatical, is she?'

'Don't be so damn rude. I'm going to give this place a real tidy up any day now.' She mopped her face with his hair. 'Listen, Col, I'm nineteen, too young for this. I'm not your bloody executor.'

'Just carry it to him, in certain very unlikely circum-stances. Hand it to Iles personally, and then get out, immediately. He'll want to stroke your body and rub away pain, beginning at quite neutral areas.'

'What pain?'

'I'd ask someone else, only—'

'No, I'd hate that.' She lay down again and put her face against his shoulder. Wet lashes brushed his skin, like being antiseptic-painted, pre-jab.

'Not hidden in some book,' he said. 'People forget which. Or they lend it.'

'This is very confidential, then?' she said.

'It's a briefing. For getting me out of trouble, not funeral instructions.'

'So, what are you going to do? Risk, yes? If there's possible trouble, it's risk. One kind of risk can bring all kinds of other risks.' She banged at the word like a boxer with a punch ball.

'It's cards on the table.'

'Oh, Jesus,' she said. 'A *mot*. Which table? The autopsy table?'

'Clearly, Denise, you wouldn't read it, would you?' Harpur replied. 'I mean now or at any later stage.'

'I've got your life in a fucking envelope and I don't open it?'

'Maybe hide it behind one of your pictures,' Harpur replied.

'Like that money in *The Grifters*.'

'What's that?'

'Anjelica Huston.'

'OK. Think of somewhere else.'

'I've got an indexed box file, for course notes.'

'That'll do. Put it under my name. It's Harpur, with an *H*, not the other one. In my jacket pocket.'

She left the bed and it was a treat to watch her walk naked to his clothes, bring out the letter and then cross the room to her file. It was the businesslike way she moved and acted. Mostly, he considered her body as gloriously sexual and gloriously lovable, and now, here she was, or it was, trudging about the place, being busy, handling stationery, stepping with regular skill around a couple of unwashed dinner plates on the floor. One of these he thought had been there last time he visited. He found the ordinariness of what she did brilliantly exciting. She sat down with the box file on her lap and leaned over it picking the index letter, her breasts neat and considerable, dark hair hanging forward and screening half her face. Harpur hated coming to her flat, because of the risk of being seen and the squalor, but there would occasionally be moments like this, when it was as if they had a real, routine life together, naked or dressed, just workaday, and he enjoyed that. She liked him to come here now and then, perhaps for the same reason, perhaps because it still unnerved her to go to his house, although by now he was an established widower.

'It's double-sealed,' she said. 'Bloody heavy-duty Sellotape.'

'What distinguished names am I filed there with? Homer? Hemingway?'

'A recipe for hot and sour soup,' she said, 'and some ancient pop paper articles on Harvey and the Wallbangers.'

When she came back to the single bed, Denise lay close to him and pushed the duvet down to uncover Harpur almost to the waist. She put her head on his chest and began to stroke his neck, shoulders and arms, gazing at his skin. He thought he knew what she was doing, because now and then he had done the same to her. She was imagining him damaged, broken up, in some way that she thought the letter might explain. Although no longer crying, she looked wholeheartedly miserable. Once or twice Denise had been menaced by people wanting to get at Harpur, and he had tried to think then – and had tried *not* to think – had considered what might happen to her body in a reprisal raid. He would stare at Denise just like this. Well, they hadn't reached her and wouldn't now. Nobody could know she was holding the letter. Nobody could know the letter existed. Senior policemen did not set down their intentions like that. It was culpable idiocy.

'How will I know when to deliver it?' she asked.

'Oh, you'll know. I heard you were bright.'

'Well, obviously, if you were killed,' she said, and did not even sniff now.

'Right.'

'Or arrested?'

'That kind of thing. It would make the Press.'

'Iles could put it all right?'

'He might. More than anyone.'

'Oh, I like the sound of him,' she said.

'Don't.'

She kissed his elbow a couple of times. This did not really get through to Harpur. 'Obviously, Col, in my head I'll be writing my own scenarios, doing versions of what's in the envelope. I could get it right by fluke.'

'I don't think so.'

'It's not to do with that crooked lad, maybe an informant, who came to your house once, trying for some deal, when I was there?'

'Which crooked lad would that be, Denise?' Yes, she was a clever girl, this one. Mucky but bright. It frightened him sometimes. She might leave him behind. 'Scenario? A purple word for what's actually in there, believe me, love. Only a bit of slightly out-of-the-way police business that I wouldn't want publicized just now.'

'That right?'

Well, more or less right. All the same, he felt glad she was filing it away still sealed and unread. Inside its envelope the letter said:

I was approached some months ago by Keith Vine, a tipster we have used, and whom you'll know of, sir, enquiring whether the two of us would like to be associated with a business syndicate he and a partner were creating. The invitation went like this: 'I wondered if you and Mr Iles would consider taking an interest in another little team.' He had heard, you see, rumours that the two of us were involved with a collapsed syndicate which had been seeking to take over the Oliphant Kenward Knapp conglom. Absurd, of course, as you'd be the first to state, sir, but this was what he believed. Naturally I ignored his proposal.

However, in view of the chief's brave wish to break the whole drugs culture before it can recover from Kenward's death, it now seems to me that it might be useful to infiltrate one of the current competing syndicates and use the information gained to destroy this syndicate from within. And perhaps destroy others through the use of knowledge acquired as a supposed member of the trade. I consider that the murder of Mrs Christine Tranter – who was linked, as you are aware, to Ralph Ember – might become explicable when I have such trade knowledge. I fear that if this crime is not quickly solved we might see more bloodshed, the very reverse of what the chief aims for. I have reason to believe that Leslie Tranter is engaged in a vengeance mission and has been seeking information on the killer(s).

Accordingly, it is my intention, sir, to create circumstances in which Keith Vine might repeat his offer. If he does, I shall pretend to accept. Possibly his syndicate and its trade are so well established by now that he no longer feels any need of police participation. Why waste a share of assured profits on an extra, unnecessary partner? Were this the case, my plan would have been dead from the start, since I'm sure he would suspect a trap if I, rather than be, initiated an approach. I have to wait for him to ask me again. And, ACC, the fact that you are reading this letter indicates he did, in fact, reinvite me.

I act alone in this because I know that, at your rank, and with your sterling views on probity, you could have no part of such an enterprise. You, sir, all credit to you, would not compromise yourself, not even for such a 'good' purpose. Vine's, and his partner's, or partners', motive for attempting to recruit police officers is, of course, to ensure no prosecutions of their business. Until I have collected all possible information on their syndicate and on the trade here generally, I shall afford them this protection.

They will naturally pay me. I would expect the sums to be large. They will understand that it would be foolish and counter-productive for me to spend ostentatiously, but they will probably expect to see me indulge in a few discreet luxuries, and for the sake of my cover I shall do this. Perhaps you will have noticed some improvement in my wardrobe, though not to your level, of course.

I write, sir, because, as with any implant operation, things can go wrong. Especially they can go wrong when the operation is unsanctioned by the Force and entirely secret. By taking money, spending some of it and preventing prosecutions, I will put myself into a highly exposed position, should my apparent involvement ever become known. I put my plans before you in this postdated manner, so that, should I find myself accused of corruption, you might be able to counter these charges, if – and this should go without saying, sir – it suits your personal book at that time. Please do nothing painfully or fatally selfless. Your features, though distinctive to a fault, are not of *kamikaze* cast.

There is also another kind of risk. We have seen the savagery with which those in this trade guard themselves and their interests. As you know, we lost one undercover officer, Raymond Street, some time ago. And more recently, for safety considerations, we had to withdraw another, Naomi Anstruther, when she seemed rumbled. If I am violently prevented from completing my trawl for information, this letter should indicate the direction that further enquiries might take, and I know you will continue them, again as long as your private interests are not endangered, naturally.

C.H.

Gazing miserably for a final moment at the envelope's stout seal before shutting her box file Denise said: 'All right, so I'm excluded from some of your most important thoughts. Yet, in a way, to keep this letter makes me proud. I would never read it, obviously, since this is your declared and determined wish. Yet I'm the only one you can trust, like Lorre giving the letters of transit to Bogart for safe keeping in *Casablanca*. That shows you really think a lot of me, Col.'

'You knew that.'

'Well, yes. But I see you looking at the mess, the dirty clothes and unwashed plates, nose wrinkling, making comments, and I suppose you wonder, What kind of sleazy young cow is this?'

'Yes.'

'Making comparisons with the way your wife used to run things.'

'Yes.'

'But then I think of the bed sheets in your place. In their now state, I mean – widowerhood state.'

'And I'm glad you don't care about conditions here, Denise – I mean, the way you don't go fussily house-proud and tidy up just because I'm coming. That one plate and the brown sauce line I'm fond of by now. It's geography.'

'Or you, not changing the sheets,' she replied. 'No bumptious hygiene.'

'I always see my life as soiled,' Harpur said.

'It could be a strength – recognizing it, I mean, even so late in life.'

'Just being soiled is a strength itself, sometimes,' Harpur said. 'One is of the world.'

'Is this what the letter's about? And Iles – is *he* soiled?'

'Don't ask him questions like that, or any at all. Hand it over. Leave.'

'Will I be able to visit you?'

'Where?

'Jail.'

'When you see Iles, you could wear some really shapeless outfit, rubbishy, and maybe neglect the deodorant and black a couple of teeth. Listen, Denise, if he gets to fancy you he'll leave me there to waste away, out of the running. This man is a colleague.'

15

As a treat, Keith Vine took his girlfriend, Rebecca, out to see the house where Oliphant Kenward Knapp used to live. This property, The Pines, would say something helpful to Becky about the kind of wealth and prime status that a sweetly run business could bring. Occasionally she needed a nice tonic. Pregnancy made her irritable, even low: he did not understand this, when she was carrying the future. He would say to her, 'Come on Beck, cheer up, girl, you've got the twenty-first century in there!' Well, that was easy for a man, no popping belly button! You had to be considerate to them, and he knew she would enjoy The Pines, in its genuine country setting out Longdean way. Beck loved style and had quite a bit of taste, even. On one side of the house, there was a long first floor room, called The Gallery. This was bound to have grand views over a great rural area if you liked all that, and, being on the west, must catch every bit of afternoon and evening sunshine that was going.

'I bet even you never saw a house with its own private gallery before, Beck,' he said. 'Kenward could loll there in jodhpurs among paintings and busts and think of wonderful projects.' In the last few years of his life, Kenward had definitely made it to what was known as 'the 400'. Keith Vine's ambition was to be among that number. This would mean a brilliantly decent start in life for the baby. Keith's father used to tell him to make sure he was a good provider, and that instruction he still regarded as holy, no less.

They drove past The Pines. It would be stupid to stop, but he had been told about a good high ground spot where you could get a full view. A spread of gardens and a paddock lay around the property. In fact, Kenward had been shot dead on an outlying part of his own land, although the grounds and house were protected by Alsatians on the loose. Apparently they had been crossbowed in advance. In the 400 you were supposed to have moved above violence, and should definitely not get wasted on your own doorstep among dead dogs. Kenward had let himself down.

Becky stared out. 'He must have spent a fortune just on the fences.'

'He'd heard county families always have a wall round. Kenward was a great one for privacy.'

'Didn't keep the bullets out.'

'He was on the wrong side of it. Anyway, the fence spoils our view of the place,' Keith replied. 'Why I'm going up the hill.' Since Kenward died, the house stayed empty. It belonged to his schoolboy son now. Executors were asking £360,000 – £45,000 up on what Kenward was known to have paid when prices hit bottom. The boy boarded at a slick school, and they would need something for the fees.

The car climbed a twisting lane behind the house. Vine could not risk asking the agents for a look around inside, although he would have loved it. Walking through those rooms he might have felt the future had arrived. But many agents were Masons and belonged to select clubs in town, and there could be a word dropped to Desmond Iles at a social evening. Never send signals when big funds move your way. Folk like Harpur and Iles would want to know where from. Folk like Harpur and Iles might want a share, even though Harpur had turned down a discreet join-us invitation that night not long ago at his scruffy old house in Arthur Street. Harpur's student bird came down while they were talking, all dewy from the bedroom and alight with sex, for a stare at the late-night visitor. Maybe Harpur had refused the offer because he did not want her to see him doing deals. Or maybe he hung back as a bargaining ploy. Police were devious, and top police even more. How they got there.

But Harpur was hard to know. Some definitely believed, regardless, that he did not take. Well, he still lived down there in that crummy street, kids at a comp, though this could be just cover, more deviousness. As a matter of fact, Kenward had had a place near him for a while, and then, suddenly, The Pines. This was how things went in private enterprise, but not in the police, not if police were straight. Anyway, Harpur would never, never, get another business invite from Keith Vine. Why the hell should he? No entitlement. The firm was up and running without him. If he came begging for a way in now, Vine would just give him the old polite brick wall. This postman only knocked once.

As soon as he parked and they could gaze down, Keith saw the visit was a bright success. Although he had known it would be, Becky's excitement was so huge it really thrilled him. Her lovely face showed such delight. At first her eyes sped over the house and grounds, taking it all in, and she gave little squeaks of pleasure. Then she went back to where she had started and looked at everything again, but now much more slowly, really appreciating and noting features. He loved this girl, the way she could blaze suddenly and forget her cares.

'Oh, that must be a fountain!' she cried.

It was not working now, but yes. The house had been built around a grass and paved quadrangle, with the fountain in the middle as a true feature. In summer, when the gallery might get hot and flies banging the glass, Kenward most likely brought a lounger out there and listened to the cool, gentle music of the water while he thought out great new moves peacefully. 'Modern and yet distinguished,' Becky said, still enjoying the house. 'Proportions.'

'Kenward was always one for that, proportions. Big for an ordinary family, and yet we'd need a nursery, a study–office, guest rooms – it's surprising how people get used to the space.'

'Library, even. A sewing room.'

'Well, I don't want any girl of mine sewing, Beck. Just replace. Except nice ornamental work, I mean – samplers.' They would probably drop to £300,000, but Keith was nowhere near that kind of money yet, not this year, and the trip was for sightseeing only. Mortgages were difficult in his kind of work. By the time he had the cash, The Pines might be sold. But there would be other worthwhile houses. In any case, although Becky had a soft spot for Nature and countryside all around, Keith did not think much of it himself. He played along, that's all. Nature didn't give a shit. It would grow everywhere if you did not fight, smothering property and civilization as Keith knew it, so much damn sap, and all so soundlessly.

'How long did he live here?' she asked.

It could not have been long. Maybe not much more than a year. He said: 'Oh, quite a while. He was known to love it, to have as it were come home.'

'Tragedy to be executed like that.'

Tragedy, opportunity. But at once he saw she might swoop down off her cheery perch to sadness again. There were times when Becky yearned to quit this whole region, even this country. Becky had education, and she liked the idea of herself under a big straw hat in the South of France, full of relaxation and getting the child bilingual. She thought things were growing perilous here, and that Keith had picked up rough business enemies. It would not help now if she started pondering about Kenward, knocked over at the very moment he seemed so beautifully established, and after an evening out at one of his clever charity functions. 'Let's get closer, shall we, Beck?' He had been determined to stay well back, but adapt, adapt. 'Maybe have an ogle through the windows. No dogs about now.' Keep her mind off Kenward and on the property and the grounds and pretty little fountain.

They went down. The big gates, always closed and electronically locked in Kenward's day, stood wide, and Keith drove in and parked. This spot would be only thirty or forty metres from where Kenward was shot. But because he failed to take care of himself, it did not mean Keith Vine could not take care of *him*self and of his dear ones. Sometimes Becky seemed to doubt that, although he had shown her the damn useful automatic pistol he carried these days whenever there was the smallest smell of trouble. Her attitude then would anger Vine. Even though Beck was bright and often helped him with major thinking, there would come times when he felt like telling her to go, bugger off alone to France or wherever she liked, if she wanted to. But she would not be alone, would she? The baby was coming, and to be split from his child would kill him. That child was continuity.

They left the car and walked slowly right around the house, staring in where they could. Some windows had curtains across. But the kitchen was on view and great, done in a kind of old farmhouse style. The units seemed of authentic tree wood, and a big, mock-ancient dresser for crockery took up one wall. It looked as if all the movable furniture and carpets had gone.

Becky's voice shook a bit with passion: 'I'd love to see the main rooms.' These had the curtains over.

'I'll find a way in,' Keith replied. Mad, obviously, but you had to go with their enthusiasms up to a point.

Then, of course, she chickens. 'Oh, Keith, but do you think there'll be alarms?'

'I doubt it, now. There's nothing inside to steal.'

'But vandalism.'

'No alarms.' As if Oliphant Kenward Knapp could have risked it. Alarms brought police and neighbours. Would he want law and outsiders nosing among the sort of commodities and loot he used to keep here? Keith asked Becky to wait at the side of the house, and went quickly to the rear. Normally, when he entered a property he left no sign. This was a basic skill, and he despised crude work. But although Kenward would not have alarms, he certainly *would* have the best locks, and you could not whistle them open. No time for perfection today. Keith broke a window, waited for a moment just in case the executors had subsequently put alarms in, then knocked out the rest of the glass and climbed through. He would have liked to welcome Becky properly at the front door, but, as he expected, this was deadlocked and could not be opened from inside without the key. The kitchen door leading to one side of the quadrangle was on bolts, though, and he opened that and called her in. She was beaming, not a thought about the hazards. This he loved her for, too.

They went slowly all over the house. The rooms and walls were empty except for curtains here and there downstairs, but the place still looked and felt really fine – everything just right for sale, the decor perfect, ceilings handsome and high and no trace of bloodstains outside.

They stood near the closed curtains in one of the big downstairs front rooms, and Keith opened them a few inches so there was a little more light to show the fine woodblock floor and a huge cement-as-stone fireplace.

'I would feel so at home here,' Becky said, and again he heard passion.

'I know it.' He wondered if she wanted to make love on this rich, yellow-brown floor. Women could be like that. It was something they picked up from modern books. The idea seemed to be that by having it off unofficially in a big pricey residence, you took a sort of possession of it, and had a bare-arsed laugh on the owners. One girlfriend had made him fast-fuck on apparently a Regency sideboard in a Northumbrian stately home, while the rest of the tour party and guide did the cellars. He moved towards Becky and put his arm gently around her shoulders. She was big now, but he did not mind at all.

'Yes, I'd feel at home, but vulnerable, very vulnerable,' she said. She stepped away from him to the window and looked out of the small gap. 'Where was he killed?' she asked.

'Close.' He tried to pull the curtains together, and draw her back towards the centre of the room. Screwing got rid of so many niggles for the time being.

'No,' she said, putting her hand on the heavy material. 'It's a grand view. But didn't he have partners, I mean, someone who might have helped scare off the opposition?'

'Well, Kenward would have a driver–guard, I expect.'

'But partners? Someone close. Depending on each other, so they'd be a strong unit? To deter. To aid.'

'He did it all alone.' Keith made a small circle with his hand, bringing in the grounds and the house, and trying to include the former furniture and pictures and the horses in the stables. It was like saying that if Kenward had shared profits he would have been unable to afford The Pines.

'What I mean – vulnerable,' Becky replied. 'No back-up,

you see, so he's blasted in sight of home. What use such a place then?'

This was that other, brainy, unhopeful voice she would use occasionally. Becky was a wonderful girl, but at times she did seem a bit fond of suffering and misery. Although he and her friends tried to help, she was not always grateful – like so in love with her wounds she forgot the stretcher-bearers.

'We ought to close the curtains now,' he said. 'The gap could be noticed.' She still did not move, though, and he saw there would be no invaders' celebration on the floor in front of the big, bogus fireplace. 'Of course, I'm not solo like Kenward myself, Beck, but into a really sound partnership. We look after each other.'

'The famous Stanfield.'

'He knows the scene.'

'Well, I hope so. I do. Nobody else? Maybe more weighty. More influential where it counts.'

It was true Stan could be a worry. Impossible to find out what was in his past, except – so he told everyone – that fucking painter. Yarns around said there had been some kind of very bitter disaster in France. Why had he needed to run to France at all? Were there enemies about, here or over the Channel, who might still bring hazard? And then, Keith wondered about the woman shot on the foreshore, probably by mistake. The rumour on this was London killers had been hired to ease a business path for someone. That would be just like Stanfield's big-deal secretive way, subcontracting in the metropolis without telling Vine. Stan had these grand connections everywhere, grand connections with expensive weaponry, who could foul up, though, by the look. If Stan had paid for that, it could start more trouble, wholly unsuitable for a good commercial atmosphere.

'Do you think we'll ever have such a place as this, Keith?'

'Would you like that, Beck?'

'Oh, need you ask? The scope. Ponies. Babe could be riding before she/he walks.'

'Better than France?

'Well—'

'Yes. Wonderful. I think I can do it,' he told her.

She was still looking out at the grounds, but said over her shoulder, sort of matter-of-fact: 'You do need someone else in your business, Keith. I mean, in addition. I believe in you, Keith. Aren't I still here – and not in France? When I say vulnerable— Look, my only point is, this kind of house, this kind of style, can make other people angry. Envy. Thus, the late Kenward.'

'I expect so.'

'Why a really good, strong alliance is needed. OK, Stanfield is fine, as you tell it. But is he enough? Keith, love, take time to build a really solid team. What would be crazy is for you to think you *must* have a house like this, a style like this, and you must have it fast – must rush so much you neglect to recruit the right support. You might leave yourself, ourselves, open. Thus, again, what happened to the late Kenward, if you ask me. OK, we'd both like babe to have it all early, but she/he isn't even here yet. If we stay in this country, Keith – and to get a gorgeous place like this, well, yes, it's a real temptation to stay, I admit it – but if we stay, we do every step with real care. Protect ourselves. Above all, protect yourself. Build that grand team, no matter how long it takes.'

This was the thing about Becky – she could sink low and gloomy, but she had a brain that really worked at the issues, and when she saw a great chance she would decide it should be taken, and she would spot how to take it. Naturally, she could not know the details, but the wider planning she was wondrous at. Listening to her and, as usual, pretty convinced by her, Keith thought it might be an idea after all to make another offer to Harpur. That was the quickest way to the protection she mentioned. The approach to him would be very tactful. When inviting, you used a style that could mean anything or nothing at all, but once they took the first bit of salary you had them. Everyone knew that netting top police brought perfect security and power.

Becky backed away from the curtains now. 'Do you know what I'd like to do?' she said.

'What?'

'Fuck.'

'When?' he cried with a laugh.

'Now.'

'What, here, Beck? You mean here?'

'On the floor.' She had begun taking her clothes off.

'My God, Beck,' he replied. He started to undress himself, real tearaway pace, for enthusiasm. You had to.

'It will make me feel we own it already, bare-arsing on their blocks.'

'Yes? Yes. How do you think up these great, fierce ideas, Beck?'

16

Ember could always tell when someone in The Monty wanted a close word with him. *Talk to me, Ralph, listen to me, Ralph. Save me, Ralph. Bail my brother, lover, husband, father, mother, priest, Ralph.* You learned to read the signs. Just a basic, club owner's skill. Even a responsibility. Another. About 1 a.m. Beau Derek came in alone, eyes frantic, and went to sit solitary, up in a darkish corner of the club, away from the bar and pool tables, idiot, the shadows hugging him supposed to be discretion, but like a declaration of intent. He was on rum, doubles, and began seeing them off fast: nerves, probably. When he came to the bar for his fourth he said, 'Got a minute, Ralph?', those almost likeable, slipshod features having slipped even further now, because of booze.

'Some other table,' Ember replied. 'It's like a conspiracy where you are. Act open.'

'What? Oh, yes, I see. Sorry, Ralph.' The drink gave throaty grandeur to his voice, made even the apology sound magnificent, like Lord Carrington in Bosnia years ago. Swaying a bit, he walked to a table under the big, framed photograph of that troublesome early 1990s Monty outing to Paris. Obviously, Beau was only Beau, a bright artisan, but Ember's rule had always been, Listen to anyone, even to nobodies, because occasionally nobodies knew something, maybe by accident, maybe because nobodies had eyes and ears, too. After all, Beau used to be close to the great Stanley Stanfield.

The club would shut in an hour or so, and business began to slacken. Ember went out from behind the bar to clear up. He worked his way slowly towards Beau's table, and when he reached it sat down as though for a casual chat, still with a handful of dirty glasses.

'Ralph, I'd like to help you,' Beau said in the same bigtime voice. Then he glanced about and whispered it: 'Like to help you, Ralph.'

Here's a turn-round, like a beggar offering you a quid. 'This is fine of you, Beau, but—'

'What the hell help can some jerk like Beau Derek give me is what you're thinking, yes? I see it in your face.'

'We can all do with help at some time.'

Beau looked down at his hands, interlaced on the table and shaking. The fingers were podgy and gnarled, and you would never think he could persuade safes. 'Listen, Ralph, you heard about Stan Stanfield?' He stayed bent over his hands. This was grief.

'Bit of a break-up between you two?' Ember replied very gently. 'That came as some shock. All those good years.'

'Right, all those good years,' Beau whispered. He took a hard pull at his rum. Ember turned and signalled to the barman for another and some armagnac for himself. 'We had a great thing going, Stan and me.' Said like this, still in the throbbing whisper, it sounded like more than a business relationship, but probably no.

'He's paired with some kid. That's the tale,' Ember said.

For a second or two Beau snarled: 'Well, you know this kid, Ralph. No need for tact. Seen them in here together, have you?'

'This is Keith Vine? Millenium man.'

'They've been here together?'

'Once or twice.' Christ, but it was like giving evidence in an old-fashioned divorce. Beau had lifted his head now, the rough little ramshackle face high pink from the rum, and sharp in places with tragedy.

Beau said: 'This is where that kid would look for him, supposed to be casual, before they set things up. Making the approaches, Ralphy. Just blatant.' Although half pissed and dazed by sadness, Beau spotted his mistake. 'I mean, Ralph,' he said.

'Some private talking, yes,' Ember replied.

'Cutting Beau out,' he said. 'I'm regarded as unsuitable. Suddenly. Yes, after all those good years. Like obsolete, Ralph.' There the voice broke up to almost a scream.

'I heard a whisper,' Ember replied. Beau's name was Derek something, and a joker had put the Beau in front of it one night, echoing a film actress, Bo Derek, and this stuck. He was small, with very thin dark hair, red cabbage skin, and of course the big laugh was he could not be less beau, or beautiful, nor could the old brown leather jacket. But he did have good things to him, and there was a very passable piece living with Beau now. When you looked at him what you saw first was dependence. The barman brought more drinks. Beau stared about.

'It's all right,' Ember said. 'Stan and Vine don't come in this late.'

'But word could get to them, Ralph. Beau and Ralph Ember – private negotiations, like you said about Stan and this Vine. Why I thought the other table.'

'We play there's nothing to hide. In fact, there *isn't*. Just a nice chat about the state of the world, a break from my pot-boying, that's all, Beau.'

'Think they're going to believe that?'

So, if he was scared, why come? Couldn't he have rung and arranged something in a secret spot? Everyone said Beau was great on the safes and could read accounts, but not a thinker, only clever. Stanfield used to do all that for both. If Stanfield had cut him loose, Beau might be tottering.

'Vine wanted me out from the start, Ralph. Am I bitter? Of course I'm fucking bitter.'

'He's getting masterful. He won't last.'

'How do I look to Melanie, Ralph? It's degrading. She sees her man thrown out like dregs. This is a girl who's had some life, Ralph, and can spot the difference between a high-flyer and horse shit.' Beau crouched forward a bit, his face just above the cluster of dirty glasses, the same sort of used, damp look to it. He tried to jolly up. 'Well, anyway, which makes me at a loose end. Scrap heaped at thirty-six? Never. Why I'm here now. I heard you might be looking for personnel, Ralph. Or even partners, if that doesn't sound big-headed. Backed out of the university temporary, because of prospects, I gather. Ralph, if you're expanding, I—'

'The university? It's because of this, the club,' Ember replied. 'Really humming lately. Taking all my time.'

'Syndicates everywhere, new confederations,' Beau said.

'I wouldn't know much about—'

'When I say help you, Ralph— Oh, you imagine tickling safes and so on, which is what you think Beau is and not much else. So, does Ralph Ember want safes done, for God's sake? Fair enough. But look, safes are one thing, but a new business needs information. This fact, Ralph?'

'Information's always a plus.'

'I can look and listen. Insight. Long-stored knowledge. You heard about that woman shot down the foreshore?'

'The funeral on TV? That one?' Ember could not tell whether Beau had picked up tales about him and Christine, couldn't tell who else might know about them. Iles probably did, and that meant Harpur, as well. They might keep it quiet, though. If they thought they alone knew, it could seem more useful. Best play ignorant with someone like Beau, anyway.

'Ralph, she's got to be connected with something.'

'Connected?'

'You know the weaponry?'

'These were—'

'When I say connected, I mean one of the after-Kenward syndicates, Ralph. Has to be. Running one, even. She wasn't in your syndicate, for instance, Ralph, was she? Though, obviously, she would not be running yours, with you yourself personally available.'

'Mine? Which syndicate is that, Beau? Syndicate for what?'

'When I heard of those Sokolovsky automatics do you know the first thing I said to myself, Ralphy? Ralph?'

'Sokolovsky didn't mean a thing to me. I thought a Polish conductor.'

'Stan Stanfield, I said to myself.'

'Stan? Stan's got a Sokolovsky?'

Beau had a chuckle and looked almost better for a couple of seconds, his harmless Skid-Row face alight and superior, eyes back from mourning. They used to say Beau only showed a real gleam when he was fighting a tough safe or on some other specialized task, like cutting through a fence. But now too the laugh lifted him. 'Stan? Is Stan going pot-shotting down the mud? Stan's too big. Related to that sea artist.'

'Did he paint the foreshore?'

'She's clever. Just a housewife it looked, ordinary home, and yet she must have some vital business role, must, Ralph. She would be a very crafty, dangerous operator. No question. Why Stan would take her out early. Look, Ralph, now and again when we had trouble in the past, threats, jostling, he'd hire a couple of lads from London who'd deal with it and then disappear. I don't say they used Sokolovskys then. That would be crazy, unprofessional, the same weapons. But always the best, expensive stuff. Their trade mark. I know these boys.'

'Are you telling me Stan would send out for—?'

'What I mean when I say I can help you, Ralph. Stan's

playing so serious. He looks around, sees other syndicates getting together and he won't have it, that competition. The likely money's too big. These outfits will be warring all the time, looking for the lot, for monopoly. It's the way of business, you know that. So Stan gets rid of the competition before it even starts properly. I know him. Hasn't he worked in France? Ruthless. He'd be on the phone to Jason the Pigtail and his little friend, Alf Impater, London South East's best. Call The Sleeping Sentinel pub any night and discuss terms with them. I've done it for him. Half in advance, the rest on completion.' Beau reached out and gripped Ember's wrist for a second, then released it quickly, as if realizing he had been familiar. 'This woman taken out one day because Stan's heard her named. Who's next, Ralph? I can tell you – who's next is anyone thinking about a syndicate.' He stared around the club again. There were only two members left, seated silent in an alcove where Ember had indoor plants for a picturesque mode.

'It's all right, I tell you, Beau. Stan never shows at—'

'I'm not thinking about Stan, Ralphy. I'm thinking of *you*, aren't I? How I said – help you. So easy to walk into this place, do the job and walk out again. Doors open all hours, the target nice and obvious behind the bar, like Aunt Sally down the fair.'

Probably those two useless sods would miss even here. 'Well, it's kind of you, Beau, but—'

Beau sat back in his chair, his hands out in front of him now, cupped, like a priest with the blessing – to signal that what followed was obvious. 'Ralph, he does a survey, and who's the next one he sees, the one above all the rest who could handle a big business role, including leadership, or especially leadership – the one who's got the scope for it and background? The one who's the biggest hazard to his nice new firm with the kid?'

'Beau, I don't think—'

'Ralph Ember is the one,' Beau replied. 'Stature. It's plain. Maybe you're already into it, Ralph. I don't know. But if you're not – if you're not yet … Is Ralph Ember going to sit back and doze in The Monty when the rosiest empire since India waits for takers? I don't think so, and Stan Stanfield won't think so. He'll hear you're giving up the university despite your famed love of learning, Ralph. When Stan's thorough he's thorough. All he can think of is success, a clean sweep. He gets rid of everything in the way, starting with Beau Derek – as he sees it. Yes, I was supposed to be in the way now, regardless of the great past.'

'Those two – they're not going to risk coming back to this domain, Beau. Police everywhere. And the chief's into a campaign, I'm told.'

'Those two or another two. What's it matter? Stan knows a lot of hirable people up there.'

'I—'

'My own feeling, Ralph, is I could come into your syndicate and be a real strength. I know how Stan thinks, how he will operate. That's what I meant, information. Not just about those two, but the wider aspects. Being able to read him, forecast. Keep us nicely ahead and in profit.'

Ember stood. 'This is interesting stuff, Beau. Speculative,

obviously, but interesting. I've got to close up now. I must shut those dangerous doors you mentioned!'

'It's no laugh, Ralph.'

'And I'm grateful – coming out here like this.'

'I'm taking risks, Ralph.'

'What I'll do is think about what you've said. I will. I don't know whether any of it could be used, in a practical sense, I mean. But I'll—'

'If they come here, Stan and Vine, look at them, Ralph. The faces. They think they can take on the world.' Beau stood, too. 'Well, I might get a call from you, Ralph?'

'If I want to discuss some points.'

Beau did not move from alongside the table. At first, Ember thought the rum had taken his legs. Then he said: 'One favour, Ralph.'

'I've got to close up, Beau.'

'Only a minute. Melanie's out in the car. It seemed better to be private at first. But I'd like to bring her in, just so she sees I know you, can have a discussion with you. She would not believe that – "You're not trying to tell me you can go direct to Ralph Ember himself?" she said. Wouldn't have it. This would show – well, show I'm not caving in because of Stan. Other irons.'

Please help, Ralph. 'A lady in the car park alone, this time of night, Beau. Well, of course, ask her in, do. A few words.'

'This is great of you, Ralph.' In a couple of minutes he came back with her, a woman Ember had seen with Beau before. She had a nice, warm, wide face and no-fool eyes. Although she was a bit older than Beau, you could see he would be worried about losing her. The hair dye was still winning, and her body looked good. She dressed young – a black bomber jacket and jeans – but she would get away with that for another month or two. The jacket was newer than Beau's.

'Here's Ralph, Melanie. We had our discussion.'

'I understand now why they talk about Charlton Heston,' she replied.

'Oh, the resemblance to Chuck!' Ember said. 'It's the poor light.'

'Ralph finds all that embarrassing. No side to him at all.'

'It's all right,' Ember said. He went to the bar and poured two armagnacs and another rum. Then he came back around and stood with them.

'Ralph thinks there could be something for me,' Beau said.

'You're so far gone you don't know what Ralph thinks.'

'I got the feel of the meeting, anyway,' Ember replied.

'Can you use him, Ralph?' she said. 'I expect your team's already picked.'

'Well, team! My team are the staff here, that's about the strength of it. I don't suppose Beau wants to be a cellar man.'

'The wider business picture?' she said.

'Melanie, love, Ralph Ember's not going to talk about matters like that with you, just brought in cold from a car park.'

'But I'll certainly keep Beau in mind,' Ember said.

She downed her armagnac. 'Talking to you, what I feel,

Ralph, is not just the Heston factor but – well, deep power. Yes.'

She leaned forward and moved her finger slowly along the scar on his jaw. He had known women do that before, women who were more or less strangers. It was as if they thought the line of stretched, paler skin gave a more intimate contact with him, his body and his past.

'Power?' Beau said. 'Of course. Why we're here, isn't it?'

'Power and strength,' she said.

'I try to keep a steady attitude to what happens around us,' Ember replied.

'Famous for it,' Beau said.

When they were gone, Ember sat for a while in the bar alone. The barman and last customers had left. Rage battered him. Hadn't he decided he had done all possible to trace Christine's killers, and could honourably abandon that quest? Then this discard bastard Beau comes in and gives names. They were not names Ember knew, but he had heard of the pub. Yes, it was the type of place you could recruit anyone, as long as you had cash as cash. The thought of hunting down people in that kind of jungle district and that kind of crook fortress made him groan and sweat. He put up a hand himself and touched the scar. Chris would not have expected him to travel to London and take on a hard villain army, surely to God. She had valued him too much for that. And, after bloody all, the vengeance function was not officially his. He had not been her husband. There was no *public* responsibility. Tranter himself seemed to recognize he had these duties and was trying to fulfil them, working at it. Of course, he was a useless fat amateur, and would fail. He could be given help, though.

Ember went to the club phone cubicle and dialled an untraceable to Tranter's house. He had often done that when Leslie was away. It seemed strange to be ringing there, knowing Christine could never reply. But Tranter answered almost at once. He must be sleepless, poor sod, although it was past 2.30. Ember put on what he hoped was a South London accent. 'Get a pencil, Mr Leslie Tranter, please,' he said. 'Right?' He gave the pub's name twice, and Jason the Pigtail's and Alfred Impater's three times. When he rang off he felt very satisfied and no longer panicky. He liked to face up to things, and he had done it, regardless. Obviously, when she touched his face like that, Melanie was saying more than, Please look after Beau. He tried never to take offence at these offers from decent-looking women, and put up with the comparisons to Chuck Heston. It was only sensible to keep people like Melanie and Foster's Deloraine in mind now dear Christine had gone.

17

After a few days Denise broke open Harpur's letter to Iles. Mostly, it thrilled her, brilliantly confirming everything she already knew and loved about Harpur, a soul collage. These few pages had so much of Colin's on–off decency, ruthlessness, his courage, fear, self-belief, love of her and of deceit, and his trust in Iles, and dread of him. Above all, Harpur's courage – but cagey, uncareless courage. It delighted her that the letter had been hand written with what was obviously a proper nibbed pen, not Biro. She brushed her fingers across the lines, feeling for the words' raised shapes, like traversing the rough and smooth of his wrist skin. Lowering her head she sniffed at his bold black ink, as if slowly nosing again into some hidden area of his body. 'Oh, Col,' she muttered, going over the letter with delight for the fourth time, 'you're unmagnificent and great.'

For her fifth reading, she spread the sheets fondly across the open pages of *Beowulf,* one of her study texts: that sterling tale of a splendid, out-and-out ancient hero. The letter's puffed-up language to describe shady tactics intrigued her: 'I shall afford them this protection', 'in this postdated manner,' 'highly exposed position'. Also, there was the 'she being she' bit about herself, and the likelihood that she would do what she was now doing and look at the letter. Fucking know-all sod: this contemptible police instinct. She thought of blacking out these black words with marking pen, but then decided this might draw extra attention to them. Someone like Iles would probably have an ultraviolet way of discovering what had been obliterated, and so find that what was obliterated was exactly correct, the pair of smirking bastards. Except one of the bastards might not be alive to be smirking if this letter were ever read by the other. She would photocopy it before resealing.

Denise saw, of course, that what Colin proposed was perilous. There would be no need for the brilliant courage if not. But although she had been upset when he first spoke to her of the letter, now Denise saw the detail of his scheme she felt almost content, and worried less for his safety. He would excel at such work. Colin was born for brazen two-timing, for gifted spying and for brave, arrogant individualism. It was individualism, though, which intelligently recognized limits. Colin knew he might need to call on Iles, and catered for this in advance of the risk. If someone with Iles's savage assets existed, it was obvious thrift to think of possible uses for him.

Excitement at reading the letter gave her a real body throb, and she decided she must see Col at once. You had to catch these moments. She believed in such impulses. They would probably grow fewer as you aged up into the twenties and so bloody on. Knowledge of these three pieces of paper made her feel as if she possessed him entirely at last, and she obviously needed to re-enact that now, in a bed or the back of a car or shop doorway. It was late evening. She might ring him at home and find whether he was around. If so, she could go over to Arthur Street. Until a few months ago, she would not allow herself visits to his house, even though he was now a widower and single. She had hated that former matrimonial bed, and had been embarrassed at the thought of scrutiny by Hazel and Jill, his daughters. Since then she had met them – and met them actually in the family house – and they seemed able to accept her without ill feeling. The bed she had come to see as just a grubby bed. All the same, she still felt self-conscious about telephoning, seeming to pursue him, particularly if he was not at home and one of the girls answered.

She drove over to his place, deciding that if his current old car were there she would knock at the door. It was not there, and she parked and watched the house from her Panda, waiting for him to come back. After about half an hour she felt that someone was staring at her through the passenger window and, turning quickly, saw his older daughter, Hazel. Denise lowered the window.

'Coming in?' Hazel said. 'I've been to the rap caff. I don't think Dad's home, unless he's changed his vehicle from the pool again, but you can wait. He might not be too long. Who knows?'

'He's working?'

'Like I said, who knows? Was there something special?'

'I was passing this way, that's all.'

'Oh, really?'

They walked together to the house and went into the big book-lined sitting room. The younger girl was in her dressing gown, watching boxing on television. She put the sound down. A kettle whistled from the kitchen. 'But why do you wait in the street, Denise?' Hazel asked.

'She could tell he wasn't in,' Jill said. 'She didn't come to see *us*, did you, Denise? Will you marry him?'

'Oh, God, think of his age and all those creepy, set ways,' Hazel said. 'That haircut and the music he likes.'

'If he asked you.' Jill said. She stuck out her tongue at the boxers. 'They're both bums.' She switched off.

'Dad won't ask her,' Hazel replied.

'How can you be so sure?' Jill said. 'Why is he with her at all, then? They seem able to make each other happy. Anyway, perhaps Denise will ask *him*.'

'Oh, *happy*,' Hazel replied. 'Married is different. Jill, you saw that, didn't you, even you? You lived here with Mum and Dad. I mean, happy! Could you stand the police life, Denise? Do you know anything about it? The sleaziness.'

'A bit,' Denise answered.

Jill went into the kitchen and came back with a tea tray. She poured out. 'Hazel thinks she's got to be all hard and weary because she's fifteen.'

Hazel said: 'The teachers at school don't say anything *against* police – well, they couldn't, because of looking after their jobs – but you can feel it, you can tell some of them think . . . think police are just crooked and political. "Of course, your father's police, isn't he, Hazel?" Always "of course", a doom. And never "in the police" but "your father's police", a *condition*, like dyslexic or lame.'

'Don't you want her to marry him, Haze?' Jill asked. 'She's fairly nice. It could be worse. Don't forget he knows all sorts.'

'Where is he?' Denise said.

'He thinks a lot of you, whatever Hazel says,' Jill answered.

'Oh, he's out on something vital and secret. That will be his story,' Hazel replied. 'Could be bingo. Nobody knows where he is half the time. That's another thing.'

'Did you see Dad on television, Denise?' Jill asked. 'A funeral. Mourning's often part of the job. There ought to be a course.'

'Whose?'

'Mrs Tranter. The foreshore killing?' Jill replied. 'And Iles, looking sort of, well, silky, and so very, very, very sad, even without a course.'

'That was genuine, you little wretch,' Hazel said.

Jill made a gerbil face: 'See, Denise, nobody can say a thing against Iles when she's around.'

'And there's a drugs angle in the killing, probably, Denise,' Hazel said.

'Who says, who says?' Jill asked.

'The buzz in school.'

'I haven't heard this buzz,' Jill said.

'Probably it wouldn't reach down to the babies' class,' Hazel replied.

'Nuts.'

'You can feel it, Denise, people on the staff and some of the kids, they think police are involved, taking a cut, selling stuff they confiscate from dealers they don't have a deal with to dealers they do. Some big conspiracy. So, no arrests. Well, kids come right out and say it to me, or hold their noses – supposed to be corruption-stink – but with the staff, they couldn't, obviously. So you fight the kid, get your elbow in his or her throat, stamp on ankles, and some teacher breaks it up and asks what it's about, and nobody says, naturally – *omertà* from TV, code of silence, but the teachers know, anyway. Probably they started the rumours.'

'You're making it all up,' Jill yelled. 'Dad might be investigating it tonight, for all they know, for all you know.'

'He might. It's what I mean, could you could stand police life, Denise? This sort of smear the whole time from all sorts. It's in their eyes and perspiration.'

'All rubbish, isn't it, Denise?' Jill said. 'What do they know, teachers? Do they understand about undercover, all that? Dad's fighting big, clever, people. It's not just joyriders. As a matter of fact, I think you'd be all right with him.'

'So do I,' Hazel said. 'I think you're suited, except he's much cleverer. But he's much cleverer than almost everyone, but not—'

'Saint Desmond Iles,' Jill said.

'We're going to bed now, Denise, but, obviously, you can wait. He'll be ratty if we're still up.'

Denise was gazing at the shelves.

'These books get you down, do they?' Jill asked.

The shelves were heavy with volumes that had belonged to the girls' mother. 'We'll definitely be getting rid of them,' Hazel said.

'Dad wants to, honestly,' Jill said. 'Just too lazy to make a start. It's not because they were hers, like precious for reminding him of her. I can see that would hurt you. Books don't mean a thing to him, hers or anyone else's. There's a good boxing book, *The Sweet Science*, I want kept, and *The Orton Diaries*, of course. The rest, Oxfam or torched.' She crossed the room to where Denise was sitting on a sofa and put her arms around her and held her for a few seconds. Denise embraced her, too. Then Jill gently kissed her good-night on the cheek. Denise saw Hazel thought of following, but must have decided she was too grown-up and cynical for all that.

'Goodnight, Denise,' she said. 'Breakfast again?'

'Please, Denise,' Jill said. 'Be here tomorrow.'

'Could be.'

'Shall I put the boxing back on for you or do you want to read one of these books, being a student?' Jill asked.

'The boxing,' Denise answered.

She had been watching for about twenty minutes after they went upstairs when Denise thought she heard tapping from the kitchen. People called on Colin very late and very secretly, and did not always look too wholesome. She had heard this same sort of tapping here before. And once she had awoken in the middle of the night and found Colin had left the bed. She went down to look for him then and dis-covered Colin talking to someone she guessed was one of his informants, a youngish, bouncy man in a combat jacket. Police life, as Hazel said. Now Denise lowered the television volume again and listened. It was the noise of a coin on glass, as previously. When she went into the kitchen, she saw a hand in a dark woollen mitten suddenly appear from below the window outside and rap three times, then retract, like a puppet popping up to do its bit before disappearing beneath the stage. After a few minutes, the action was repeated. She walked to the window and looked down. Denise made out a quite burly man crouched there and thought she recognized him, the jacket and the close-cut fair hair. About twenty-five, he was staring up at her from a square, strong, big-chinned, astonished face. She opened the door to the garden and looked into the darkness: 'Hello,' she said, 'didn't you come to the house before?'

'Oh,' he said, 'look, I wasn't expecting a—'

'Colin's not here.'

'You can never tell with him. He uses so many different worn-out cars. There's three in the street that might be his.'

'You could come in and wait,' she said.

'Yes. You live here now?' He hesitantly entered the kitchen, and she locked the door behind him. She had not switched on the light, and was walking towards the switch when he said, 'Best not. No curtain here, is there?'

'Oh, right.' She left the kitchen dark.

'Just neighbours and so on. Could be misunderstood.'

'Right. The tea will be cold. I'll make more in a minute.'

'You live here now?' he asked.

'You go into the other room,' she replied. He left her and she put the light on. When the kettle boiled again she went back into the sitting room for the teapot. He was seated on the sofa, his face turned away from where the curtains failed to meet. He had undone the combat jacket, but looked tense. The boxing had ended, and he was watching a black and

white Woody Allen film, not smiling. She made the tea
and rejoined him. 'Need Colin urgently?' she asked.

He nodded towards a sideboard cupboard. 'Usually
there's something in there for cooling this.'

She found some whisky. He gulped to make room for an
addition. She did the same. Last time, when she interrupted
them, he and Colin had claimed he was a book dealer,
interested in Megan Harpur's library. This was the man in
the letter, Keith Vine, ex-informant and probably present
drugs magnate, but Denise thought it best to stick with that
earlier tale. He had come to make a proposal, maybe, though
not about books. Colin was waiting for it, and would not
want him scared off. It delighted her to help with Colin's
work. Another lovely bond.

'A great collection, isn't it?' she said, waving a hand at
the shelves.

'Distinguished.'

'But I mustn't go on and on praising them or you'll think
I'm trying to jack the price up.' She laughed.

He had a smile, too. 'Well, Mr Harpur and I – we're very
near an agreement.'

'Yes?'

'Oh, yes. We understand each other – about the literary
commodities, I mean. I come here in this rather, well,
secretive way so we don't get other dealers trying to muscle
in. No kitchen light – that sort of thing.'

'Yes, Col explained.'

'Do you sort of live here now then?' he asked. 'I mean,
making the tea and so on.'

'When Colin comes in, I'll leave you to it,' she replied. 'Is business good?'

Momentarily, his face glowed, and not just from the whisky. 'Brilliant,' he said. 'He's got to believe that.' She felt he had forgotten his role for a second and was answering about that other, actual, cash-bright business. Then he said: 'Book collectors – real fanatics. Luckily.' He had a full laugh.

'First editions, some,' she replied.

'First editions, last, I'm fond of them all.'

'Here he is now,' she said. She watched Colin's face as he came in, but it showed no shock. Perhaps he had taken a squint through the curtain gap. Perhaps he had spotted a strange car parked in the street. Perhaps he was just Colin Harpur, used to showing nothing.

'Come about the volumes, Mr Harpur,' he said.

'Ah, grand. And Denise has been entertaining you?'

'Jill wants two books retained,' Denise replied.

'What?' Colin said. 'Yes, right.'

'If it's going to be all business talk, I think I'll go to bed,' Denise said.

'Oh, right,' Colin replied. 'We have to do these deals so late, and so on—'

'To fool the book world competition. I had it explained.'

'Good.'

'Well, I feel sort of guilty, turning you out,' Vine said.

'I'd be bored,' Denise replied. 'Probably.' Or maybe not.

When Harpur came to bed more than an hour later she was still awake, still excited. 'I had to come over, Colin,' she said. 'Really had to see you.'

'Lovely. Any special reason?'

'Just love. A feeling of real closeness.'

'Grand. You read the letter, then?'

'The letter?'

'Under *H*'

'Why, is it raunchy, or something?'

He rolled into the bed naked. 'You *haven't* read it?'

'If you think it could turn me on, maybe I will, when I'm a bit down.'

'No,' he said, 'don't read it.'

'To do with your visitor?'

'Sale of books? Why would I write to Iles about that?'

'That's true.'

'They're on their way out.'

'What?'

'The books.'

'Really? What did you talk about, Col?'

'Well, the books, naturally.'

'Some approach by him? Something settled?'

'Yes,' Harpur said. 'About the books.'

'It took a while.'

'A lot of titles,' he replied. 'That's the thing about books. All different, you know. I love it when you just turn up.'

'I've never done it before.'

'I know. I love it.'

'I feel entitled,' she said.

'Of course you are.'

'I felt tonight I really knew you, was really, well, yes – close.'

'You *did* read the letter?'

'Look, Col,' she said, 'I came for lovemaking, not this drip, drip, drip of the same question.'

'I love your needs,' he said, running his hands slowly over her shoulders and upper arms. He had never thought of any woman's shoulders as elegant before, but hers were elegant.

'My needs get sharper,' she replied.

'That's all right. That can be coped with. What do you love about me?' he asked.

'Just the way everything adds up.'

'Adds up to what?' he said.

'Adds up to make you you.'

'That would be true of anyone.'

'No. It would add up to make them *them*, and I want you. Want you here, for instance.'

'Here?'

'Where else?'

'Well, since you ask—'

'Of course. There as well. But later. We've got some time? The literary figure's not going to come back, tickling your casement again, is he, asking whether Taylor's *The Rule and Exercises of Holy Dying* is really a first edition?'

'That a book?'

'Col, just concentrate on the rule and exercises of unholy staying alive, will you?'

18

Keith Vine wanted to celebrate – but not by crazy, pointless partying. This was a business celebration, so it ought to contribute to the business some way. Leadership meant using everything to make the firm stronger, even your relaxed times. He thought The Monty. It would show Ralphy Ember he was losing or had already lost. Yes, the poor, feeble sod might read the signs and give up. Ralphy had this famous streak of collapsibility, like a deckchair. Vine must try to bring it on. This also was what business leadership meant: if you could annihilate the competition without a direct fight, it was better – no waste, no hurt. Probably Ember would realize what sparked this celebration: he might be yellow, but not stupid. If Keith Vine looked so dominant and at ease, it could only signify he had the police incorporated, a real coup. In*cop*erated! In*coup*erated! What else *could* it signify? There was Stan Stanfield as partner also, yes, quite a strength, but not everybody thought as much of Stan Stanfield as Stan Stanfield did. Not even Panicking Ralphy would be scared out of his ambitions by the idea of running against Stan. But Ember would know that if Harpur or similar was suddenly aboard Vine's outfit, the hopes for his own had sunk. How could you fight a business interest that came from nicely high in the police force, all that official ferocity, good tradition and special insight?

Keith Vine's Becky was not very keen to go to The Monty. She never was, but he persuaded her, and they drove there late. Clearly, you did not get many pregnant women in the club, especially not at this hour, and to walk in there with Becky when she must be near her hugest would certainly be a statement to Ralph and all his people. No question, Keith felt proud to be with her. This declared that, even excluding the business, he had something wonderful going, a proper future, the boons of a fine woman and a coming child.

'How they treating you, Ralph?' he called at the bar.

'They're not,' Ember said.

'Oh? Well, what will you have? Let's do some Dom Pérignon, shall we? One of your good years, not the stuff you made yourself last Tuesday,' Vine replied. This bit of old crosstalk made things even better than he had hoped. It was good to be buying Ralphy a drink and a quality drink: that lowered him a point right from the start, turned him into someone you were kind to, like a better-grade down-and-out. 'But something soft for Becky,' Vine said. 'Things being as they are.' He loved speaking about the child, and in words like those, which carried affection and responsibility, but without getting loud.

Obviously, he could not tell Becky exactly what he was celebrating, but she was clever, too, and would probably pick up the message. He longed to let her know he, personally and alone, had managed to draw Harpur into the firm – what family life should be all about, sharing the pleasure of professional triumphs. Especially he wanted to tell her because she was the one who had given him the idea, the day when they were in Kenward Knapp's place. If she had not spotted then that the business needed somebody else, he would have continued turning his back on Harpur, because Harpur had once turned his back on him. Childish. Yes, Becky had a brain. Becky was a total with-child gem, and desirable even at this very late stage.

'When's the big day?' Ember asked.

'A week,' Becky said.

'Wonderful,' Ember replied. 'Start of a dynasty.'

'Right,' Vine said. That was a jibe by Ember, but true, also, even if Ember did not realize it, blindfolded by cheap sarcasm. This child was a big future, going into the next millennium. The baby was another way of indicating Vine's grand business status, because obviously he would not begin a family, a dynasty, unless certain he could give his first child a brilliant start. As he saw it, he did not have a dukedom to pass on as some might, but he would provide his child with the title to a fine, secure conglomerate.

Naturally, Vine could not tell Becky straight out Harpur had been recruited. At this level, full confidentiality was key, confidentiality even from her. Harpur would not appreciate advertisement. So Keith had wondered how he could give Beck some hint that, thanks to her, the syndicate was now immensely stronger, had depth and long-lastingness. She deserved that, the dear girl. Another reason for this trip to The Monty. It would be more than just an evening out. Being so sharp, she would spot the full meaning. To be relaxed in there and doing some decent spending would also show Ember that already Keith regarded him as no real competition. You would never lounge about on the territory of someone you feared, or even took seriously. Tonight's visit had symbolism.

There were quite a few people in the club, mostly small-timers talking and scheming at the bar or playing pool. A big, mixed party were drinking heavily and singing old-time music-hall songs at the far end. They were into 'Daddy wouldn't buy me a bow-wow', with a couple of the women on the table barking the tune and wagging their behinds. Ember could be too tolerant. He was getting education, but still did not have much idea on class and due behaviour. The only real behaviour he knew about was how to stack wealth, and he was not bad at that, Vine would admit. This money and the possessions made him very cocky when he was not blotted out by panic, and it was important to wear him down. He had a syndicate going, almost for sure.

Vine and Becky sat at one of the best tables with the bottle of champagne, and orange juice for her. On the wall near was that mahogany-framed enlarged photograph of the inaugural club outing to Paris, when two members kidnapped a tart in Montmartre for thirty-six hours and broke the arms of a pimp who came searching. This joyful picture was taken early in the stay, before Caspar Nottage had been clawed down the face by the girl, or Bespoke Vincent's nose was multi-broken in the pimp tussle, and both looked boyishly excited, like school kids on their first trip abroad. The various excursion pictures helped give a really good community flavour to the club.

Panicking Ralph

Vine felt relaxed. And he needed Ember to spot this. 'I want to get out of here, Keith,' Becky muttered.

'Give it a little while.'

'There's something wrong.'

'That fucking singing? They'll go soon.'

'No. Ember.'

'What?'

'Knowing something. He's tensed up.'

Vine laughed: 'This is Panicking. Half his life he's tensed up. His skin gets too tight for his body. It's a condition. He'll leave himself to science.'

After a while, Becky seemed to relax again. They were bound to be jumpy as their time came near. But she still looked great. People here would see right off her maternity clothes must have cost no end. When she first grew big, she bought some old-style second-hand things from an antiques market. They were very nice, in the way a lot of these past modes could be, bygone elegance, but he would not want her to wear them to The Monty. Folk here did not understand the beauty of former fashions. They looked at clothes and saw price tags. Especially for maternity garments. A man had to make it very clear he was a true provider, and what you wrapped your future babe in told your credit rating more than a bank could.

'As if Ralph knows something – something that could do you, us, damage,' Becky said suddenly.

'Such as?'

'Oh, Christ, Keith, would I know? What do you tell me?'

'I'll get the sod over,' Vine replied.

'No, please. Please, Keith.'

'I can't have you scared by someone like Ralphy.'

'Keith, don't be so—'

Vine turned and called to Ember behind the bar: 'Ralph, it would be a real pleasure if you'd join us. Bring another of the same, would you? On my tab, of course.' The singers had moved on to 'My old man said follow the band', and Vine had to bellow it all twice, taking away some of the casual ease he wanted. Now and then, he thought this club was a pit. He knew Becky always did.

Ember gave a little wave. Vine could not be sure whether this meant Thanks or Get Lost, but it was a careless gesture, really, because as Ralphy's jacket tightened for a second in the movement, Vine saw the outline of a shoulder holster. Well, that was absolutely all right. He would not come to a place like The Monty without carrying something himself, the eight-shot Makarov.

After a few minutes Ember strolled over to the table carrying an orange juice and another bottle of Dom Pérignon, plus a glass for himself. He sat down, and they all toasted the baby. 'Last time you were here it was with Stanley Stanfield, yes, Keith?'

'Oh, Stan,' Vine replied. 'This bloody din, Ralph.' He nodded towards the singing party who had reached 'They're all single by the seaside', with the girls on the table doing leg kicks now.

'They're celebrating, that's all,' Ember replied. 'No harm. The mother got off. A police witness had the dates wrong and failed to turn up. Seeing much of him these days?'

'Stan?'

'Stanfield, yes.'

'Well, we bump into each other.'

'We're not stopping, Ralph,' Becky said. 'I'm supposed to keep decent hours.'

'Exactly,' Ember replied. 'So, what's Stan up to these days then, Keith?'

'What's the big fascination with Stan Stanfield, Ralph?' Becky asked.

'An interesting lad. Gets about,' Ember replied. 'The great strength of Stan is he sees openings. Forget the ancestor who knew Charles Dickens, but Stan does see openings.'

Vine thumb-indicated the high-kick girls and said: 'We all do. Someone's been chatting to you about him, Ralph? I mean, brought him to your mind?'

'This is just general interest in his career,' Ember replied.

Vine said: 'I'll let him know, Ralph. He'll be flattered.'

'If you bump into him.'

'What, Beau's been in here talking, has he?' Vine asked.

Ember's face went fond. 'Stan and Beau, those two used to be quite a team, yes? This was a prestige team that looked unbreakable.'

'What you saying, Ralph?' Becky asked. 'Come on, cough it up.'

She was clever, Becky, but she did not know how things worked. If she wanted to say something she would say it like that. In many ways this might be a nice, forthright way of behaving, but now and then you'd think she'd never heard of subtlety, even though she had education, too. With someone like Ember, it was best to circle and listen. He had this dirty skill that told you something without telling you. The bastard could talk about Beau and never mention him, but made Vine mention him instead, this was the point. People like Ralphy learned these smart ploys on the wrong end of interrogation. Most said Ember had never been convicted of anything anywhere, but this did not mean he had never been questioned. Probably he was never convicted because he had taught himself the way to kill interrogation. Vine knew he must sidestep Ralphy's sly genius.

'Beau, a great lad in many ways,' Vine said, 'yet maybe gone a bit adrift. Poisonous. He's taken a hate to Stan, you know. Yes. Oh, feels shut out suddenly, apparently. Shut out from what, don't ask me. Beau's a tradesman, a great tradesman, but some trades go out of the limelight, don't they? Inevitability. Think of folk who made grapeshot. This must have been one hell of a bustling business, Nelson's time and so on. But suddenly, it's Exocets. And because Beau's angry, his method is to put these tales around.'

'Which?' Ember asked.

Vine decided Becky might have it right, and it would be a good idea to get out of here. His relaxation was starting to go, regardless of the vintage champagne. He had come here to scare Ralphy with an unspoken message, but all the messages were coming from Ember, and Vine did not like them. He was not in charge of the night any longer. This bastard sat at *their* table, but he behaved like the host, filling glasses, helping the conversation along, smirking at Becky and her belly. Perhaps he was tense, as she said, but he was

not tense in the genuine, Panicking Ralphy, coming-apart
style, bursting out through his flesh. It was dangerous tense,
and crafty tense. This sod Ember might know something, as
Becky said, and he might know something Keith Vine did
not know, maybe about Stanfield, the secretive bastard. You
should be able to trust a partner right through, but Stanfield
hid behind that big fucking stupid moustache and might try
all sorts, and you would never guess until disaster moved in.

'Beau's bound to understand how Stan thinks,' Ember
said. 'So long working together, and his contacts, that kind
of thing.'

'But what's it all about, Ralph?' Becky asked. 'You're
telling us something important? Which contacts?'

'All businesses run on contacts, love, don't they, Keith?'

'Contacts? Oh, crucial,' Vine replied. He was nodding and
agreeing with him like some dumbo sidekick. Occasionally
Vine would suffer these terrible reversals. New, cruel views
of himself would be enforced by a sudden show of power
and even contempt from some old hand like Ember. But,
Christ, Panicking Ralphy could do that to him? Yes, Panicking Ralphy could, because Panicking Ralphy had a
background and a club and property and knew all the
biggest business people of the last ten, fifteen years and was
not inside. When he felt like this, Vine would always hear in
imagination that poor trick he had of calling himself Keith
Vine while mulling things over or talking to someone, and
especially to Becky. *Keith Vine thinks this, Keith Vine wants
that* – like he had grown so big he was something apart and
majestic. But what a prick to talk like that. He was just a

shaky bit of riff-raff. 'I think we should be on our way now, Becky,' he said.

'What? Already?'

This was how she could be, the silly fat cow, changing all over the place. Now she wanted to stay, obviously thinking she could make Ember come up with something that revealed. This was the trouble with her, she did not realize someone like Ralphy had the sort of business brain that could blow her out of the water. 'You must get your rest, Beck,' Vine said.

'Oh, pity,' Ember replied.

'Can you let me have a bill, Ralph?' Vine said, standing and going for the fifties he had crumpled for casualness and put loose in his trousers pocket.

'On the house, Keithy,' Ember replied.

'Christ, no, I can't have that, Ralph. Two Dom Pérignons.'

'The Monty can stand it. And such a real treat to see you and Becky here. If I bump into Stan before you bump into him I'll mention we were talking about him and old times, shall I? Plus that lad you mentioned. Beau was it?'

*

When they had gone, Ember sat for a while, finishing the second bottle of champagne. The singing party had left, too, helping one another out to taxis. One of them had bled on a pool table after a fall, but Ember did not make anything of it. A party was a party. Only a couple of people lingered, mumbling unhappily at the other end of the club. They would be moaning over some job that had produced peanuts, and/or the slaughterous price their fence gave. Gospel of the useless. The club had too many of them. He must close up shortly. Now and then, he would hang on like this, enjoying the quiet as the tobacco and booze fumes subsided. He felt no special satisfaction, though: to hammer some dropping like Vine was a very tiny victory.

As with any of the big London clubs around St James's, The Monty probably looked better when most of its members were absent: almost noble. At these times, he could imagine the club's previous, very decent existence near. Important legitimate deals had been discussed here then, even clinched. These kinds of constructive agreements helped the city develop and take its present good shape. Ember considered his civic work continued all that.

He recognized that The Monty had possibly slipped socially. Now, instead of genuine businessmen, the club allowed membership to Vine and his sort. Conversation with Vine had to be a string of frightening half-revelations and unspoken threats. Vital to down him. The pregnant girl with him though! Just right out with whatever she thought. Ember smiled. He quite liked a bit of cheek. Once the baby had come and things went back to normal, she might be worth a fairly serious approach. Again he realized how much he was going to need somebody now Christine had been so savagely taken away, and a jumpy jerk like Keith Vine couldn't really be enough for Becky, surely to God. Ember prayed she could stay safe, not like Christine. Cheek was nice, yes, but perhaps she should try to learn when to keep silent, or how to say things without screaming them in headlines. In a way, she was like Christine's husband, Leslie Tranter: both bystanders who wanted to be more.

After ten minutes Ember stood and announced he must close up. His sojourn with the Dom Pérignon had begun to go sour. He should not have thought about Tranter. Jesus, hadn't he deliberately sent him to hunt those two London hirelings? In his tubby straightforward way, Tranter might blunder into that South London pub and start asking well-informed, intelligent, stupid questions and naming names, without any idea of the hazard: just the way Becky had asked well-informed, intelligent, stupid questions earlier.

'Are you all right, Ralph,' one of the lads said as he ushered them out.

'Fine, fine,' Ember said.

'Sort of turned in on yourself? Big business worries?'

'Along those lines.'

'If you need help.'

'I've always got you in mind, Brian,' Ember replied.

'Plus myself.'

'Yes, of course, Cliff. You two lads are a famous team.'

'But not too famous,' Brian said.

'Discreet,' Ember replied. If ever he wanted an empty supermarket trolley stolen he'd call them. He followed the pair out, locked and alarmed the doors. Driving from the car park he found himself scrutinizing vehicles in the street very carefully: he had casually won the tussle with that little prick, Vine, but it had unsettled him, made him aware that a fight was near. No car followed. He could go back to his thoughts. Of course, he had known before this that he might be sending Tranter into peril. At the time, though, Ember had decided that if anybody should take the risks it must be Les, the husband. Ember saw he had been slinking out of difficulties again, and this cowardice looked sickening. Often he worried to see how people not properly part of things, though close, could flounder around dangerously in areas they failed to understand: Becky, blurting out her tactless queries; Tranter and his poignant do-it-yourself efforts to trace Christine's killers. Les and Becky needed looking after, even if they both certainly had sharp brains. Perhaps he should stop Leslie taking his innocence and his unbalancing rage and big soft body to London. Good God, hadn't they shared a lovely woman?

But then, nearing Low Pastures, he felt these onslaughts of self-blame start to dwindle very nicely. Sight or even thought of his property would often restore his morale. Simply, he *couldn't* stop Tranter. He had passed on the names from Beau Derek and mentioned The Sleeping Sentinel. If Ember checked now or in the morning and found Tranter had not left for London yet, so what? Do another anon call and tell him the information was wrong? Would Tranter believe that? It had been too specific. And if Tranter was absent, should Ember deduce he had already gone hunting in South-East London? More likely he would be out of town selling his animal aids. He had lost a wife but still had children to support.

Despite this return to good sense, Ember found himself forced briefly to consider one other option. Should he get up to London personally and at once, find those two before

Tranter, and try to finish them? Perhaps he did owe Christine a vengeance mission, after all. Didn't he? Didn't he? Tranter would then be unable to endanger his pathetic self.

Almost immediately, though, Ember decided this was not an idea that fitted with what made Ralph W. Ember Ralph W. Ember. He believed he could be strong, resourceful, decisive – certainly – but what he could not accept was wild risk-taking, gung-hoism as the army called it. Yes, he often had a conscience and he could show tenderness, but he also had duties, to himself and to his family. Just as Tranter had duties to his dead wife and family. Plus Ember was a businessman. It would be feeble to make a present of himself to those gunmen, and on their own ground. The terrible difference between him and Tranter was that he, Ralph Ember, was unquestionably the target, just as he had been unquestionably the target when Christine was hit. Ralph Ember was a principal, Les and Chris accidental spectators. For Ember to go looking for those hit men would be to do their work for them. Probably, they would see instantly that Tranter did not rate, this Oliver Hardy in marquee trousers. They would spot he had been involved without knowing it, and might be satisfied to scare him off. Not true if Ember himself went: they would recognize he was hardly someone to be scared off, wouldn't they? They would know Ember was formidable – had been due to be killed because he was formidable – and must be killed now, for their own safety. To give them the opening would be simple-minded.

19

At home alone for a late lunch, Harpur took a telephone call from Keith Vine, the agreed communications drill. If Vine wanted contact, he would ring at around 3 p.m. on school-days, and Harpur made sure he was there then two or three times a week. Vine sounded low, as if he'd had a recent setback or fright. 'Col, we ought to get rid of those books,' he said. 'For credibility.'

'What do you mean, Keith?' he replied, knowing.

'Your girlfriend. I'm there as a book dealer twice now. She'll puzzle why they don't disappear, sold.'

'Oh, she's said nothing about it.'

'We need to confirm my profile. What I mean, Col – I don't want her wondering what our arrangement really is. I'm sure loyalty's her second name, but she could still wonder. We've got business opposition on all sides, you know, and I can tell you it's tough, strong. Just lately, I've had a fresh glimpse. We can handle it, of course, of course, but if some whisper gets out and I lose you, well, this firm's suddenly so much weaker. You're a strut, Col. Oh, yes, a strut. No, I'd never say this girl would deliberately spread the word, and you're entitled to whatever companion you wish, clearly – a winsome arse, if you don't mind me saying. But these intelligent kids, they talk. It's by nature. They believe in expressing themselves, which can quite often be

Bill James

great, I don't deny. Becky's the bloody same. But things get heard. For instance, this girl's in the university, I understand. So's a possible, very possible, business opponent, as you know – coffee and general conversation in the common room, all that, though I had a tip he might be putting it on ice for a year, because he's so busy. You see what I mean, Col? *Busy.* Like Winston Churchill dropped his oil painting for World War II. I'd say, suddenly, this lad's got maximum confidence in the future of some business operation, wouldn't you? No time for anything else. Perhaps he's been recruiting. Perhaps he's all at once a lot stronger. This is my impression. I must be able to counter him, and can't risk injuries to my outfit, Col.'

'But I—'

'So, it's important I'm through and through a book dealer, to her. That girl had a damn good look at me. You won't believe this, Col, but some women say I'm memorable! Well, I don't blow any trumpets, but this was two good looks at me, and then, second time, a chat. We mustn't have suspicion hanging on in her head. You yourself wouldn't want that, I'm certain. Maybe not even a girl so close to you would feel understanding for this kind of business link. But if the books go, like sold, I've got what I said, Col – full credibility. Look, I can tell it's sensitive for you. Tender connections. But why not regard them as the closed past and take this new one out for a big meal, like on the proceeds? Maybe jewellery. Jewellery they go for more than books, believe me. I never heard of a song 'Encyclopedias are a girl's best

158

friend'. Naturally, I'll give you the money for the outing. I mean, out of your first wages.'

Harpur could not tell him that Denise might already know of the 'arrangement', from his letter. Sometimes he wondered if he had meant Denise to know, without having to tell her. Of course he had heard of the subconscious, but did not go much on it. Harpur needed to think he was in control of himself, right through. '*All* the books?'

'Col, if you want to keep a cherished few, absolutely all right with me. This could happen with people selling a library and would not damage cred. A former wife's prayer book, say, or Sunday school prize. These commemorate.'

Any number of times Harpur had assured himself and the children he would dispose of Megan's books, to make the room less like a big browbeating study. Always he had drawn back. It seemed very final, and an insult to her, a betrayal. Another betrayal. To Harpur, the books as books, and books in general, meant almost nothing. This was why hers signified. Megan's volumes spoke of Megan, only of Megan. Because of that, Denise would probably like to see them gone, too.

'How?' Harpur said.

'I've got a van hired.'

'Already?'

'Oh, I knew before I asked you'd see the point, Col. This is partnership. Listen, I want her to be there when it's done. Naturally. This would really clinch my image – consummation of the deal. But she needn't come with us afterwards.

I'll learn a couple of things about books today so I can discuss collecting – which will bring more—'

'Cred. She can't come with us? Why's that?'

'Regrettably, Col, we pyre them. I know a quarry. Some petrol. Open them out a bit, they'll go up like a stolen car. It's a routine night sight in the country.'

Harpur felt his mind jolted back to the crematorium at Megan's funeral. 'Burn books?'

'Only the ones you don't want, Col.'

'Books, though.'

'What? World War II period again, yes? You're thinking of that Goebbels and his library bonfires. Famous symbol of barbarism, I know. Well, I hope nobody would ever call me barbaric. But what else, Col? Where else?'

'You want me to come?'

'I thought joint. See them to their end, as an act of respect.'

'Yes.'

'Tonight? Late?'

'Fine.'

A while after Vine had rung off, Harpur walked to the book shelves and pulled out a couple, held them in his hand. He felt like a trespasser. Obviously, there was nothing he wanted to keep, but he needed to touch some volumes, get the weight and shape, a kind of late communion. The girls came in early from school and surprised him while he was still holding two books, though not open.

'What's up, Dad?' Jill asked 'Ill? Teachers' meeting. The last class was dropped.'

'You still think about Mum now and then, do you, Dad?'

'Well, of course he does, of course we all do,' Jill said, 'but what's that got to do with books?'

'Good news,' Harpur replied, 'they go tonight.'

'Oh,' Jill said.

'Why?' Hazel asked.

'Well, didn't we all say we wanted to get rid of them, love?' Harpur replied.

'They don't really do any harm, do they?' Hazel said. 'It's upset you, as well? Why you're handling them?'

Jill was in an armchair, still wearing outdoor clothes, crouched over her schoolbag, head lowered.

'What, some dealer?' Hazel asked.

'That's it,' Harpur said. 'Fortunately, a true books lover.'

'They'll be resold all over the place,' Hazel replied. 'A lot are rubbish, yes, and dead as dead, like most books, but she liked them all together and with one another on the shelves. A collection's about the person who collected them. Bits sold here and there – it destroys something, Dad.'

'You're taking money?' Jill asked, speaking down at the school bag.

'Not much,' Harpur said. 'We'll split it.'

'I don't know,' Jill replied. 'I don't know if I want it.'

'You will,' Hazel said.

'Take out the ones you'd like to keep,' Harpur said.

'Is that what you're doing now, Dad? Choosing mementoes for yourself?' Hazel asked, hope in her voice.

'What? Oh, yes.' Fondly he gazed at the two books he was holding.

'You've never even heard of them, have you, Dad?' Jill asked.

'These? Of course,' Harpur replied. 'Oh, I definitely couldn't let these go.' He ruffled the pages of one. 'She's put pencil notes.'

'Say what they're called then – without looking again,' Jill said.

'This is a real, true dealer?' Hazel asked.

He had an appointment with Leslie Tranter in the evening, and left when he had given the girls their meal and washed up. Leslie and his safety worried Harpur. Tranter might easily stray into regions he did not know and could not manage. It would have been Tranter asking questions around the foreshore love cars. If you suddenly found out your wife had another life, another life leading to her death, it was natural to look for detail, even posthumously. Tranter, tap-tap-tapping on those steamed windows, might have discovered something, something more than Harpur did. This would be easy, because Harpur found nothing – only that someone else had been asking. Tranter might start nosing his plump and helpless way into trouble. Harpur had spoken to him immediately after the discovery of his wife's body, of course, and decided Tranter knew nothing. But that was then.

And so Harpur had telephoned to fix a meeting. The arrangement was firm, yet when Harpur arrived now, Tranter did not seem to be at home. The house was in the Rouge-ment area, a pricey, spacious district, where Desmond and Sarah Iles also lived. There were a lot of trees and hedges, and some unmade-up roads, to give that rural touch and prevent skateboarding. It was still only 8.30 p.m., yet the house appeared totally dark. What Harpur took to be Tranter's Granada estate car, and an Escort that must have been Christine's, stood side by side on the drive, up near the front door. A little way from it was an old cream and brown Dormobile, presumably the one Christine and Ember had used for evening love sessions in the multi-storey. Harpur could not make out the registration in the dark, but it more or less had to be. He waited, and grew increasingly anxious. People like Leslie who turned amateur investigative could attract reprisals. Harpur wished the estate car were absent: then, Tranter might have been on a sales mission somewhere. Now, there had to be a possibility he was in the house. Alive and uninjured in the house? He and Christine had children, and Harpur fretted about them, too. But perhaps they were away at school, or with relatives, until the first shock of the killing had passed. Yes, perhaps.

Harpur left his car and did a walk past the house. It was a big, white-painted, detached place, with two gates leading on to one of the unmade-up side roads, and had a wide gravelled horseshoe-shaped drive. There must be money in pets. Harpur kept going. It was the kind of road where people would hit the phone if they saw someone loitering after nightfall. He wanted no posse here.

The prospect of entering the Tranter home chilled him. Normally, Harpur adored breaking into homes on his own. On his own and illegally. An authorized, properly manned police search of a property had no charm. He liked to breathe

the essence of a place, and you could not do that if personnel were reprocessing the air. What he enjoyed in a dwelling was to read quietly from its privacies the nature of the owner. He compared the skill to psychiatry. A psychiatrist looked at the furniture of the mind and made his findings. Harpur just looked at furniture, and in and under and behind furniture: wardrobed clothes could speak; desked papers obviously could speak; beds, shoes, dirt could speak. But tonight, gazing at Southbridge, the Tranter five- or six-bedroom residence, he feared he might come upon something, somebody, some body, which could not speak at all.

Returning to his car, he sat and thought for a while. What was it he feared for Tranter? Had his wife been pulled into something through the link with Ember which Iles mentioned? Naturally, Harpur had known about that, too, and so had Francis Garland; but possibly they were the only ones, the only police that is. Ember might have been with her when it happened, might not. Harpur had sent Garland very early on to question Ralphy on this in oblique fashion, and, inevitably, Ralphy had replied in oblique fashion that he knew nothing of the woman or the death.

The case reversed all usual expectations: these two men, Tranter and Ember, had been close to the victim, yet neither was a suspect. Harpur himself would question Ember only if there were some good, unskirtable evidence. A waste of time, otherwise. And, with Ralph, there never was any good, unskirtable evidence: why he stayed free, nearly respectable, and supremely loaded. Probably he was at the foreshore with her, and someone, more than one, came looking for a settlement with him and botched it. They might come looking for Ralphy again. And, as an extra, they might come looking for anybody who seemed to be looking for *them*, and whose fat frame was a potential nuisance.

He gave it another half hour, then left the car again and this time went fast up the drive in the conifer shadows and paused behind the Dormobile. From there he did a long, close scrutiny of the house. As far as he could see, it had no alarm. That would have killed it for him: in theory he knew how to cancel one, but had never tried, and would not have made his first attempt here. Looking for weak points, he made a slow tour. He decided there were none, except, possibly, the front door. It was visible from the road and from neighbouring houses, and he had hoped to avoid that. Southbridge had double glazing on all windows downstairs, and probably upstairs. This always made things tough: a lot of glass to break. When he tried the door to the kitchen from the garden it felt as if there were bolts, as well as the lock.

The front door had an ordinary Yale, but his plastic card did not shift the catch. Very uneasy at being stuck in front of the house, he had another pause. Always he had a pause before smashing his way in somewhere: damage pushed criminality up more than a notch or two. Double glazing did not extend to these colourful, floral, leaded front door panes. Harpur broke one and waited again. He knew how to work in reasonable silence, but if you broke glass some of it was bound to fall inwards. He heard a few pieces hit what sounded like an uncarpeted wood floor and smash again.

Anyone awake inside would hear it, and quite possibly anyone asleep. Nobody came, though. He reached through and let himself in.

As soon as he shut the door behind him, he felt that customary, wonderful build-up of delight at penetrating someone's nest. All the earlier queasiness disappeared. He stood in the dark at the centre of the big hall and knew once again that, whatever his children said, or Megan used to say . . . and say and say . . . yes, he knew his chosen profession reached and satisfied the soul, brought him unmatchable sessions of towering exhilaration. Peering around the hall, he noted the pieces of good heavy Victorian furniture, the two barometers on the white walls, a scatter of what might be Afghan rugs on the parquet. Harpur could feel the fine enlightened style of these two, Christine and Les, and sensed the pathological boredom with it all that would have rushed her towards Ember. She had been tugged by the Rat Alley scar along his jaw, the off-key handsomeness, his grubby pomp and sadly frail dignity – and by the lean body after her husband's. Until what had happened happened, Harpur would have said Christine might have picked worse than Ralph. How did they first meet?

Very swiftly he went through the house. He had his pencil beam flashlight, but only put it on when skimming over the contents of a desk, and when he searched a dark recess under the stairs. His terror that he might find Tranter dead somewhere in the house began to subside. He had even feared he might find the children dead. The house, upstairs and down, looked undisturbed. The tone of the place was the same throughout: plenty of white, plenty of space, smart rugs, a preference for nice biggish Edwardian and Victorian pieces. They had obviously been keen on solidity and a sense of continuance, except, as far as Christine was concerned, in the actual marriage basics.

There was nothing and nobody in any of the beds, nor in any of the built-in cupboards. He did not enter the roof space, but put his torch beam on the decoration near the trap door, and spotted no scuffing. In both the front bedrooms he stood for a while at the side of the window before searching and checked that Tranter was not returning along the road. Leslie might have been tempted into a walk to the local from this lonely house. Harpur decided he must work even faster.

He was on his way back downstairs for another, more thorough, look in the desk when the telephone rang on three extensions, two downstairs, one in the main bedroom. Harpur felt encompassed by the din, and off balance for a moment. Then he went into the sitting room and picked up the receiver from the coffee table.

'This is Mr Leslie Tranter again?'

Harpur thought the male voice came very disguised and probably through cloth. He wondered if he could get away with a grunt, as if just woken from sleep, although it was still early. The caller might be in a street booth from which he could see the house. The darkness here had to be explained. He yawned a yes.

'All that information given previously was wrong, Mr Tranter. Do not act on it. Please. To do so would be not only dangerous but in error. Destroy the notes.'

Harpur yearned to put questions, but knew he must not. He waited.

'It would be best to let matters lie now. Yes, I do think so. She's dead.' There was a silence, as though the casual bluntness of his own words had upset the speaker. 'Nothing can change it. To attempt vengeance is to invite chaos and more suffering, Mr Tranter.'

Harpur stayed silent, trying to identify the voice, but able to decide for certain only that it was an assumed accent spoken through a layer or two. Ember? Well, it could be. Or not.

'Please, can I take it you agree, Mr Tranter? Please.'

Harpur brought out a handkerchief. He had sensed finality in that repeated 'please', and felt the call might end. He had learned almost nothing, and must risk his voice and a question now. Pulling his handkerchief over the mouth-piece he tried to sound West Country. 'Which information?'

No reply came for a moment. 'But you know which.'

'Yes, but which parts?'

'All. Look, Christ, who's speaking? Where's Tranter?'

'Leslie Tranter speaking.'

'Why are you talking through cloth?'

'Why are *you*?' Harpur replied.

The receiver at the other end went down: not slammed down, but lowered slowly, and just as final. It must be a call from a house, the speaker not wanting to draw attention by noise.

Destroy the notes. Was that something to salvage? *Destroy the notes.* Harpur went back to the desk and began to work through several heaps of papers, searching for unexplained names, of people or places: starting points for Leslie, and maybe finishing points. That's what the speaker seemed to fear. Harpur found nothing helpful. He saw that in his concentration on this kind of information he might be missing other important papers. For instance, there were interesting-looking figures on a couple of sheets, possibly accounts. No time to study them, though. Of course, the call might have been too late. Tranter could have the notes on him. Harpur left, walked quickly to his car and mobiled Denise at the flats, 'Can I pick you up? Something to show you,'

'But I'm struggling with *Sir Gawain and the Green Knight.*'

'Give in to both. Then you'll be ready when I get there,'

Wearing a studded black leather jacket and black trousers, she was waiting for him on a corner a block away from Jonson Court, and they drove towards Harpur's house. 'The dealer's coming to take Megan's books. You might want some for your studies. Plus you'll probably enjoy waving the rest goodbye.'

'This time of night? Which dealer?'

'You met him,'

'*That* dealer. Your grass? Vine? He's nocturnal?'

'He wants to prove he really is a dealer.'

'Mad.'

'Humour him.'

'Because he's useful?'

'He's useful. Look, choose any books you want to keep. Let the rest go.'

She slewed in the seat and stared at him. 'Christ, he'll dump them?'

Harpur kept quiet. He knew she was still staring but gazed ahead, intent on his driving.

'My God, Col,' she whispered, 'he'll *burn* them? This is *books.*'

'Don't get weighty. You're thinking of that German lad, are you? Goebbels, was it?'

'I wouldn't be surprised. But just like that? Burned? Have you read *Fahrenheit 451*?'

'What's that?'

'The temperature at which paper burns,'

'Yes, but—'

'It's a book.'

'A book about burning books?' Harpur asked. 'Biased?'

'It shows books are well, sort of . . . life.'

'*Mein Kampf*?'

When they reached the house they found Hazel and Jill still up and the books gone, except for *The Orton Diaries* and the volume of boxing journalism that Jill wanted. These two volumes stood together at one end of a shelf, about the same size library Harpur's parents had when he was growing up. 'Well, that's all right then,' he said, 'Once the shelves are down, this room will look twice as big.' He felt relieved Vine had come early and gone alone with the consignment to wherever he was going. Keeping up the play-acting, he said: 'He'll pay me later, will he?'

Jill said: 'Hazel phoned Iles.'

'Well, he reads, Dad. Makes all those corny quotes. All that. Even his house is called after a famous poem, yes?'

'*Idylls*', Harpur replied.

'Tennyson,' Denise said.

'There you are then, Dad,' Hazel said. 'That's a poet, isn't it?'

'Mr Iles took them?' Harpur asked.

'She was crying on the phone to him', Jill said. 'You know the way he is about Hazel.'

'He loves books, that's all,' Hazel yelled.

'He was here ten minutes after the call. Two journeys in two cars. His wife came. The baby in a carrycot. We helped load, obviously. Hurrying, in case the other one arrived. It was great, Dad. Like an adventure, and the baby being here, but sleeping all through. The books all round her cot in the car.'

'He'll keep them together,' Hazel said. 'And he'll read them.'

'If we want to go and look at any in his house, we can. Or take those we want,' Jill said. 'Like when we grow up, if we need them for education. Oh, God, what a thought. And Denise would be able to look at them as well, a student. Unless you don't want Denise near him, Dad, on his own property. I don't expect you do. Or Hazel, probably.'

'Don't you think Iles is great, Denise?' Hazel asked. 'I mean, this is an assistant chief. You'd expect some kind of animal, and naturally he can be. But this other, sweeter side. And reading. Can you imagine? An assistant chief, but *reading*!'

'Great,' Denise replied.

'There you are, Dad,' Hazel said. 'Listen to Denise. You're upset about not getting money for them?'

'Your dad's not like that. But you already know.'

Harpur said: 'Is Mr Iles coming back? Or is he too busy *reading*?' On the whole he hoped Iles would not reappear. He hoped Sarah Iles would not, either. He did not want Iles to run into Vine. And, for old times' sake, he did not want Sarah to run into Denise.

'You just scoff at him,' Hazel snarled. 'But he can do good things.'

The children went to bed. At just after 1 a.m., Vine arrived with the van. Harpur brought him into the room and said: 'Had a better offer.'

'That's the book business,' Denise said.

'Right. It happens all the time in our game,' Vine replied.

'But I expect there are interesting libraries you can pounce on elsewhere in the small hours,' Denise said.

'No offence meant, but I see it as sad that people today are no longer interested in the books so carefully assembled by parents, even grandparents,' Vine replied. 'I fear the former . . . well . . . yes, the former *reverence* for books – by no means too strong a word – I fear it's gone.'

'I can always get turned on by *Aaron's Rod*,' Denise said.

Vine glanced sympathetically at Harpur. The two of them walked to the van. 'Sorry, Keith.'

'Who?'

'A friend. You wouldn't know him.'

'That's all right. Obviously, I couldn't care less. Fucking

books themselves, just an eyesore. As long as I convinced your bird I'm a genuine dealer.'

'No question,' Harpur replied.

He would have liked to make love to Denise on the sitting room floor, or against the shelves, as if to proclaim this domain was truly theirs now. They had done it here before, behind the sofa, with the books glowering down at them. Denise would not have it now, though, and insisted on going to bed. 'It would be crude and cruel, Col – a bit of second-hand symbolism. You owe her better.'

'You bloody kids, full of quibbles and preaching.'

20

It had taken Ember nearly twenty-four hours to decide after all that he must warn Tranter – if possible stop him going to London and The Sleeping Sentinel. The hazards for that lumbering fool were too great. Ember was often badgered by such vile attacks of conscience and decency. And so he had weakened suddenly and telephoned Southbridge from The Monty. It was the evening after he resolved on his drive home to do nothing. Of course, the reply had terrified him: an unknown or disguised voice at the other end, trying to be Tranter. Ember might have gone out to the Rougement area immediately to investigate, but there was one of those occasional nasty outbreaks of fighting at the club, and he could not get away until very late.

Had those sods come looking for Tranter before Tranter could go looking for *them*? They must have heard of Leslie's nosiness and pushiness and dangerous amateur anger, and visited his home to end all that. Once more Ember's loving debt to Christine was transformed into very late concern for Leslie – maybe much *too* late. Possibly the debt to Christine and the debt to Tranter were identical, and he could only protect Leslie by taking out the hunters – the same hunters who killed Christine. Ember was half thankful for that fracas at the club: the delay gave whoever answered time to get clear. Ember knew he might have been too scared to come earlier.

Southbridge appeared dark. He drove past slowly, turned and came back, taking another careful look. It seemed a decent enough place. Gazing at the Dormobile, he experienced violent sorrow. Wrong, so wrong, that it should languish, imprisoned by Leslie's stout hedges, as if Tranter possessed her more now after death than in her life. Ember parked. He must get closer and perhaps inside the house. At this prospect, early panic sensations did start – that crippling ache across his shoulders and down his back, and the sweating, of course. He sat for a while, partly to postpone the invasion, partly in case his car had been heard and drew someone to a bedroom window. Strange that before this he had never even seen the place where Christine lived. Yet now she was dead, he would try to enter it, and not on her account, but Leslie's.

He left the car and walked quickly back towards the property. As long as you were careful, footsteps produced little sound on these unmade-up pavements. He turned into the Southbridge drive and used the shadows from a line of conifers for his approach. Behind the Dormobile he paused. Sadly and with love he ran his hand over a rusting section of the bodywork. Lately, all physical touching related to Christine had been tragic: manhandling her body across the mud, and now this. The house seemed to have no alarm system, but he thought all the windows on both floors appeared double glazed, and that could mean problems. The front door might be the most likely for entry. People rarely double glazed leaded panes of stained glass, and even if they did it was less noisy to break one of these small rectangles than a complete window. The sweat and ache in his shoulders continued, but not too bad. His legs felt reasonable, and he had no urge to check his jaw scar for leaks. The front door was overlooked by the upper storeys of a couple of neighbouring houses, and it caught beams from a street light. But too bad.

He moved forward and entered the small porch. Immediately, he saw that one leaded pane had already been broken and fear welled. This reaction made no sense. The phone call had told him someone other than Tranter was inside, so he could have expected signs of entry. But his panics never squared with logic. Before he was really aware of it, his hand reached up and ran desperately along the scar. Obviously, he had been so right to come here, and so wrong. Almost everything in him urged retreat, while it was available. These were the sort of flee signals he so often received, and so rarely resisted – the sort of signals that had brought him a prime career and kept him safe and on the right side of the wall. Despite the time gap, an intruder, intruders, might still be in the house. And Tranter could be here, but not alive. His children – his and her children – might be here, but also not . . .

This thought dazed him and took all the rest of his diminished strength. After that, he could not have run, would never have reached his car. He stood huddled against the door, supporting himself on it, and after a moment threw up massively in the porch, just one roaring disgorgement. Christ, he could taste the club's special Kressmann Armagnac as it went by, and smell it afterwards. Would vomit identify him? The din might have reached neighbours and because he could not retreat Ember decided the only way to hide was forward. He put his hand through the broken pane, let himself in, then closed the door. He sat down on the parquet floor among glass fragments, his back against the door, and puked again – less, but enough. Oh, God, what a way to treat dear Chris's property. He tried to stare through the darkness of the hall, in case someone came to investigate the noise.

Of course, in its shoulder holster he carried the Walther automatic which he favoured these days. After a couple of seconds, he would certainly be recovered enough to bring that out to readiness, but did not feel up to it now. In any case, he had double or triple vision. The outlines of furniture and a couple of barometers – it *was* two, wasn't it, his eyes could not be that bad? – these outlines that he could just make out around the hall and on the white walls danced and faded hellishly, then danced again, and he would be useless with a gun. Yet, despite this eye trouble and the persistent nausea, he loved the feel of this hall. It seemed to him so right for Christine, spacious, genuine, cool.

After a few minutes he was able to stand. He rested for a while longer against the barometers wall, and now brought out his automatic. He had the gun in one hand and a small flashlight in the other, but did not use this yet. Very slowly he began to move through the ground floor rooms, searching each for any evidence of trouble. In a sitting room he saw on a coffee table what might be the telephone where his call was taken. Nearby stood a handsome bureau desk, possibly even pre-Victorian. He opened that and, switching on his flashlight briefly, went through some of the neatly pigeon-holed papers, but found nothing that interested him. What *would* interest him? Something in Christine's handwriting, probably. He saw none of that. Most of it was routine domestic stuff, plus one or two pages of notes about what Ember took to be the cat and dog business, just unexplained figures and hieroglyphics, possibly even a kind of code. If the figures were money, they seemed very big for flea powder and feed machines. But look at this house. That seemed very big for someone in such trade, too.

He gave all the rooms, upstairs and down, a good search, and a recess under the stairs. In the front bedrooms he glanced out from the side of the windows in case Tranter or anyone else was approaching on foot. But where would Tranter have been at this hour? At any rate, he was not in the house, nor were the children, thank God. And, thank God again, nobody else was here, either. In what he took to be the main bedroom he could catch thin traces of Opium, her rich perfume, and, when he opened a wardrobe and put the torch on for a moment to search, found many clothes he recognized and which had always looked so great on Christine. Turning, he saw something else familiar. On the dressing table was one of the distinctive Monty blue champagne flutes, containing a single artificial white carnation. The flute caused a deep shiver to pass through his body. When he had recovered he put the automatic into his pocket, then picked up the glass and pressed it for nearly a minute against his face before replacing it. Sad, sad, sad. He had given that glass to Chris the first time they met. With the end of his tie he wiped it very throughly now. God, but it took him back.

Christine had come to the club one night with a divorced lad she was seeing something of in those days, Brendan Haldane, always called Item, and Ember had managed a couple of little conversations apart with her, while Item was talking private business elsewhere in the bar. Possibly he was working for Kenward at that time and liked big-wheeling. All the same, Ember could not believe Item was enough for Christine, and edged the chat with her around to suggesting lunch one day, not at The Monty. Often Ember considered beautiful women looked unfulfilled when with other men. God knew how or where she had first met someone like Item: her marriage must really have gone bad for her to turn to him. Well, of course, it *had* gone bad: he learned something of that later. She had needs, and Leslie did not meet them. She was bound to look elsewhere. Ember would never think ill of her for that, even though she had first chosen Item.

That evening, Christine had hesitated over Ember's lunch suggestion, and then, maybe to switch topics, said how she adored the champagne flute she was drinking from. Immediately, and really only as a joke, Ember handed her one, told her to put it into her handbag, and said she could repay him by coming to lunch. She had hidden the glass, and, eventually, just as Item was returning, agreed to meet Ember. Within a couple of weeks, she dropped Haldane, and soon afterwards he disappeared altogether, though Ember had never heard he was inside or taken out of circulation otherwise. Presumably, Christine told Leslie she had bought the flute somewhere to act as a bedroom vase. Tranter was unlikely to come to The Monty and see its family. It was because he never visited the club that she had been able to attend with Item.

This flute greatly moved and delighted Ember now. His visit here had been a triumph, after all. It meant so much that she had chosen to place this gift from him near the marriage bed. She could have fixed her eyes on it while Leslie, just back from his animal travels, told her of sales and motorway tailbacks. She might even have gazed at it reminiscently while the two of them— But no, no, he would not let himself think of that again. He went downstairs. Very soon he must leave. It was not far off dawn. He found a floorcloth and thoroughly mopped up the hall and porch leavings. No question of returning the cloth, and he carried it with him to his car, distributing the vomit in unremarkable helpings along the hedge of a neighbouring house. The cloth could go into his incinerator at The Monty later.

The joy brought to him by sight of the flute began to decay as he drove home. For reasons he did not understand, he often suffered second thoughts as he approached Low Pastures, usually good, but sometimes not. Christine was still dead. Yes, that champagne flute signified glorious faithfulness to him, even when she was sleeping with someone else, yet it made her loss more agonizing still. The question of Leslie remained. It had been a relief not to find him butchered in the house, but where was he? Had he followed those lethal directions? He might have gone by train or coach, so as to have no identifiable car with him in London. Would he arrive at The Sleeping Sentinel later today, spouting harsh, careless questions? Had he been there already? And if so, was he still alive? Would he suddenly and eternally drop from view like Item? By the time Ember reached his house, he could no longer recall why he had felt happy. Things were as bad as they had been.

It was almost 6 a.m. when he crawled into bed and folded himself around Margaret's behind. She woke up. 'Problems, love?' she asked.

'Vendetta riot. Took some putting down. It stopped twice, and then broke out again. One lad wore a coloured cravat instead of a black tie to the other lad's mother's funeral. Disrespect. Oh, knives eventually.'

'My God, Ralph, are you all right?'

'Very little damage, in the circumstances. But upset. Margaret, a fracas like that – I'm afraid it shows we're still not quite The Garrick.'

'Never mind.' She turned. 'I want to make love with a hero,' she said, deep kissing him.

Luckily, he had cleaned his teeth and done a heavy job with the mouthwash.

21

With his first money from Vine and Co. Harpur bought himself an Avantage Swiss wristwatch, narrow and elegant, a make advertised now and then on the back page of the *Daily Telegraph*. He wanted some luxury which was not too noticeable, but noticeable enough for Vine and Stan Stanfield. As well as telling Harpur the time, it had to tell *them* he was aboard, and enjoying it. Of course, Iles would spot the watch and cost it to within a hundred, and Denise might, too, so he wore it only when he was meeting his new colleagues. His daughters also saw it, but probably would not realize the price had been £2,700. They looked, did some admiration to humour him, then forgot it. He bought a couple of fine silk shirts as well. A watch like this needed to lurk half under class cuffs. He loved the sight of their brilliant combination, and began to resent days when he had to leave the watch at home. Wealth would suit him, he decided. God, he *was* enjoying it.

So far, he had done nothing to earn his wages. These two lads knew how high-level recruitment worked. Probably Stanfield had instructed Vine in the delicacies. Stan had seen a lot, appreciated protocol. Always, the first fee had to be up front, ahead of any service. It was thought coarse to link the money direct to an actual task right from the start. The first fee signified goodwill, and promised far more to come, once work began. The first fee told of fine trust and an understanding. The first fee had strings and more strings, but for a brief while looked as if it had no strings at all, only sound sentiment. The first fee was three thousand in fifties, without any advice note to say what period it covered. Vine passed it over in a loose wad. He said if there was one thing he despised it was money in envelopes, because that always made a transaction seem shady. And he thought the notes just like this, open and ready, encouraged happy spending, which was what he and Stanfield wanted Harpur to take pleasure in now, after such a long and skimping time on police pay. Vine could be right. Harpur split the cash, and he was conscious of the fifties' pleasant weight in his jacket pockets, one portion on each side. They brought him the lovely sense of being protectively enclosed, cherished, embraced by funds. Perhaps with later fees he would be able to buy a classier jacket.

And then the first task came. It sounded simple, but Harpur realized from the start it might turn out not to be. Vine said a major delivery was due, and they would like him to be with them to take it. 'We switch rendezvous points every time, Col. Well, as you'd expect. Not just your fine boys we have to worry about, is it? We're talking about forty, fifty grand's worth of stuff and forty, fifty grand we're carrying from street profits to make the purchase. Not a bad combined haul for some evil pirates.'

'This will be just a gentle trip out, Mr Harpur,' Stanfield said. He had the big, fair, roguish moustache, but respectful voice. The story went he did more than all right with women.

'Plus if you could check first we're not under surveillance by your drugs section, Col. We change rendezvous, yes, but once or twice we've both, that's Stan and me, we've both thought we might have had something behind us on the way out. Once we actually aborted. Oh, I don't know— I mean, it could be nothing at all. There's been no move on us, and we've done some very pricey transfers already, obviously. But now and then your people bide their subtle time, don't they, thinking the longer they wait the bigger the catch?'

'Would you know if your drugs lads were doing anything, Mr Harpur?' Stanfield asked. 'They're secretive, these specialists, as I understand, trust nobody, not even you and Mr Iles. No, not Mr Iles.'

'They handle their own operations,' Harpur replied. 'But I'd probably have heard. They report to me, ultimately.'

'You could do a little check, Col?' Vine asked. 'Sort of turn detective.'

'As I said, they're in some ways an independent unit. But I'll give it a go,' Harpur replied. He had to try to read these two, especially Stanfield. They were not the same. Possibly Stanfield had not wanted Harpur brought in. It could be a Vine proposition which Stan had eventually accepted, but still disliked, even if he had coached Vine in how to do it. Stan's jolly moustache, his heavy politeness, and all the ancestor bullshit overlaid a brisk brain. It would have been Stanfield who decided Harpur should make this little test trip with them, and who forced Vine to agree. This was Stan's condition for accepting Harpur, so Harpur had better go.

Had to go. He'd taken the signing-on money and spent it. The strings.

Vine said: 'We want you to see how the business functions, that's all, Col. Like work experience? If some day we run into trouble – which pray God not – but if so, such trouble could knock out one of us or both, that's Stan and/ or me, say lying low or even worse. Well, a business has to plan for such contingencies, however unlikely, and in that case, Colin, you might have to get out on a delivery alone.'

'Educational,' Stanfield said.

'Glad of the chance,' Harpur replied.

With a big laugh, Vine said: 'Yes, well now, don't learn so much you think of going off on your own, Col. We've got enough competition.'

'I'm a company man,' Harpur replied.

They held their meetings in Stanfield's flat or at The Martyr hotel car park. The three thousand had been handed over so matter-of-fact in the car park, but tonight they were at Stan's place again. They could not go to Harpur's or Vine's because of the children and Keith's girl. Stanfield lived alone – had women in for a spell, naturally, but nothing long-term. To cut risk, Harpur and Vine always arrived here separately, of course, and left separately, of course, Harpur first, also of course, so Vine and Stanley could talk about him privately afterwards. The flat was creepily chintzy for someone as cosmopolitan as Stanfield. There was a moquette suite, like one Harpur's parents used to have, but without antimacassars, and a brown–beige, sensibly dark fitted carpet. On what looked like a Utility-style 1950s sideboard he even had a tantalus displaying square-shouldered decanters, though he offered no alcohol. They drank coffee from mugs. Two framed, dim seascape prints hanging on one wall looked as if they had been taken from an art book. Harpur wondered whether they were by Stan's supposed nineteenth-century forebear, and such an aid to his prestige now.

Stanfield was sitting alongside Harpur on the settee, and suddenly turned towards him in casual style and put a hand in under the lapel of Harpur's jacket, to where a shoulder holster would have been. 'You're not carrying anything, Mr Harpur?' he asked.

'I'm among friends, Stan,' Harpur replied.

'Great, great answer, Col,' Vine said, from his armchair. He thumped the moquette arm in approval. '*Among friends.*' Keith seemed to regard Harpur's words as a triumph over Stanfield. 'Col's not one to carry a weapon except when weapons are necessary.'

Stanfield sat back. 'Myself the same. But Keith, now – he likes a bit of metal against his tit non-stop. Deems it big-boys him, don't you, Keithy?'

In its way, that had been a comradely, permissible thing to do, the frisking by Stanfield – not much different from shaking hands or asking after someone's family. And in its way a clever thing, too. Stanfield would not really be interested in whether Harpur carried a gun up there. He wanted to know if Harpur was wired for sound. Clearly, this was not something he could ask or investigate direct. It would be a deep insult. So, this ploy. Didn't he know, though, that science had advanced? All the cabling-up was no longer necessary. If Harpur had been carrying a bug, this primitive grope would not have found it. But he was not carrying one. He had nobody to transmit to or record for. This was Harpur solo, white-knighting again in the shaky cause of worldwide virtue.

'How will you check whether your drugs boys have us in mind, Mr Harpur?' Stanfield asked.

'What the fuck's this Mr Harpur, Mr Harpur, Stan?' Vine replied. 'He's Col, Colin. Aloof, that's how you sound, Stan, unconfed.'

'I'll call a little general update meeting,' Harpur replied. 'Ask for a general situation survey. I often do that. Nothing noticeable.'

'They'll tell you?' Stanfield said. 'Everything?'

Harpur shrugged: 'I'll ask them.'

'What else can he do, Stan?'

'Police – they sit on their findings, hoard them until it's time to maximize the *gloire.*'

'That's Monsieur Stanleeeee telling you he worked in France, Col. But Monsieur Stanleeeee had to come back, for undeclared reasons.'

'I might be able to browse a file or two, on the quiet,' Harpur replied.

'We're taking delivery at Medal Park Services on the motorway this time,' Stanfield said. 'Tomorrow night at ten. Pick you up somewhere at nine-thirty, Colin?'

'That's better,' Vine cried. 'He's opened his distinguished heart to you, Col. First name terms at last.'

*

Naturally, the delivery never took place. They drove to the services and waited in the car park until 11.30. At 11.15, Stanfield made a call on the mobile phone, but could get no answer. Probably he was ringing his own home number. 'Some late crisis,' he said. 'It's happened before. They get a problem and can't tell us.' He waved the mobile. 'They don't like talking on these things, and I can't blame them, really. Think of Prince Charles and the lady. It will only be a postponement. But a tragedy it has to happen the night you're here for familiarization, Colin.'

Harpur was fond of motorway services. He liked the notion of people speeding randomly to these no man's land, all men's land spots, and then almost instantly dispersing every way, bladder-drained and garrisoned by an exorbitant bun. It all had to be a symbol of something. From first mention he had thought this rendezvous might possibly be make-believe. Stanfield would never allow somebody so far unproved to eye such a major buy. The delivery people would kill Stan if they discovered he had brought a possible give-away. Harpur's Avantage and the shirts made their grateful, minion statement, but he knew Stanfield would stay unconvinced. He had obviously wanted to see whether Harpur would whistle up an ambush. If he did, there would be nothing for the posse to discover except a senior detective in strange company, but Stanfield would have discovered plenty. If Harpur did not, Stan might be able to believe he was genuinely in, not just a crippling Vine error. There had been no need at all last night for Stanfield to disclose the meeting spot. They could simply have driven him there, sealed orders. Stanfield had wanted Harpur to know in advance, though, so he could pass on the dud location, if he was a plant.

'I made some gentle enquiries with our drugs section,' Harpur said on the way back. 'I'm pretty sure you're in the clear.'

'*We*'re in the clear, Col,' Vine replied. 'This is an equal partnership.'

22

Ember had the message that when he motored down to see the supplier for their first big consignment he should bring at least one of his partners with him, and if possible two. Actually, the word used was not partners but principals. 'Bring one or two of your principals, would you, Ralph?' – spoken in that lilting, jump-to-it-serf boardroom voice. Hearing this by phone, Ember had been puzzled for a second, even enraged. Then the explanation: 'Ralph, I'm spelling principals *a l s*, not principles *l e s*, of course. I'm sure you've got more than one or two of *those*, Ralph – the *l e s* kind, I mean, i.e., moral standards! Ralph W. Ember is famed for them. No, I refer to your main colleagues, your other directors, principals in the firm.'

Ember chuckled and said, 'Of course, of course, Barney.' That was all right, then. The sweet, coke-tankering ponce was not saying Ember lacked ethics. Or *was* it all right? Ember had planned to keep Harry Foster and Gerry Reid, the outfit's rough-edged other ... well ... other, yes, maybe ... *principals*, definitely out of view. They had their different flairs, no question, but at first sight and sound they could knock a bad hole in people's confidence.

'Important to make their acquaintance, Ralph, and vice versa. If you were laid up with a nasty migraine some time, or hammer-toe, one of these fine associates might have to

190

be your proxy at a meeting, and it helps if there's been earlier face-to-face. Thus, no identity worries. I mean for either side.'

'Wise.'

Of course, what sodding Barney really wanted to do was what Ember did not want him to do, and this was measure the status of the firm by vetting the full team, an audit. Foster and Reid would love it, as good as getting a peerage. Instead of lining up street dealers for the off, they would meet class company. He had told them to wear suits and decent ties, and they looked well intentioned enough, like ushers at a low wedding. Both swore they would let Ember do the talking, but you could not rely on it, not with a Mouth-Mouth like Gerry Reid. Gerry thought he had a gift and aplomb. Many must have told him no, yet he kept brave faith in himself.

They drove down in Gerry's Nissan, forty grand news-paper-wrapped in the boot. This money and the recruiting fees he had paid Reid and Harry was from all sorts of little enterprises way back in Ember's career, and probably safe to spend now. It had pained him to have it lying uninvested, even in these days of low inflation. Now, it would start earning. Eventually, everything he staked would come back to him, and come back bigger. These two realized that. The income ratio would be two shares to him, one each to them, until Ember's floating funds were repaid. There were years' damn dangerous work in this outlay, and he wanted the money used sweetly. He also wanted the deal it secured to be the start of a long, good relationship.

In the car, Ember said: 'Barney's tough as tungsten but acts ladylike. Not gay – languid. Aims to sound like a marquis. Don't laugh. He makes half a million a year.'

'Well-known English type, what's called "the officer class",' Reid replied. 'La-di-da voice, but so brave going over the top againt the Boche. Me – well, out of a different stable in County Cork. But I admire that type. That club – The Cavalry and Guards, Piccadilly. I'd love to belong to it. I mean as well as The Monty, of course, Ralph.'

'Importing how?' Foster said.

'We don't ask,' Ember replied. 'It comes to him, he sells to us. That's all we have to know.'

'*All we know and all we need to know,*' Reid said. His grammar could be all over the place, but he had a bullshit poetic side, like most Irishmen.

'Get to the source and we'd cut out his percentage, Ralph. Why help him to half a Big One plus?' Foster asked.

Jesus, this is somebody who should not be on the trip at all, and he was already trying to fucking run things. That was Harry. This kind of aggression had its worth, clearly, but in the right place, like some trouble spot. Harry was not good on tact and judgement. He had wanted to bring Deloraine with him today, 'for a nice run'. This was a tasty piece, unquestionably, but Ember would not allow it. He did not even like it that Foster would tell her where they were visiting. Ember sincerely meant to find some time for Deloraine soon, but not on this kind of major outing, for God's sake.

'We just do the deal and come away,' Ember replied.

'Remember that Les Howard in *The Scarlet Pimpernel,* on

TV?' Gerry Reid said. 'Squeaky talker, yet real brave, right under their Froggy noses.'

Earlier this morning there had been a few moments when Ember considered putting off the journey. Should he get to London and The Sleeping Sentinel fast, to look for that other Les, Tranter? This burden still troubled him, as though Les himself had dropped his huge, pushy weight on Ember's back. When you had pulled a man from the water you felt bound to him, and especially when he was the husband of a lady you had fucked on a regular basis. But you could not mess with the timetable of someone as majestic as Barney. The date and time had been fixed when he rang about these brilliant principals. 'It'll be an all-round delight to see you and yours then, Ralph!' Oh, Christine, Christine, am I your hubbie's keeper? He hadn't even been *her* keeper, not with any success.

Barney had a place in quality Hampshire boating country a bit west of Southampton and the Isle of Wight. You could not get anywhere greener or more high-class maritime. This was a village on the river, and included a nice collection of yachts just outside Barney's front windows, with that smart sound of rigging against masts in a breeze. Giving directions, Barney said his part of the village was called The Wharf, and Ember had been expecting something like one of the disused docks near Valencia Esplanade. This was different. This wharf meant a neat little white jetty kept in first-class order, where four glistening craft were moored in the swift brown water today. Ember did not know much about it, but he thought none would have cost less than three quarters of a million. One of them was sure to be Barney's, or perhaps more than one. Probably the yacht named *Modesty*. That would be just like the smug bastard.

'This his business fleet?' Foster said. 'How he brings it in?'

'Christ, of course not. This is pleasure. Sport, Harry. Style,' Ember replied.

On a couple of the boats people moved about doing sea-type things that Ember always loved to watch: coiling ropes, carrying buckets, laying out oilskins to dry in the sun. They had a sound appearance of leisure and wealth. Ember used to think he had a fine life, with the club and Low Pastures, but when he saw vessels and houses like this he knew he had not started yet. This scene gave you scale and stoked up your ambition. The radar on some of these cost more than The Monty. They parked down near the water, and Ember thought it looked bad to be carrying a newspaper parcel tied with thick hairy string in this setting.

Ember had met Barney a couple of times before, but not at home. He was the kind who liked to be in shirt sleeves and slacks only, so everyone could see he was not carrying anything. Barney had gone above all that a long time ago. He thought he could take care of any untowardness by force of personality and his reputation. He did not object if others were armed – did not object, and did not even seem interested. Probably he regarded guns as artisan.

At the door, greeting them, he cried: 'I love it, love it, Ralph. The package. So deftly understated.' He had on a scarlet shortsleeved shirt and black jeans. His face was at that classy stage between tanned and weather-beaten, and Ember had an impression that even his elbows would taste briny. 'And these must be your best chums, then.'

Ember introduced them.

Barney said: 'There are some who argue business and home don't mix. But I'd say friends are friends wherever, indivisible. I've no time for silly demarcations.'

'How I do agree, Barney,' Reid replied. 'These arbitrary supposed ground rules!' He was looking with admiration around the long untidy hall, where a couple of very old-style bicycles with flat tyres leaned against a wall and two petrol cans stood on the central shelves of a big glass-fronted rosewood china cabinet, which was otherwise empty. Above the cabinet hung a heavy framed oil painting of rural lanes. 'Magnificent,' Reid said. 'As striking as any modernistic gallery.' He waved at the picture. 'The art in standard form, and then you have these exhibits to as it were comment – splendidly witty bikes, and them cabinet shelves, the void-ness of the top and bottom highlighted by the red cans. Red always brings out voidness, don't it, Barney?'

'I think the games room,' Barney replied. He led up the fine, wide stairs to double doors in a corridor on the first floor, and they entered. 'Oh,' he said. A couple of middle-aged women in worried-looking print dresses were playing darts at one end. 'Here are Camilla and Maud. They look after me. Oh, yes. Meet some new chums of mine, girls.'

The room had a high-backed church pew against a wall, and Barney led over to it. The four sat alongside one another and watched the darts. There was no other furniture in the room. Old cream linoleum covered the floor. Ember had the money on his lap. It was unpleasant to think Barney did anything with Camilla and Maud. They were friendly, full of happy giggles and active, but no real bodies to compensate for their age and clothes. Now and then you would come across people like Barney. They made the money and had enough imagination to set themselves up with the usual big possessions – the great house, the boat, probably a noble car or two somewhere. But then they seemed to lose energy. Wealth bored them. That did not mean they grew slack at bargaining, but they wouldn't bother with décor or accessories, and made do with women who might have been around long before the riches came. Somebody with a name like Maud was bound to be from the past. She eventually won the darts, and with some charming gestures and a speech Reid went over and presented an imaginary trophy, his round face and blue-black eyes aglow with friendship, even gallantry. This was one of Gerry's strongest aspects. He could switch it on and lull all sorts, as long as they did not know him.

Ember was at the far end of the pew from Barney, and, when the women had gone, passed the newspaper package along like a collection plate in church via Reid and Foster to him. It was an inconvenient way of sitting and talking, making easy interchange impossible, but Barney was host, and it would be crude to object. He undid the parcel, let the newspaper and string fall to the floor, and then counted the money twice. Ember had the idea this paper and string might stay there for months. He leaned forward around

Panicking Ralph

Foster and Reid to watch the counting. Barney took his time, murmuring figures to himself, and put the fifties into piles of ten grand each on an unused piece of pew to his left. The thoroughness of it, and the way he turned his body to half conceal the stacks, struck Ember as almost insulting. He began to wonder whether Barney was after all genuinely aristocratic, not just jumped up. How else did you explain his contempt for manners, his willingness to screw boiling pieces, and the indifference to everything domestic?

Finishing the check at last, Barney said: 'I'm going to let you have 2.5 kilos of moderately cut but excellent produce in exchange for this honorarium, boys. Since you've made such a journey, and for the pleasure of seeing you all.'

'Sixteen grand a kilo?' Foster replied.

'To you,' Barney said, 'but don't tell others, or I'm bankrupt. Look, we had the customs the other day talking about a confiscated 1,300 kilo load being worth £250 million. That's getting on for £200,000 a kilo.'

Foster said: 'Oh, customs. They knit themselves medals. Let's talk trade, not trumpet calls. Sixteen grand a kilo? I heard of—'

'This is excellent produce, Harry,' Ember said.

Foster said: 'All right, say it is, but—'

'What's decent, cut produce street-trading at in your purlieus, then, Harry?' Barney asked. 'Sixty pounds a gramme? More?'

'About sixty,' Ember replied.

'But we don't sell direct on to the street,' Foster said.

'Would I think you did, looking at you?' Barney asked.

'Are you alley and corner people?' He had a kindly guffaw, which clang-echoed in this bare room. He gazed at Foster's plastic shoes. 'Hardly.'

'That's what I mean,' Foster said.

'What, Harry?' Barney asked.

'We're not talking about two and a half thousand sixties just for us,' Foster said.

Because of the pews, he was right up there alongside Barney, getting these points in so direct, whereas Ember, isolated at the other end, had to try to keep things amiable by shouting across Reid and then Foster's wide shoulders and chest and slabby wedge of black hair. Ember felt something of a panic starting.

'Two and a half thou times sixty!' Barney cried. 'That would be lovely gain, indeed, yes.' He clapped his hands, once at the unreal beauty of this idea. 'Pay forty grand, bring in a hundred and fifty. One could say that would rate as profiteering, wouldn't you think, Harry? Wouldn't *you* think, Gerry, Ralph?'

'Our street dealers will be taking five hundred a week, sometimes more,' Foster said.

'That's about par,' Barney replied. 'You'll be selling to them at what a gramme – forty, thirty-five? Say forty. That's sixty grand clear in your confederate pouch for one transaction. After all, the risk is elsewhere, Harry. You're not in the firing line, are you?'

'Firing line?' Foster said. 'And you, Barney, would you say—?'

'Possibly you could do 2.75 kilos, Barney,' Ember called.

Panicking Ralph

Barney leaned forward, the forty grand tucked into his lap, and smiled along at Ember. 'Ralph, Ralph, I'd heard you did a tough deal, but, well – 2.75. Well!'

Foster said: 'We make sixty but then we need forty of it for the next lot.'

'Oh, probably more at the start, Harry,' Barney said. 'You'll be wanting to expand, I expect. You have to invest to gain.'

'Well, there you are then,' Foster said. 'And these figures are make-believe, anyway, because we're going to be paying back Ralph for capitalizing and so on. Months, maybe years.'

'Eventually you'll be making such meaty withdrawals, won't you, though, Harry? This is a trade where expansion is virtually automatic and extremely rapid. But let's suppose for a second you were equals and you stayed at the forty. This is if you were unambitious, which I'll swear you're not. That's twenty profit every delivery – say fortnightly. Let's be modest – I love modesty – say seven grand each as profit every three weeks. One hundred and twenty thousand per principal a year if you were splitting simple three ways. All right, you won't be at the start. But you'll soon clear Ralph's investment. Then, wow! Are you used to a lot better than that, Harry? What's your other occupation, co-starring with Kevin Costner?'

Foster said: 'I won't be buying any yacht on my share.'

Barney looked fondly at him for a while. 'You know, I wouldn't have thought of you as a boat person.'

'No? So what sort of person did you think of me as then, Barney?'

Reid said: 'Barney thinks of you as a salt of the earth person, Harry, and so do all of us. But not a sea salt person.'

'Right,' Ember declared, with a decent laugh. The panic still held him, but was not advancing.

'And then this fucking room, this fucking house,' Foster replied. 'No proper furniture in here, so we're strung out like waiting for a vicar. No curtains. That tip of a hall. What's it all about, Barney?'

'The best part of this type of work is you get eye-openers,' Reid said.

'I hope I'm someone who listens well to what he hears all about him,' Barney replied. 'And especially when what's said comes from someone like Ralph W. Ember. I'll go to 2.6 kilos, on account of his civilized plea and for general good fellowship.'

'Thanks, Barney,' Ember replied.

'But, look, don't take it as a precedent. Now, please. A man has to live. That's going to put you on a hundred and thirty-five, hundred and forty a year, Barney said.

Foster said: 'Yes, but, look, Barney—'

'This appears to me like the kind of deal to please all sides,' Reid remarked. His voice was warm and jubilant. 'The kind we're here for, Barney. The kind that, having heard the sort of fine operator you are, showing proper consideration for all parties, the kind of deal I would have expected.'

'Thanks, Gerry,' Barney said. He leaned out again to gaze at Ember and grew grave. 'You've got opposition where you are, Ralph. I have to say it, these are sizeable people – Stanley Stanfield, for one, plus possible police commitment. Now we're in full business contact, naturally I want to keep you hale and safe and productive. And, meeting you as a fascinating unit, I know you'll do superbly. They have Eleri ap Vaughan operating through them. A magnificent list.'

'I'm going to have a little approach there,' Ember replied. 'Possible poaching.'

'And do keep that killing in mind, won't you, Ralph?'

Ember's fingers went up to his scar. 'Killing? Which?'

'Oh, this is a supposed housewife, isn't it?' Barney replied. 'Hit by Sokolovsky .45s.'

'I've heard of this one, Barney,' Reid said.

'Yes, I might have, too,' Ember said.

'On TV,' Reid added. 'This is significant, then?'

Barney sat back in the pew and had a long, not too religious giggle. 'You know about this, do you, this lady? You're leading me on.'

'What about her, Barney?' Reid said.

Ember wanted to ask, also, but was not sure about his control, for the moment.

Foster said: 'Are you telling us you know more about our realm that we do, Barney?'

'A woman called Tranter,' Barney replied. 'Something Tranter. I know the surname because of the husband, of course.'

'What "of course"?' Foster asked.

'Tranter,' Barney replied. 'Leslie Tranter.'

'Yes, what about him?' Foster asked.

Ember saw Barney turn and stare at Harry, then stare at Reid, and after that at Ember himself. Barney seemed to be thinking of giving another disbelieving giggle, as if whatever it was he knew about Tranter, or thought he knew, had to be known to the three in the pew with him, too. Ember suddenly recalled those coded notes and possible big-money transactions on the sheet of paper in Tranter's desk. Despite his state, he managed to get a wafer of a smile to his face and hold it there for enough seconds.

'Ah, I see Ralph's in the picture,' Barney said.

'What picture?' Foster asked. 'Ralphy, what fucking picture?'

Ember ignored that *y* on the end this time and brought up another smile. Christ, he could not let Barney think they had great wildernesses of ignorance. Looking at Harry and Reid, Barney must already be wondering what the hell he was dealing with.

'Leslie hadn't been toeing the line is what I hear,' Barney said. 'That your information, too, Ralph?'

'Something of the sort.'

'Wait a minute,' Foster said. 'We've got the right lad, have we? Big, fat object? Yes, on TV at the funeral. The papers said he works with some pet-feeding invention and flea powder.'

'Powder, anyway,' Barney replied.

Things turned quiet for half a minute. 'What?' Reid asked. 'Barney, you mean our sort of powder?'

'This is a lad who travels all over, estate car half full of, as you say, flea powder,' Barney said. 'Can you think of better cover for a business courier?'

'Christ,' Reid replied. 'A mistake and some mog's wash-licking ten grand of coke.'

Panicking Ralph

'Look, Ralph, have I said too much?' Barney asked suddenly and in a whisper. Some sense that made, when the other two were nearer him. 'Is there a confidential reason you haven't told these boys about L. Tranter? Barney's doing his famed bull in the china shop bit?'

Yes, there was some confidential reason. The best. He hadn't told them because he did not fucking know it. 'It didn't seem all that relevant to our present problems, Barney,' Ember replied. 'These lads have enough to think about.' Jesus, if Barney knew so much about Tranter, did he know also about Ember and Christine? If he did, no wonder he would assume Ember was aware of Tranter's other business outlets. That is, of course, if what Barney said about Les was right. 'It can't do any harm to tell the boys now, Barney.'

'You probably have it fuller and more accurately than me, Ralph. So, please, put me right if necessary.'

'Certainly,' Ember replied. He was recovering again.

'Kenward Knapp had been successfully branching out from your realm, building new markets far away, hadn't he?' Barney said.

'That's how it appears,' Ember remarked.

'Tranter was invaluable for that, the established, routine voyaging and so on. But then Kenward is knocked over. Suddenly, Tranter has no employer. He's been doing fine and spending right up to it, so there's a big house to maintain payments on. Plus probably debts from his legit business, where he's in no-win competition with all kinds of very big outfits. Leslie decides to go independent.'

'You're not telling me that fat lad becomes a major dealer?' Foster asked.

'There's no weigh-in for this game,' Barry replied. 'Have I distorted anything so far, Ralph?'

'Not that I've noticed,' Ember said.

'But after this point, I'm not so clear,' Barney said. 'It looks as if Tranter did what he had to do – what you boys are doing now, if I may make the comparison – and what he had to do was find a supplier.'

'You?' Foster asked.

Barney had another great chuckle. 'No, no indeed. I don't know who. Perhaps Ralph does.'

'Not exactly clear,' Ember replied.

'No,' Barney said. 'This lad knows how to cover tracks. But, anyway, hereabouts, things seemed to go wrong for him. He appears to have given offence. I'm not sure where. Perhaps he got stuff on credit and didn't come across.'

'Who gets stuff on credit in this trade?' Foster asked. He pointed at the money, now removed from the pew and sweetly cradled in Barney's lap.

'Rare, yes,' Barney replied. 'But it can happen. Tranter would look such a sure-fire trader, he might have been able to swing it.'

'Don't we look sure-fire?' Foster asked.

Barney fondly gripped Foster's shoulder, despite the quality of that suit. 'None surer, Harry – you, Gerry and Ralph. But, simply, Barney has an invariable rule. Cash. *Please do not ask for credit, as a refusal often offends.* Have you seen those notices in chip shops?'

'He plays naughty and they shoot his wife?' Reid asked. 'People do that?'

'If they'd warned him and he ignored it,' Barney replied.

'But his wife?' Reid said. 'Why not Tranter himself?'

'They want their money,' Barney said, as though he understood perfectly. 'If they kill him, it's gone for good. If they kill his wife, he gets scared they'll kill his kids next. He pays and thereafter behaves himself.'

'My God,' Reid said.

Ember saw Gerry begin to wonder what kind of world he was walking into. Ember wished he could say something to comfort him, and comfort himself. No. Had Christine known about Leslie's other business? Had she concealed that from Ember? This would be such a grief. Was that how she met Item?

Barney stood and paced a bit. The lino looked as if it would not take it for long. 'Or another possible. Somebody on your patch hears Tranter is thinking of going alone in the trade. Now, suppose one of the new syndicates wanted Tranter to continue where he left off with Kenward, giving a bigger geographic spread to the business, only working for *them*. But Tranter's suddenly set on becoming his own man, Tranter Inc. Because of this, the principal of a firm feels betrayed. This would be somebody else who'd want to give Tranter some pressure, without damaging him personally. He's a business asset. The same answer. Hit wifey, set up tremors for his children.'

'This someone?' Foster said, doing an impatient snarl at the coding. 'We're talking about Stanfield?'

'I have to say it could be Stan Stanfield, indeed, yes. Stan would have the high-gloss London contacts on call, people with Sokolovskys.' He turned and faced them, square on, like that vicar Foster had mentioned. 'But it's possible, of course, that Ralph can settle all this for us, shine his bright mind and his beams of genuine information through my fog.' Barney threw his arms wide, in supplication.

'No,' Ember replied. 'This part of the situation remains appallingly unclear to me, also. I think you've given a fine summation, Barney.'

Barney sat down again. 'My only motive is to let you know – or to remind you, rather, since Ralph already is obviously very much in the picture – to let you know the degree of hazard you might meet back home.'

'We'll be fine,' Ralph replied.

'I know it, know it,' Barney cried.

In the car on the return, with the kilos in a nice little cake box on the back seat alongside Ember, Harry said: 'Barney offers 2.5, you ask for 2.75, we settle for 2.6. There's not some split-the-difference going on between you and him is there, Ralph? You agreed 2.6 so fast.'

'Talk to me like that, you novice shit, and I'll throw you out of the fucking car on the motorway,' Ember replied. Harry loved to dig deep into a subject, which could be great, but one day the sod would cut all his toes off.

'We're a team, don't forget,' Reid said. 'We all got to be watching one another's backs, in view of that bleakly threatening sketch drawn by Barney.'

'What does bloody Barney *really* know?' Foster replied. 'Anything much?

Reid said: 'Well, he knows he took forty grand from us, and he knows he got a big house and a big boat. These kinds of people, they usually have their information rather right, Harry.'

23

And then a bit later, as they were getting up towards Winchester, Foster said: 'Stanfield.'

'Surprised?' Ember replied, with a rosy chuckle. 'But we knew he probably had a firm with Vine, didn't we?'

'Barney rates the bugger, that's obvious,' Foster said.

'We all rate him. He's Stanfield, and he's the opposition,' Ember replied. He put some good snap in his tone: 'We'll deal with it.'

Gerry said: 'Yes, but getting that woman shot, Ralph. Great big, tear-through .45 shells. This is filthy.' As ever, Gerry was driving. They went on for a while, quiet: not like Gerry, to leave an idea unexhausted in the air. Usually, he talked every subject dead, laying on the clapped-out rhetoric, needful or not.

'Ah,' Reid said, like some huge discovery, and nodded at the sign to Winchester: 'A town with an historic public school, am I right, known for producing endless intellectuals through the ages? Privileged, maybe, but what we got to ask is, Can privilege ever be entirely eliminated?'

'We don't know for sure he fixed her death,' Ember said. 'Barney's say-so only. Harry's right: how does Barney in Hampshire know so damn much about our territory?'

'Just filthy,' Reid said, speaking over his shoulder to Ember. 'Shot in the back. That's what I mean about a school like Winchester – for years, indeed, centuries, trying to give this country a lead, teaching kiddies how to shape their moral thinking and live proper, yet we still get the Stanfields who has a woman blasted, although fuck-all to do with business. Ralph, I'll have to mull this.'

'How do you mean?' Ember asked.

'Weigh it up,' Reid replied.

It almost made Ember hoot to hear this chat-along go heavy.

'And he will, Ralph. That's Gerry.'

'Oh, we've known from the start he might turn dangerous,' Ember said. 'He's Stanfield. We learned nothing fresh.'

'More than dangerous,' Reid said. 'Savagery. A man who kills women for nothing. I'd see this as a soiling of all decent standards, Ralph, Harry. No fluke we was passing this area now. Winchester College reminds us of esteemed values, and Stanfield got to be pulped as soon as poss. In any case, if he'll blast a woman, what will he do to real trade opposition – us three? Yes, indeed, Ralphy, we *have* learned something, and I don't like it.' The gassy, platform lilt had gone, and Gerry sounded nearly hard.

'Look, he doesn't stroll about acting target,' Ember said.

'He can be reached,' Gerry replied. 'Anyone can be reached. One of the first lessons I learned.'

'I didn't know you were at Winchester, Gerry,' Foster said. He slewed in the passenger seat to talk to Ember. 'Gerry can be like this, if he . . . if his soul gets outraged. This is the thing about Gerry – soul. He has to cleanse. Obsessive. Well, all sorts get like that. I heard Lane's the same. Mission. You and others look at Gerry and think just gab and smart driving, yet he has this hidden core of fair play.'

Reid said: 'I blush. Anyone would respond like me if they heard about butchering a harmless woman, yes, Ralphy? I don't make no special claims.'

Foster said: 'Like Gerry suggests, we get rid of Stan because he's a degenerate, but also – very also – he could bite lumps out of our business, destroy us. That Stanfield wants monopoly. He's the sort. He thinks working in France plus this alleged painting ancestor give him the right.'

'The fucker's dead,' Gerry replied.

'Well, of course he's fucking dead,' Foster replied. 'Christ, he knew Charles Dickens. He's dead, but he's still an influence.'

'I don't mean the artist. I mean Stanfield. As good as dead,' Reid said.

'Well, let's consider all the aspects,' Ember replied hurriedly. 'Let's think priorities.' It appalled him to hear Reid, appalled and shamed him. And it enraged him to be on the end of that question, *Anyone would respond, yes, Ralphy?*, like being taunted. What kind of an anyone was he, Ember, still dawdling on the vengeance duty? Here was this low caste scullion – shit, Reid did not even *know* Christine – this Mouth-Mouth spouting of the need to avenge her, and calling him Ralphy, like giving some feeble kid life lessons. Gerry Reid handing him a sermon on obligations! Perhaps the noisy talk was as far as it would go. Ember did not think so. This was turning out no hoot, after all. Reid made the destruction of Stanfield sound like tactics as well as vengeance, but anyone could see it was vengeance that pushed him harder. People could surprise you. Ember always regarded Harry as the one with full venom, yet now here was Reid talking execution, Reid who would not even carry a gun.

'Look, Gerry, I think you'd better leave Stan Stanfield to me,' Ember said.

'I've sort of promised myself, Ralph,' Reid replied. 'This will plague me till I see him off. Sorry.'

'Gerry's like that, Ralph. I could tell you of other incidents.'

Ember said: 'But Gerry, you checked on Untidy Graham for us, a great piece of work. I can't ask you to look at Stanfield as well.'

Reid laughed. 'Untidy? That was nothing, Ralphy. Anyone could see he was off religion permanent and had come back to the fold. No hazard at all.'

Of course, there was the other side of it. Of course. Of course. Some parts of Ember thought, great, Gerry would do the job for him. Gerry would knock over the organizer, and Leslie Tranter might knock over the hired butchers. Ember would not have to stir, yet the total tit-for-tat package could be unmistakably delivered. This was the kind of nice and natty hazard-free triumph he had so often thrived by: how he had been able to buy The Monty and stuff the loft with loot.

Yet he could not think like this now. When things were to do with Christine, even Christine dead, he had to reach fine manliness, had to be clearly Ralph Ember, not Ralphy. Well, he was never Ralphy, but particularly not now. Reid had no entitlement to feel like that about Christine. She had been Ember's, and any vendetta was his property alone. But, before this trip, he had thought that his one massive cowardly betrayal of her among the foreshore bullets made any failures that came after of no account, including failure to avenge her. He was irredeemable. And so there had been his yellow ploy to shift Tranter on to the hunt.

Now, though, a change. Suppose what Barney said was true, then Christine would undoubtedly have been killed, even if Ember had not scampered. She was not hit instead of him, and he had not abjectly turned her into a shield. She herself, had been the target. It was he, Ember, who had been the spare article on the foreshore, not Christine, and *he* had been put in peril because of *her*, not vice versa. Ember saw there was nothing at all he could have done to save her, not against two polished tradesmen advanced enough to use Sokolovskys. Consequently, as Ember viewed it now, his honour remained as brilliantly intact as his body that day. He was Ralph Ember, cherished lover and distinguished businessman.

He must act in accord. Already he had behaved with valour by going to bring her body back from the mud. Even trying to send Tranter into those London perils was not as disgusting a trick as he might have thought once or twice afterwards. Tranter was no longer the fat, wide-open innocent Ember had believed. Tranter would know why Christine had been hit, and would see he had to protect his business future, as well as avenge his wife. Tranter was a weathered operator and must realize what he was up against if he made for The Sleeping Sentinel on a trade and vengeance mission. True, at the foreshore he had been clearly panicked by the sight of Ember's gun, and had tumbled into the reen. A weathered operator, unused to guns? But perhaps he had been lucky in his trading, lucky and very skilled, never running into violence – until Christine's murder. In any case, even the most experienced people could panic sometimes. Ember knew all about that. Since meeting Barney again, he had grown almost elated. Ember felt his whole character was restored, as if new. It could be developed into something renowned and glistening, yes, as renowned and glistening as anybody produced by historic Winchester College, as long as Ember could reach Stanfield before Gerry, and slaughter the sod.

Ember said: 'So, it's going to be a race between us to Stan, is it, Gerry?'

'Could be,' Reid replied.

24

'You'll be wondering what we'd like you to do for us, Colin,' Stanfield said. 'You're the kind who once he's taken the money will feel he must give some return. It's a credit to you.'

'Come down off your fucking easel, Stan,' Vine snarled, staring up at him in the half light from the ground. 'So bloody grand.' He did some mock pomp. ' "It's a credit to you." ' Bollocks. Col knows this game. He knows that the time will come and come in its own due . . . well . . . time, when he can offer us some worthwhile help. No need to say in that slimy, back-to-front way he might take the pay and do nothing.'

Now and then Harpur wondered if these arguments were set up. Villains aped police, and this could be the old hard and soft routine from interrogation suites. Probably they'd decided they still had to ease him along.

'What we can reasonably ask is limited, Col, isn't it?' Stanfield said. 'And we want to be nothing but reasonable. We certainly cannot ask you to do any work where there's the smallest chance you'd be identified.'

'Thanks,' Harpur replied. Stanfield did know how to call up gorgeous unction, his big face grave and jam-packed with empathy.

'No need for thanks, Col,' Vine said. 'Identification would

be curtains for you, but also curtains for this arrangement and maybe for the syndicate. Don't let Stan make you feel grateful. That's one of his creepiest tricks. This is equal partners.'

'Thanks, Keith,' Harpur said.

Stanfield laughed. 'Keith can be *so* fierce, can't he?'

After a while Keith laughed, too: 'I can take a joke,' he said.

'Of course you can, Keith,' Stanfield replied. 'You can take any fucking thing.'

They were on neutral ground this evening, an old World War II anti-aircraft gun site in woods on a hill above the city.

'What we'd like, Col, is your aid in knocking out the competition,' Stanfield said. 'Obviously, this would be clandestine.'

'Obviously clandestine! Or clandestinely obvious. But you know what he means, Col. If we take out the other main firm, this is additional business for us, more dividends for the partners,' Vine said. 'We won't get bother from the Monopolies Commission.'

Now and then Harpur used this spot for meeting Jack Lamb, his most gifted and revered informant. Such overlaps did occur. Cops and crooks moved through the same world and all of them needed secrecy at some time. There was a limit to secluded places. Vine had suggested the gun site. Was he telling Harpur he knew about Lamb? Anyway, no more trysts here with Jack.

Vine said: 'Don't turn cross at this next remark, Col, but

with the extra you could move out of that bloody ordinary street. Is it a place to bring up lovely daughters?'

Harpur and Stanfield stood leaning forward against the semi-circular perimeter concrete wall of a gun emplacement, like lookouts. Their closeness and stillness seemed to give a bond, and anyone watching would have thought comradeship. Knees up to his chin, Vine sat hunched on the floor, his back against the wall. Harpur said: 'It's difficult for me to operate on drug squad territory.'

'We know that, Col,' Stanfield replied. 'We talked of it before. But this would leave the main part of the action to them. Although you'd be helping the squad, they wouldn't know it. That's the deftness of the thing. Look, I'll give you in detail how we see it. There's risk – of course. But if any of it strikes you as beyond the reasonable say so at once, and it's off.'

From their feet Vine grunted: 'Col's into risk every duty day. Is he going to chicken? You insult him, and you insult me, who brought him in.'

Often, up here, where the defending guns used to pop away, Harpur would stare down on the city and wonder whether his efforts to guard the inhabitants were as hit-and-miss as those ack-ack batteries had been, more miss than hit. The bombers still got through, and probably so would the coke and the Ecstasy and the heroin and hash, for ever. 'What we hear from the streets, Col, is that another firm's trying to press-gang our pushers,' Stanfield said. 'We depend almost absolutely on our street personnel. What we're seeing now is the kind of grubby scramble that's bound to happen when a system like Kenward's ends. Such disorder has to be decisively countered. Decisively it must be dealt with, yes.' Stan could get a pleasant psalm-like rhythm to his threats. He was looking down at the city, too, no doubt seeing a valuable market, but menaced. 'I'm talking about Panicking's syndicate, naturally,' he explained.

'My own view, frankly, very frankly, Col, is blow the sod away, no messing. I still don't see why not.' A pity Vine seemed to have given up his usual camouflage jacket. It would have brought the right military tone, the way some of Jack Lamb's outfits did when he and Harpur had met here, or at the foreshore defence post. Instead, Vine wore a three-quarter-length, very superior suede coat, which must have cost up towards five hundred. Once you were into this trade business was never anything but good, and the cash needed to be spent. Harpur hoped Keith's girl was getting a proper slice of it.

'Important to be positive,' Vine said. 'If we got rid of Ralphy, we'd have you acting in a well-placed police position for us, in fact, the best, and you could contain any enquiries, surely. Not that I'd leave traces, anyway. Nothing to compromise you. Would Keith Vine do that? Panicking would just be gone, and everything restful again. I mean, are police going to fret much if somebody knocks over Ralph Ember? You've been trying to get him for years. But, of course, with Stan it has to be subtlety. French influence – all that shady stuff they like: smart-arse Froggery, instead of clean and simple.'

'Ember's formidable,' Harpur replied.

'So is Keith Vine,' Keith Vine said, yelling at Harpur up the outside of his trouser leg. He had this strong big-chinned broad face and short fair hair, and in his combat jacket always reminded Harpur of young tough troops you used to see on television film from Northern Ireland. 'Col, tell me who else would have the skill and balls to bring in a big catch like your good self for this infant syndicate? And I could describe other matters achieved in my career, but, no, these might only embarrass you.' He grinned in that boyish style, suddenly all forgivable impishness. 'I've got to remember, you're still a cop. Just believe me, Col, Panicking would be no problem.' He stood, as if needing to get some stature behind his large promises. Harpur might not know all Vine's mighty achievements, but he had killed a sub-postmaster once, no question, though someone else posthumously and conveniently collected the blame. Keith might be up and coming.

'Yes, Ember's formidable,' Stanfield replied. 'Why I'd say aim our attention elsewhere, and not head-on, in any case. That's the kind of thing I had in mind when I said no crazy risk. Maturity.'

'Col, Stanley's so fucking oblique he'd fall off the side of the world if it was still flat.' Vine gave Harpur a light, matey punch on the lower arm. 'I know, I know, you think this is two lads mocking up aggro the whole time, the way *your* lads do, to lull the third party and get him softened. No way. We'd never treat a partner like that.'

'Gerry Reid,' Stanfield announced.

Vine waved his arms about, like a money market dealer.

'He thinks hit Gerry and Panicking will drop into such a fright their team's finished. See? Oblique.'

'Not hit,' Stanfield said. 'Not hit the way Keith talks about hit, anyway. Am I going to ask Colin Harpur, a senior officer, to take out Gerry Reid, for God's sake?' Stanfield had a really good laugh over this one, his big, woolly moustache bobbing in the gentle grey of twilight like a coupling ram. 'We pay Colin, yes, and I hope adequately, but still not that kind of money.' The moustache was a clever stroke, and did a lot to make Stanfield seem solid and good natured. He was fair, too, and big built, almost glamorous, despite the moustache. You could imagine him as a gifted chiropodist or green-grocer. Harpur thought even Denise liked his style. 'We remove Reid,' Stan said, 'but we remove him in a different fashion. Done right, it could also land the rest of their firm for you, Col – that's Panicking and Foster. But you know how they're implicated?'

'Of course he knows. Do you think he slept his way to chief super. He gets voices, don't you, Col?'

One of them had been Keith Vine's, but Harpur only muttered: 'I hear a lot of rumour.'

'We all hear rumour, Col,' Stanfield replied. 'This is right-through real, though. Those three have been for a consignment. It will be down Hampshire way. I have to piece together fragments and what you'd call rumour.'

Vine struck the concrete parapet with his fist. 'For instance, scheming to take our street dealer, Eleri ap Vaughan, that's what really pisses me off, Col. Stan, too, but me especially. Eleri's got a wondrous list of subscribers, built up so lovingly during Kenward. I expect you know. This is middle class and above – folk where money's always on tap. People with their own companies, legit companies, and able to get their hands on the petty cash, only not so petty. Or inheritances. What every pusher dreams of – nice, ripe regulars with a genuine devotion, which brings them back week after week, but which is never so out of control it fucks up their jobs and stops the income. These are customers who don't have to mug and thieve for habit cash, perhaps getting caught, Col, and then buying from the screws not us. Dentists, managing directors, professors, surgeons, solicitors, MPs, and TV executives, of course. Eleri's a really clever lady, saw the opening in the market way back. Keith Vine prized being associated with this clientele, Col – the most worthwhile side of the business, and anyone could bring up a child on such gains without guilt, important to me now Becky's very near her time. And then Panicking starts working on Eleri to go over to him with her list. That Chuck Heston profile and putting his dick in her hand I bet. I mean, Eleri's gone sixty, pulling the pension. She's not going to get much more heartfelt romance, the age, the gut, but here comes Ralph W. Ember, who can always turn it on in a good cause.'

Stanfield said: 'Yes, it *is* irritating, Col. I thought, let your drugs boys know the three of them have been down to Hampshire. This is most likely to a guy called Barney, who'd get the Queen's Medal for Imports, if there was one and it covered cocaine.'

'You could say one of your voices gave you the tip, Col,' Vine said.

Panicking Ralph

These two were drawing him in, tucking him up. All right, he had expected that, had schemed for it. As he became more and more enmeshed, though, he increasingly wondered whether he would be able to free himself at the due moment and get the result he wanted, and Lane wanted. Could he deliver a cleaner, safer city? Very occasionally Harpur saw himself as a solitary and even noble force for good, like Moses. But would a jury believe he had joined this confederacy only to penetrate and destroy it, and not for loot? In any trial, of course, Vine and Stanfield and their prime bully-boy lawyers would be telling judge and jury otherwise, full voice. These days, judges and juries competed to think the worst of police. Harpur's nice little letter to Iles via Denise would not count for much. *Tell the court, please, about the £2,700 Avantage wristwatch you used to wear on carefully selected occasions, Detective Chief Superintendent. And do you have it on now? No. Why would that be, Detective Chief Superintendent?*

'The drugs squad wouldn't act on that – on reports of a possible collecting journey,' Harpur said. 'Too vague.'

Stanfield agreed, so grandly: 'Obviously they wouldn't. They've got to find something, haven't they, that way of theirs? The very point, Col. We want you to leave incrimination with Gerry, then suggest to your boys a search of his den might produce evidence – based on information received, source traditionally unrevealed. This is why we couldn't really do it to Panicking. He's got all this civic grandeur now, writing to the papers, caring fan of the environment. Your drugs people couldn't risk an on-spec invasion of Ralphy's prestige spread, Low Pastures. But Gerry, in that condemned house down the Valencia, another category, yes?'

'How I hate and despise these class considerations,' Vine cried.

'So do we all, Keith, but they're a fact, a terrible, distressing fact,' Stanfield said. 'And they're especially a fact to police. Col's dear chief would shit a brick if he heard sniffer dogs and heavies had been doing a chancy forage at Low Pastures, wouldn't he, Col?'

Harpur said: 'If Gerry's supposed to be—'

'Into the really big time it would need to be something weighty that your drug squad find. Absolutely true, Col. You're quick. He's got to look like a major trade figure, which is what he is, not some little go-between.'

'This package is going to be half a kilo give or take a gramme,' Vine said. 'Risk, but we regard it as an investment. We put out to bring in. This is street value thirty grand.'

Stanfield went on a little stroll across the rusted rails in the concrete base, where ammunition trucks must have trundled during the blitz. He stopped and spoke over his shoulder, as though embarrassed: 'What we wouldn't want, obviously, Col, is for this to fuck up and Gerry get a gift of that much from us.'

'Christ, such a crafty way to put your evil over, Stan. You're offering Col outright intimidation, yes? What's he going to do, tell Gerry and split the thirty with him? Innuendo, you live by it, Stan.' Vine was shouting, his voice winging out across the countryside.

Panicking Ralph

'You'll ask why can't Keith plant it, Col,' Stanfield replied. He walked back and took his place next to Harpur again. 'Fair question. I'm not dropping him into anything when I say he's the world's greatest break-and-enter lad. You know it. He can go in and out of a place and the owner could never tell, unless Keith's lifted all the jewellery and Ming vases, obviously, which generally he has. You'll say, if Keith placed this material it would have a better chance of staying unfound until your lads turned up, because, even though an expert intruder yourself, you might accidentally leave a hint, and Gerry would read the message and go searching.'

'Stan's a mind reader, Col. He'll tell you what you're going to say before you've thought of it.'

'Well, I wouldn't ask any of that,' Harpur said. He turned and faced Stanfield direct, like someone cutting the crap and going man to man. 'Look, it's OK, I see the strategy, Stan. You want to involve me, that's all. You still don't trust me, do you, not right through? This will put C. Harpur all the way into the team and no exit. Like taking me to the delivery, the delivery that wasn't.'

Vine yelled again, sadly pained this time. 'Col, you're already all the way into the team. Christ, this is the kind of suspicion Stan always builds in people. I've got to say it again – equal partners. Of course, you're entitled to your doubts and worries about how we work, and especially how Stan works, this dark fucking roundaboutness. You're a cop, so you wonder. But, believe Keith Vine, we don't set tests, Col. You're one of us, among friends.' He struck Harpur another kindly little blow on the arm.

'Absolutely,' Stanfield said. 'It's like this, Col. There's a special reason why you, an officer, should go in personally.'

'On this he's right, Col.'

Stanfield brought out some photographs from the pocket of his long black city-financier overcoat. Daylight had almost gone now, but Harpur was able to see these pictures had the slight haziness that could come when stills were taken from a television screen. There were four, and he appeared in two.

'You know where we are, of course, Col,' Stanfield said. He held the photographs fanned out, like pick a card.

'Christine Tranter's funeral.'

'You make no progress on her case?' Stanfield said.

'Not much.'

'Know this big lad?' Stanfield asked, pointing.

'Leslie Tranter.'

'What do you see when you look at him, beyond a lot of suit?' Stanfield asked.

'Get on with it, for God's sake, Stan,' Vine said. 'I hate it up here. Fucking trees just standing there, not giving a shit. Cut the mystery.'

'A grieving and aggrieved widower,' Harpur replied.

'Yes, he's that,' Stanfield said. 'And?'

'Cat and dog benefactor.'

Vine said: 'Our information, and of good credibility, is he couriered for Kenward.'

'Tranter?' Harpur replied. The amazement was real.

'And the point is, still deep into the trade,' Stanfield said. 'Brilliant at it. We think Ember and his people wanted to take him over. But Leslie's begun to ask himself, Why work for others? He wants to go alone. It's a Thatcher legacy. Ember asks and asks him, but Tranter refuses. This obviously enraged Ralphy. He's got enough competition from us. He decided to bring Tranter into line, and Gerry Reid is told to get Christine done.'

'Reid shoot someone's wife?' Harpur replied. 'Gerry won't even carry a gun.'

'Of course not. He's your standard chauffeur,' Stanfield said. 'But he could arrange it. Gerry knows London people. He's done a lot of job-driving there with top-notchers.'

Had they devised a tale to explain Christine Tranter's death, a tale to suit them somehow, though not a somehow Harpur understood? Or did they genuinely believe Tranter had crossed Panicking?

'What we were thinking, Col, is you might find something in the flat to help you tie Reid to that murder,' Vine said.

'Keith's a glorious burglar but not a glorious detective. He might not recognize the give-away material. This is how the other two could be brought in as well, Col. All-round victory. Gerry did the leg work and actual engagement of craftsmen, yes, but Ralphy gives the instructions. Harry Foster's bound to have known about it, too. Accessories? Conspiracy? That's for your expert decision. But I think we're handing you something very promising, wouldn't you say? Wipe them out.'

Vine had begun to pick his way down the hill towards the cars, cursing ferns. Stanfield put the photographs back in his pocket. 'We'll let you have the package very shortly, Col. Maybe even tonight. When you go into Gerry's, don't hide it in any of the plant spots usually picked by drug squaddies, will you? Gerry might do a daily routine check. Not behind books, if he's got any, or under carpeted floor-boards, or behind a lav cistern, obviously.'

They followed Vine. 'Where does this information come from?' Harpur said. 'If I'm going to stick my head into Gerry's place, I've got to know the strength of it, haven't I, Stan?'

'Yes, I agree with something Ember said: Kenward was like Tito,' Stanfield replied. 'While alive he might not have been universally loved, yet held a difficult realm together and ensured stability. As soon as he goes, we get a kind of Bosnia, with, as it happens, Ralphy bringing an era of vio-lence and death, or even deaths, Col. That's my abiding fear.'

*

Thank God, thank God, he was seeing Denise tonight. She could always restore Harpur. Sometimes his dependence on her made him ashamed. After all, she was a kid still. How the hell did she manage to salvage him? But she did.

'God, you look bad, Col,' she said, when they met. 'Jittery. The storm before the storm.'

Whereas she looked pretty good and quite dressed up. That is, not student gear, but a dark blue blazer with close-cut blue trousers. She was small-featured, slight, small-boned yet had a solid they-shall-not-pass presence when standing still, and a big-stride walk, as though eager to meet whatever was due and get at least her share. Clever kids were so sure they could handle the future, imagined it had been designed with them in mind, poor little sods. 'I'm fine,' he said.

'Fear not, I've got the letter safe, you know.' Denise squeezed his hand comfortingly as they walked. He felt grateful. Duplicity had exhausted him – the labour of maintaining his, and struggling to read Vine's and Stanfield's. He had wondered non-stop whether he was fooling both of them or one of them or neither. Such bad uncertainty was the norm for undercover work, but it took a while to get used to again. Although Harpur had studied the faces, both of them knew how to look friendly, perhaps really *were* friendly, and half of Stanfield's face lurked hidden by that fucking moustache, anyway. Harpur was sure to find out one day how Stanfield really saw him. And Harpur had better be ready. In no estimate did he suppose either or both gave him absolute trust. But how low did belief in him have to fall before things went terminal? Stanfield might have had no faith in Harpur from the start, regardless of Vine's enthusiasm. And breaking into Gerry's flat could be meant as a finale. Harpur passed the little test at the phantom delivery, but Stanfield might still be unconvinced. Who'd be waiting inside Reid's place? A timely word could easily be fed anonymously to Gerry and teammates. Or Stanley and Vine might be there, very ready – or, more likely, just Stanley. If you wanted to dispose of a spy, where better, than a business rival's fortress? You did two lots of damage at once.

'Yes, Col, I checked the letter was OK only yesterday.'

'Letter?'

'Oh, don't come so cool. You know the one.'

'Oh, that letter. Good.'

'But why do I mention it now, I wonder?' she said, acting baffled by her own drift of thought.

He could do without an answer so remained quiet.

'Col, I suddenly had this – this impression it might be needed.'

'Well, I gave it to you in case it might be needed.'

'Yes, but I mean it might be needed *soon*,' she said.

They did have good instincts, people of her age – still fresh and unconfused. 'As long as it's available,' he said.

'You'll triumph. You will, you will, you will.'

Now and then in his job Harpur could grow dazed and almost destabilized by doubts, and it was then – now – he craved the assurance Denise gave: not just making love to her but talking to her, listening to her, watching her, teaching her, learning from her, this girl of nineteen. Particularly, he learned arrogance. Although she was far too bright to think him infallible, she believed him less fallible than he did himself, and a lot less fallible than Iles did. It might be one reason Harpur had gone for someone so young, someone still prone to error and reverence, despite her brain. Nothing in his wife's attitude towards him could ever have been mistaken for reverence. Always he felt stronger for seeing Denise. Often he had felt destroyed after talking to Megan.

Denise suggested the cinema tonight and chose a rerun of *The Remains of the Day.* He was astonished to find he disliked the idea of sitting for a couple of hours in a dark, easily accessible spot. Stanfield must have troubled him more than Harpur realized. He feared for himself and he feared for Denise, who would be close. But this was their night out, and he would not let her see his unease – if he could hide it. Hadn't she already shown the range of her antennae? She slept throughout the film, with her head comfortably on Harpur's upper arm, and early on he unhooked the lighted cigarette from her mouth before it fell and charred her lap or his and ruined the remains of the night. It should not have been alight anyway: this was another no smoking cinema. Normally, he would have enjoyed the sense of taking care of her. Now, he felt encumbered and, in any case, had no confidence he *could* look after her. His mind did not stay on the film. He watched the aisles and glanced behind every time he heard people moving. A pity. Generally, he was gripped by tales with butlers prominent, like this one or *Changing Places*. They made him believe he was not the only serf working doggedly in drab clothes.

He was glad when it finished and the lights came on. They went back to his house. Harpur's daughters were in bed, and he and Denise ate supper alone in the kitchen.

'The very window where our famous and authentic book dealer originally tapped for entry, Col,' she said. 'Keithy. See anything of him now?'

'Never.'

'Oh, you do, do you?' Denise replied. 'He's got some sort of hold over you, Col? But I'm sure that whatever it is you'll screw out of him more than he takes from you.'

'You've got a very harsh idea of police work.'

On the way upstairs they looked at the sitting room. 'I like what you're doing to it,' she said. Harpur and his daughters had removed the bookshelves and begun to redecorate. Paint pots and wallpaper rolls stood around, and the curtains were down. Himself, he was still disturbed each time he saw it all, and worried over the changes.

In bed she was lovely with him: jaunty, demanding, as ever talkative, and, also as ever, that thrilling mix of need and generosity, of tenderness and violence. She held him hard with her legs and he lost his face in her breasts. For the moment, this passed as a fine imitation of safety, and she smelled consolingly of Lifebuoy soap.

'Stay there, stay there,' she said.

'Oh, yes.'

'You'll win, Col. Your brow is a victor's brow, waiting to be crowned. I feel it cool and masterful on my skin.' She put her hand on the back of his head and pressed his face down harder on her.

'Yes?' he asked. 'Yes. Yes.'

'Yes. We used to fuck like farewell, but not any longer. Now, like for ever,' she said.

'Yes?'

'Of course. You wouldn't doubt it, would you?'

'Never.' Yes, sometimes. Occasionally, he thought she was troubled about being welcomed into the household by him and his daughters. In a way, it pleased her, but also . . . Households generally she spoke ill of, including the one she was brought up in. He believed Denise planned permanence for her and him, though maybe not in family terms. Once, she had said, 'I see a lifetime of you and me,' and then explained she might conceivably wander into a relationship or even marry elsewhere, someone more her age, and this would clearly be important, but would not come between her and Harpur. He was not sure if he could take that.

'Hear tapping again, Col?'

'How would I?' He lifted his head from between her breasts. Yes, a minor coin on glass from downstairs.

'It's got to be Keithy recycling his act,' she said. 'How about rechristening the bugger *Coitus interrupt us*? Do you think he's brought a replacement consignment of books?'

Or some other consignment. Harpur pulled on trousers and a sweater.

She pointed. 'You ought to wait a minute, or he'll think you fancy him, Col.'

He sat on the bed for a short while then went down to the kitchen. Yes, it was the same procedure as those earlier visits by Vine, and, as Harpur watched, a mittened hand holding a fifty pence piece between thumb and first finger appeared outside from beneath the window and beat its short message, then withdrew. Harpur opened the door. Vine entered carrying a supermarket bag. 'Col, I had to come round right away because I feel I was rude about your house and this district at our earlier meeting.'

'This the stuff for planting in Gerry's place?' Harpur replied, nodding at the bag.

'Daughters like yours, wherever they're brought up, will be genteel and ladylike, I know it,' Vine answered. 'Myself, as to housing, I'll have to be a cash man. But you, Col, such a credible mortgager, with brilliant status. You simply up the borrowing a bit and get yourself something really distinguished. All nicely mixed in with your standard earnings, self-laundering.'

'We'll stay in the kitchen?' Harpur replied. 'There are no curtains in the sitting room. Redecorating.'

Vine sat down and put the carrier bag in front of him on the pine table. He was in the suede coat. Once more, Harpur missed his combat jacket. In the suede he looked less sound, like a salesman who had just blued a good week's commission on himself.

'Accommodated upstairs again tonight?' Vine asked. 'Same one? Well! This is wholesome, no question. But you're entitled.'

Harpur prepared whisky and water for Vine, and gin and cider for himself.

'Yes,' Vine said, running his hand over the bag. 'This is the material. You'll want to open it and test, I expect.'

'Why?' Harpur asked.

Vine did the great boyish grin. 'Oh, look, Col, you're bound to think a possible trap. Dealing with Stan, anyone would be jumpy. You won't believe it, but Keith Vine is jumpy himself when Stan's around,' Keith Vine said. 'Do you imagine I like that?' For a second his voice went up to almost a shout.

'Trap?' Harpur replied.

'Set you up in there. Don't tell Keith Vine you haven't considered that possibility.'

'But why would anyone want to trap me, Keith?'

'You're sure to ask does he trust you, aren't you, Col? And to be frank, you're sure to ask do *I* trust you. In fact, you did more or less ask.'

'Would you bring me in if not?' Harpur said.

'Right. But you'll be wondering if things have changed.'

'Why should they, Keith? Equal partners.'

'And then again, I'm Keith Vine, not Stanley Stanfield. You know how he is, full of bullshit eminence – the painting ancestor, and having worked in France a fucking fortnight. If Keith Vine arranges something, such as making you an offer, Col, it doesn't follow Stanley will go along. Even the opposite. He's got to be Stanley, hasn't he, regardless, so mature and wise? He has to rule and overrule, the sod.'

'I thought we were getting on pretty well, he and I,' Harpur replied.

'Oh, he can do the charm, I don't deny.' Vine brought out a package about as big as a CD, wrapped in red and gold gift paper and sealed with tape. He pushed it across the table to Harpur. 'Open it if you like.'

'No need.'

'It could be self-raising flour. Then you'd know for sure you're liable to meet someone when you call on Gerry, wouldn't you, Col?'

'I don't think Stan's like that. Not underhand. I've known him – I mean, I've known *of* him and his work pattern for a long while, don't forget.'

'From dossiers.' Vine got up and went towards the sitting room. 'Do you mind, Col? I'd like to see what you're making of it, now the lit's gone.'

Harpur remained at the kitchen table. After a few minutes, Vine came back and said: 'I expect it took some doing to root out all traces of her like that, the various titles, all high calibre. But you're so right, Colin. We have to adapt, grab what's going, as it were, paper over the sadnesses.' Vine sat down and finished his whisky. 'Stanfield gets the women all right. Keep an eye on yours. Oh, he thinks about Becky – I mean, for when she's back to a nice shape. And ability, I don't deny. Can't. I taunt him, but this is a wise scheme of his. Drop this on Gerry, get him taken and knock a hole in Panicking's confederacy and composure. It's oblique like I said, yes, but practical. Stan and I will go up The Monty, too, and offer a bit of gentle terrorizing, that way Stan has. Again, very French. Well, you and Desmond Iles do the same at the club sometimes, don't you, Col? Ralphy can be broken right down if he's given clever stress, and from a couple of angles at once. This is normal business practice. His syndicate's as good as finished.'

Harpur showily downed his drink and did not pour any more, for himself or Vine.

'There's genuine flair in Stan, no question, Col, and it's not self-raising flour in here but—' His blunt, hard face throbbed. He began talking faster and yelling again, the words a bit tangled: 'What I mean is he can cause real, full-out hate – in those close to him – business-partnership close – couldn't be closer. Yes.'

'Noise.' Harpur glanced at the ceiling, towards his daughters' bedrooms, and his own.

'Sorry,' Vine said. 'I might curdle something?' He stood.

'How I see it, Col, there'll come a time when Keith Vine no longer has to crawl in your backyard and tap your window late at night. We'll emerge eventually as true business folk, admired and envied, and with almost full respectability. Kenward was on the way to it when he sloppily got his head shot off. Very big in charities, and his son at a passable boarding school. And then Panicking, too, he's on the way. But we'll soon fuck him up.'

*

Harpur wondered whether he should log what was going on, as back-up to the disaster letter held by Denise. He was at his office desk next morning jotting down a couple of dates and places when Iles came in gleaming with contempt and self-pity. He wore one of his gorgeous navy blue double-breasted blazers and a harsh, vermilion and gold tie meant to unnerve people.

The ACC said: 'I wonder if you've ever thought, Col, about the full implications of fucking another man's wife over at least weeks and possibly months.'

This was not a question, and Harpur occupied himself gathering up the notes he had been making, and put them in a drawer.

'What's happening, Harpur?' Iles asked. He sat down, legs over the arm of his chair, and began to feel each of his front teeth with an index finger, testing for stability.

Harpur said: 'The chief's looking better, don't you think, sir? The mission he mentioned is very dear to me and I'm sure to you.'

'When I say "the full implications of fucking another man's wife", this is a point I could just as pertinently put to Francis Garland, of course,' Iles replied.

The ACC had left the door open and Harpur stood now and went over to close it. Things might get noisy.

'When I ask, "What's happening, Harpur?" I have in mind that you might be working something private. I mean more private than you usually work things. Undercover? That kind of exercise. My wife said to me yesterday: "What about Harpur, Des? You never talk of him these days." Oh, it might surprise you that I used to bring your name into ordinary conversation – tell her what you'd been up to at work, and so on. I'd refer to you like that to show that I did not regard you as some unmanageable demonic threat to my poise, never to be mentioned, just because you'd had her for a season.'

'Thank you, sir,' Harpur replied.

Iles said: 'But then I realized she was right and I hadn't referred to you lately, because you didn't seem to be doing much in the police line.' The ACC frowned, pained by some recollection. 'Col, Sarah suddenly said to me, "Harpur hasn't dropped out of view, gone undercover or something like that, has he, Desmond? My God, have you put Col somewhere foully perilous, to get rid of a sexual rival? Have you, Des? Have you?"' The ACC had given up prodding his teeth and tried to imitate Sarah Iles's voice floating up efficiently into jagged passion and anxiety. Then he reverted to himself: 'She mentioned King David in the Bible.'

'Him I've heard of,' Harpur said.

'You and Sarah did a lot of Bible study together?'

'I was brought up on the Scriptures, sir,' Harpur replied.

'Nice. Notice anything there about adultery?'

'David wanted a woman called Bathsheba, so he had her hubby put in the hottest part of the battle and killed,' Harpur replied.

'Yes, poor old Uriah the Hittite. But in our case Sarah believes it's the husband who's trying to get the opposition killed.' Iles went womanly again and began to scream in a high wail: '"Have you put him undercover, Des, you bastard? Have you? Have you?"'

Harpur said: 'This must be bewildering for you, sir, since it's so unfounded.'

Iles stayed quiet for a while and then resumed as himself again: 'Well, yes, it's absurd, isn't it? Isn't it?'

'You'd never do that to me, sir.'

'Are you doing undercover on your own account, you sly sod?' Iles asked.

'Undercover work is a complex matter, sir, requiring support and general planning.'

Iles said: 'You fucker, you *are* doing undercover, are you?' His voice wavered again, but into the tone of a plea now. 'My God, Harpur, come out of it. Come out of it at once. I don't want you killed. My life with Sarah would be finished. She'd take our child away. She'd blame me for ever if they rumbled you and did an execution. You're precious to us, Col.'

'Thank you, sir.'

'And likewise Francis Garland is precious to us, I expect,' Iles said.

'I'll let him know, sir.'

25

Seated at his little desk behind the bar at The Monty Ember decided he had the killing of Stanfield as well worked out as he ever would. He still did not believe all that much in planning – still knew that everything could be turned chaotic by some sudden change, or by a rush of paralysing fear: yes, he especially knew about that. But there had to be some sort of outline, and the timing must be fixed and stuck to. Tomorrow or the day after, at the very latest.

It was a quiet night in the club, and for a while he left things to the barmen. In front of him lay stock cards, like doing his accounts. He *was* doing his accounts, but a different kind, a sublimer kind. It must be soon, or that also-ran, Gerry Reid, might act first. Oh, there had been those foul moments when Ember wanted someone else to handle the retribution. Never Gerry Reid, though, nor anyone like Gerry. Chris's husband would have been a different case, had proper obligations himself. If Mouth-Mouth Reid somehow did Stanfield just on a casual impulse, or even only tried to do him and failed, it would degrade everything there had ever been between Christine and Ember. Dignity, identity - you had to guard them. If that great love were soiled, soiled any further, Ember himself became less. He would be eternally Panicking Ralphy, virtuoso of the yellow sidestep. The possessions and wealth could not counter this, nor even his unmatched family. It thrilled him now that as he worked out his scheme for the execution he felt no panic whatsoever. His mind and body stayed magnificently steady, authentically Ralph W. Ember. He was someone who had once in a while failed in the past, had even collapsed on occasions, but lately he had bravely emerged from all that, hadn't he?

When he glanced up, Stanfield and Vine were just entering the club. Ember gave a minute cry. He gripped hard the wrist of his right hand with his left, preventing it from rising instinctively to check his jaw scar. That disabling ache took his shoulder and neck, and an instant icy sweat pool formed in the small of his back. Jesus, who was he kidding, knock over Stan Stanfield?

'Ralph,' Vine cried, 'you're looking really corporate and splendid.' Then, leaning across the bar at Ember, he shoved that bloody Hapsburg chin forward and snarled very sotto, 'How's Eleri, you scheming shit? You really think you can get away with that?'

Ember remained on his chair at the desk for a little while. Had to.

'And how's Barney, come to that?' Vine asked. 'Does he need any help with those two old inmates? Tell him you're fully booked – Eleri, God knows who else. You could get suffocated by falling rouge.'

'Don't mind Keith,' Stanfield said, in that flat boardroom voice. 'He's throwing his weight about, being almost a dad, and this new suede coat. We all know your worth, Ralph, never doubt it.'

Panicking Ralph

Vine and Stanfield went and sat at that table they usually took alongside one of the outing photographs. The two of them always enjoyed a few giggles at this one, knowing the fucking shambles in Paris that had come next, as if what else could you expect from The Monty troupe let loose abroad. Of course, Vine and Stanfield had not been on the trip. Vine was nothing at that time, not even a Monty member. And Stanfield would have regarded the trip as touristy, having been Frog-domiciled once, Mr Bloody International. Or more likely he could not risk going back into France.

Tonight they had this all-conquering glow on them. Well, they almost always did. Now, it was more. Not just the coat. Ember saw that all they were here for was to turn him weak, to start bringing him to surrender mode. This visit would be only a part of it. They would have some other, rougher ploy. But this one was working all right. They knew him and would expect it to.

All at once, Vine grew polite and amiable, and when he called for champagne like last time, it was in an almost kindly voice, as if talking to his favourite goldfish. It was to confuse, that's all – just tactics. What they were after in him was disintegration. These were two true business people. He sent the barman. Himself, he wanted to concentrate on Stanfield's face and head. This was where Ember would put the bullets. He loved the idea of them banging into Stan's bilingual mouth. As the best therapy for his shaky state now, Ember had decided he must force himself to look at Stanfield as a target, not as a terrible threat. If he could do that he might pull back from his panic, return to that decent quota of honest rage and commitment over Christine's murder. It would come, it had to come, please, God.

'But join us, do,' Stanfield called.

'Leave your tycoon duties for a few minutes, Ralph. It will relax you.'

'Not long.' He moved a couple of bits of paper.

Ember thought he might be able to stand up fairly soon. He definitely could get himself to rights. Definitely. For instance, the way Stanfield's lips had opened to make the word 'join' was a true comfort. Ember visualized one or maybe a pair of Walther 9mm rounds intruding there. He liked to think binary. Stanfield would not be saying 'join' then, but possibly screaming, 'No, Ralph!', or, 'Please, Ralph!' or, even better, 'Mercy, Ralph!' He need not say anything at all. Simply, the lips ajar and troubled made it more pictur-esque. Clearly, the bullets would find their way in under the moustache, regardless, among his tongue and teeth: this was a powerful, Jerry-made gun, designed with a possible World War III in mind, not just Stanfield. Ember knew the chest was the official area for decisive aiming, but the chest was dull. He needed to be able to visualize Stanfield's face splin-tering and his moustache with nothing left to hold, like ivy that lost its wall in demolition.

This was not the first time Ember had rebuilt himself by fantasizing the death of an enemy, and he had learned that the pictures must be detailed and credible if they were to work. Yes, he could do the detail now, see the exit wounds in the back of Stan's neck when he turned for another derisive look at the outing photograph, and imagine everything about him deglamourized as he crumpled. And credible? Of course, of course it was bloody credible. He could do it. Ember stood, pushed aside the dockets and came out from behind the bar, his legs like pillars, his mind still glowing with fine red pictures, unique tributes to Christine.

He sat and drank and talked with the pair for almost an hour. From them now came the same bonhomie as Vine had turned to a minute ago – nice easy conversation about nothing very much at all, but, naturally, showing along the way that they knew exactly where Ember's children were at school, including the one in France. Nobody mentioned Eleri ap Vaughan again, or Barney. They did not need to, did they? How they managed things. This duo started the worries early by letting him hear those two names, and then kept him worrying and gnawing himself inside in case the names surfaced again and suddenly put an end to all the Dom Pérignon friendliness. Vine bought a bottle, then Stanfield. Ember was not going to put out this time. If the sods had so much coming in, let them see to it.

Of course, someone mad and unprofessional might have tried to finish Stanfield here. He could be spread all over the picture he found so quaint, and Vine with him. It was the people in the photograph who would be laughing then. Ember had the automatic aboard. These two, they were so into confidence that they never brought a guard. These were two very large-scale company leaders now, but they went about exposed, even knowing what happened to Kenward. They thought the world loved them, and, even if it did not, they could self-protect. They were *so* available. But you did not make a mess like that on your own ground and offer yourself up to the law, not even when the cause was praiseworthy vengeance. You owed yourself and the memory of Christine more consideration. And this was definitely not another stalling dodge. Acumen.

The barman walked over and said there was a call for Ember in the payphone booth. They would notice that, obviously. This was someone who did not want to speak on The Monty's listed number. But Vine and Stanfield said nothing. They probably knew they'd done enough damage.

When Ember took the call, Beau Derek said: 'I'm just across the road, Ralph. I was coming in tonight to see how various matters progress, if you understand. But then I spot a certain vehicle in your car park. Vine's. He's there?'

'They.'

'Ralph, are you, well this is—?'

'I didn't invite them. They just turned up. It's no business meeting, no reconciliation. Nothing like that.'

'I put this booth number in my book, Ralph. I thought wiser.'

'Yes, good.' Beau could do safes and read accounts books. Don't expect him to be good on security as well. Didn't he realize that if someone put a tap on the official club phone they would also do the booth?

'He's with him, is he?' Beau asked.

'Jolly mates.'

'Right,' Beau replied.

'Why the call? Problems?'

'The London end, Ralph?'

'I'm thinking about it.'

'But haven't been yet?'

'I'm thinking about it.'

'My information said someone had been up there, hanging about the pub. You remember the pub I mentioned? But it sounded bigger than you. I thought her husband. But how would he know where to look?'

'Mystery,' Ember replied. 'The thing is, I've got other things to cope with here. Large concerns.' He could just see the top of Stanfield's head from the booth.

'Yes? What kind?'

'Sensitive.'

'What, to do with those civic things you're involved in? Pigeon shit on the town hall and exhaust pollution?' Beau went quiet for a second. 'Ralph, I'm disappointed about London. Neglecting it. These were good insights I gave you, gave to you, personally.'

'I know, and I'm bearing it all in mind. When the time comes.'

'Of course, you could say, the London end, they're just the paid help. Often I think bigger myself.'

Christ, Beau was after Stanfield, too, so rejected and injured?

'Ralph, you haven't gone over to him, as well, have you? He can woo.'

'Not me. I told you, they're here out of the blue.'

'He used to be a great colleague, but now, poison. Sniffing at my woman.'

Ember thought he heard a bitter sob on the line. 'In hand. All in hand,' he replied.

When he went back, Stanfield and Vine were leaving. 'Someone ravishing on the line, Ralph?' Vine asked. 'Eleri looking for extra supplies of stuff because the Baptist Convention's in town?'

'Don't mind him, Ralph.' They went to the door with their usual king-of-the-castle strut, smiling around to other customers and waving, like a royal walkabout.

*

Checking the outside of the building as he always did near midnight, Ember came across Stanfield's body against a rear wall, part hidden by the old water butt. The beam of Ember's flashlight picked up shoes and legs and then the identifiable rest. He switched off. Christ, was his mind all right? Had he done this without knowing it, without remembering it? Had his body and brain blessedly found an answer at last and provided him with sub-conscious guts? Stanfield's head was damaged, and possibly even more than Ember had planned. But not a shooting. Beaten from behind two, three, four times with something useful. He went closer and put the light on again, keeping the beam limited. During his dreams of seeing off Stan, Ember had imagined him deglamourized. And probably you could say he was that now, lying in a couple of grimy pools and with several wind-blown, give-away newspaper sheets skidding across the wreckage of his skull. Yet Ember had to admit there was something majestic to Stan, even when dead and hammered. His body lay folded against the water butt with a few squeezed-in empty lager cans near, and his eyes were wide, so it could not be compared to a lying in state, not a pope or monarch. Just the same, he had dignity, maybe more than when he was alive. His battered head hung forward a little now, as though in acceptance of whatever had happened to him. Not just dignity: a sort of grandeur and contempt for anything mean and small-scale, such as a frenzied wish to stay alive. By falling here he seemed to have risen above all that.

Well, of course, Ember knew after a couple of minutes he had not done this. He could tumble into racking spasms, but not spasms of unconsciousness. And, in any case, Ember's reverie had been entirely gun-based. Christ, had Beau been waiting? Or did Vine suddenly grow sick of Stanfield's boss complex and his lech plans for Becky – or decide he had to have Stan's share of the business? Or had Tranter discovered things in London and returned to settle with the mastermind? Or Gerry had got there first, after all? Or perhaps Jack Lamb wanted to hold on to his girlfriend, and thought that at his age this was the only way? Or—

Christ, what did it matter? When you were as large-scale as Stan you set up a range of hates. Someone had done him and Ember had not, though the duty had been his inescapably. Crouched over Stanfield and quickly going through his pockets, Ember mourned. This was not for Stan, the all-time peacock bastard, obviously. Ember mourned the death of his chance to restore himself. The glorious, secret status of avenger had been briskly ripped away from him, and on his own property. His fears transformed themselves gradually into the anger he had been seeking earlier. To use The Monty car park was an unforgivable act of whoever had killed Stan, leaving Ember with a body to be lost quickly and in secret. An attempt to frame him? He could not call the police or ambulance. He was of a breed which never called the police, anyway. Things got sorted privately. Even if that tradition did not exist, how could he bring police to the death of a business rival slaughtered on his own ground? No question Harpur and Iles would know about this competition, especially if they were in the trade themselves, as was often said. Ember would be their first and only suspect, and those two had a still passable talent at getting their first and only suspects sent down for ever. Of course, if they were in the business, perhaps tied up with Vine and Stanfield, they would be even keener to have Ember stuck away.

He found nothing in Stanfield's pockets. This probably meant he had been carrying plenty, and whoever had killed him took everything: no time to sieve it here for valuable items. That might indicate a simple mugging, or it might be intended to indicate a simple mugging. If it were a simple mugging, why couldn't Vine have helped stop it? Where *was* Vine? The emptiness of the pockets could signify that the killer was not interested in money and valuables only. He might have taken papers and gone to read them in safety somewhere. Would Stan carry business documents?

The Monty was not due to close for another couple of hours, and cars were still entering and leaving the yard. He could not do anything with Stanfield immediately, except pull the body deeper into the shadow of the wall and push it further behind the water butt. Headlights might still pick it up. But not many of The Monty's clientele would want to do more about that than take an identifying look, and possibly check the pockets for money or cards, and his wrist for a watch, his fingers for jewellery.

Ember went back into the club and, in his private room, looked out some dungarees. He knew what he had to do. This was like a rerun of that terrible waltz with Christine on the mud. But now it would be reversed. Instead of reclaiming a body, he must drag Stanfield out there into one of the gullies. Instead of recovering a body, he had to lose one. The sea must take it away. Perhaps there would be no need to go on to the mud. The tide might be in, and he could simply place Stanfield in the water and hope he disappeared on the ebb. There were good currents out there. Occasionally people were swept away and their bodies never found. Yes, to escape another trip out on the mud would be convenient, yet something in Ember hoped it would not happen like that. He needed the neat circle of incident. Dumping Stanfield at that special site, far out on the flats, was to be his substitute for vengeance, just as recovering Christine had been his substitute for courage. This, then, was what his accounting added up to now.

He did not change into the dungarees yet and returned to the bar. Would there be risk? It was not all that long since his letter to himself with the keys and information for Margaret had come back in the post, but should he prepare it all again? Probably not. The hazards were less acute this time, weren't they? Weren't they?

Beau Derek had come in and was sitting alone where he always sat, at that table half hidden by the pool players. Still stupid, still an advertisement, but Beau would not change. No wonder Stanfield got rid of him eventually. As far as Ember could tell, Beau looked as always – miserable, poor, puzzled – and not excited by some recent very notable event, like Stan's destruction. Ember strolled over there, as if gathering glasses again. He did not sit down, but talked standing.

'I looked later and the car had gone,' Beau said. His voice seemed all right, too. 'There were things I couldn't say on the phone, Ralph, not even the payphone line.'

'As I told you, Beau, I'm keeping it all very much in mind, including possible business openings for you in the future, the near future.'

'He'll kill you, you know, Ralph,' Beau replied. He spoke earnestly, as if still believing Stanfield were alive and dangerous. Beau could thesp, as well as do safes?

'Well, look, I—'

'It's how he thinks. The only style he knows. Stand in his way, he'll remove you. It's around that you're poaching Eleri. This will anger him, Ralph.'

'I don't say I am, I don't say not, but I'll just have to face things as they are.'

Beau nodded a bit – wonderment. 'Christ, you're cool. This is Stan Stanfield we're talking about, not some novice.'

No, not some novice, but a novice corpse. 'I know Stan,' Ember replied. He was trying to get a look at Beau's shoes and the bottoms of his trousers for blood. Nothing showed elsewhere. 'I can't afford to be frightened by Stanfield or anyone, Beau,' he declared. 'I trust that's not my style. I don't want to sound bombastic or foolish, but I've a career to preserve, a position. You can't do that by dropping into terror every five minutes.'

He moved away, picking up more glasses. Beau said: 'The big one in London – he's back home, I hear. Nothing accomplished.'

But Ember acted as if he had not heard. Beau had had as much time as could be allowed. There were mud obsequies to be arranged.

26

Inside Gerry Reid's place, Harpur had all his usual feelings of delight and privilege at busting a home on the quiet. He had watched several nights from the street, waiting for a chance to enter with his rich private bundle. Tonight the flat was dark when he arrived. He loitered a while, and then, at a little after 11 p.m., had decided it might be safe. Gerry was probably at a club, or staying with a girl. He might not be back until 2 or 3 a.m., or not till tomorrow.

Harpur was using a totally anonymous car from the pool, no radio, no notorious registration, and he could park close. Although it was an area he loved, he must not be identified on foot now. He would be known around here. This was inner inner city, and took a lot of police time, a lot of Harpur time. Gerry lived in a faded street in the faded Valencia Esplanade district, the whole quarter due for demolition and generally known these days simply as The Valencia. 'Esplanade' had come to sound cruelly chic. Pimps and their tarts patrolled here, as well as pushers. Iles came down for a girl or girls now and then or oftener. Word might reach him in pillow talk, or back-seat talk, or waste-ground talk, if Harpur were spotted by one or two or three of those very young whores the assistant chief prized. Word might reach Gerry, too, and he could probably make a guess at what had been happening, and would really check his flat for something planted.

Reid had a whole floor of what had once been a grand, handsome villa. Because of blight, rents stayed low around the Valencia. No curtains were across, so Harpur could not use lights, except the pencil torch briefly, but he saw enough to prove Gerry kept the flat in brilliant order: cleaner and neater than Harpur's own house and, of course, much cleaner and neater than Iles's. Gerry dressed in the same tidy style, and, by all accounts, his getaway driving also had delicacy. It was only when he did one of his speeches that the shambles took over, and this might be said of so many.

Harpur stood for a moment in the middle of the main room, simply getting the feel of the place and thinking his way inside Gerry Reid. It was still the surest way he knew of reaching an alien soul, much better than interrogation. Too many blocks on that these days. The detective was dead, as Iles sometimes said – meaning standard detection skills had been made valueless by timorous courts and radical politicians: the kind of politicians Harpur's wife had admired, and browbeat his daughters into admiring. Luckily, he still had breaking and entering.

It was for a good purpose. He felt as interested as Stanfield in destroying Ember's syndicate. And, by helping destroy it, he could move further into Stanfield's confidence and destroy his and Vine's firm next. All for the chief's sake. The grand mission. Of course, Iles argued that if you took out the local firms worse outfits from London or Manchester would move in. The ACC was often in touch with Nature and had told Lane and Harpur She abhorred a vacuum. But this was strategy or even philosophy beyond Harpur's rank.

The flat was on the second storey, and from the front and back windows Harpur could watch the street and what had been the house's large gardens, now a parking yard and unofficial dumping ground. He made frequent, thorough surveys. Gerry hated guns, but there were other ways of disposing of a trespasser. And, in any case, there was nothing to say he would return alone. His friend Foster *did* believe in firearms, and so did Ember when pushed. Harpur must not be discovered. He felt glad he had given Denise the letter. If he disappeared here tonight, he wanted it known what he had been doing – known and continued.

But he was not going to disappear, get eliminated, here tonight, was he? That was melodrama, self-pity. He could watch all approaches and listen for feet on the stairs. He felt at ease, as he always did in an enemy's den. It was as if he had come home – to someone else's home.

Abruptly then, playing with the word 'disappear', he felt a thought ram itself into his mind and take his strength for a few minutes. Why *not* disappear? But disappear now, immediately – drive home from here, with the package? Harpur sat down in what was probably Gerry's favourite armchair, a big black leather swivel job. Often, in someone else's room, Harpur would try to set himself up as he imagined the usual occupier of the place regularly did. That could sometimes produce a kind of fellow feeling with his target, and an insight or two. Now, though, Harpur found he was looking for insights into Colin Harpur, and into this sudden, dazingly strong tug towards gain.

The coke package lay on his lap. Naturally he had opened it as soon as Vine left the other night. There were three sachets inside. He had gum-rubbed himself with a bit from the bottom envelope, in case the top was real and the rest makeweight – self-raising flour – a famous gambit. He got immediate flesh deadness. This was pure cocaine, or near. Vine's estimate of the value might be modest. For the first time he could recall, Harpur felt tempted by the chance of turning a fine personal profit from police work.

He spun around in the armchair and then spun again, alight with joy and brilliant excitement. Call it a high – just by having the stuff resting on his crotch and thinking what it could make for him! For *him*. He could escape the departmental thinking that corralled him now and had done all his working life. He could walk away with upwards of thirty grand. He could individualize himself. There would be ways of selling it. Of course there would be. He knew them, and where the best prices were. Loot had never looked easier, and the only people hurt would be villains: a classic hijack. Absolutely no call for loyalty to those who had sent him here.

Afterwards, would come wild peril, of course. But he could tell Stanfield and Vine he had left the package and, as arranged, he would give the drug squad a hint that Gerry might have a nice load at home. There would be a raid, and nothing found. Harpur would be ribbed a bit and told to improve his tipsters. Nothing grave: policing was not a science, and nobody expected all information to turn out kosher. In any case, Stanfield and Vine would know the tales – and believe the tales – that sometimes the squad found and decided not to disclose, but to sell on to one of their favoured dealers and split the take. Harpur could sow that notion. The quantity of stuff made it very credible, because the shares would be juicy. But, naturally, Harpur must be wary with this one: Stanfield and Vine might have contacts in the squad and intend to buy back the coke after it had been confiscated and used as evidence. Such things happened, and not just in *The French Connection*. As long as they could wait, Stan and Keith would get it at bargain price then: they would virtually be fences in that deal, and fences were traditionally allowed a heavy slice for risk. Anyway, police salesmen could not argue too loudly about a price for stolen stuff. If this were Vine and Stanfield's business plan it would make the dropping of so much produce on Gerry much more understandable: a sensible long-term investment only. Harpur would have to feel his way, gingerly, gingerly.

He walked to the windows front and back and had a good survey. It still looked clear. He sat down again, spun again. He wondered whether Reid ever did this. It did not matter. He had definitely lost interest in being Reid. To become someone else no longer seemed at all fascinating. He was C. Harpur and safely loaded. Yes, safely. There was, after all, another quite feasible aftermath story available – that Gerry must have discovered the planted stuff. Harpur could tell Stan and Vine he tried to stay out of sight in the Valencia, but might still have been observed near the house, even going into the house, and Gerry would have been notified. On top of that, although Harpur had broken nothing getting in, someone like Gerry, ever alert for what he would call victimization, might spot a sign that said the flat had been entered. He would search and search and search. And, lo, he found. At least, Stanfield and Vine could be made to believe he had found. They should have let that impeccable burglar Vine make the plant, after all. Hadn't they foreseen this very problem?

He stood up and put the package on the chair, ready, then gazed at it for at least a minute. The notion that he could instantly tonight establish himself as himself kept coming back. People talked of long-haul prisoners getting institutionalized. Harpur had been institutionalized by a police force. Even when he ignored rules, it had always been to further the police cause. Now, for example, he was in Reid's place, seemingly acting solo, but only to help the chief's mad, hopeless quest for purity.

Harpur went to the front and back windows once more. Still no Reid. He began moving around the place, looking at Gerry's things, occasionally using the flashlight. Job habit, strong even now, he told himself. He knew, though, that he was giving himself time to change his mind. Amid all the exuberance, a part of his brain could not believe he would do it: would not abruptly turn his life around, as he had turned himself around and around in that chair. The chair, though, always brought him back facing where he had started from.

There was a smart long teak table against one wall in the

living room. Part of it appeared to serve as a desk, and Harpur went through some papers, most of them junk mail. Harpur examined all of this carefully. It was a standard trick to leave sensitive documents on top of the desk, not in a secret drawer, but mixed up with innocuous, boring material. Theory said searchers missed what seemed to be unhidden, and sometimes theory was right. Harpur found a half sheet of blue lined notepaper with three names on it inside a glossy brochure from a firm wanting to know if Gerry fancied an Edwardian-style octagonal conservatory built on to the property, 'bringing a new dimension and the flavour of a bygone, more elegant age'. One name sounded as if it might be a song or a pub, The Sleeping Sentinel. The other two were Alf Impater and Jason Little, 'known as the Pigtail'. They did not mean anything to Harpur, but he wrote them into his book, then replaced the paper.

Conceivably, Alf and Jason were the London hit party Stanfield said Gerry had hired to kill Christine Tranter. If The Sleeping Sentinel was a pub, it could be their headquarters. The Yard might know all three names. Many London gangs used a favourite, soiled local as their boardroom and operations centre. And thinking of these corrupt dens, stiff with villains, Harpur realized that if he took the coke package now, he would be a villain himself, unentitled for ever after to feel cleaner than those heavies in their sleazy habitats. Feeling cleaner had always been vital to him. It might be the lingering result of all that Gospel Hall teaching as a child. 'Come out from among them and be ye separate, saith the Lord, and touch not the unclean thing'. They had made a lot of that text from St Paul. It meant, Flee contamination. Tonight he might be joining up with the contaminated, touching the unclean thing as its new owner. He would no longer be a white knight, but a snowman.

He replaced the sheet and stacked the papers as he had found them. That list seemed improbable. Not even someone like Gerry would risk writing down such names. There were only three, and easily remembered. Even if he *had* thought he should make a note, would he retain the paper after the job had been done? He had forgotten it? Possibly. Gerry Reid would certainly be liable to carelessness, no matter how tidy his flat might be. But Gerry was also an experienced lad who for most of his busy life had kept out of jail. He could not be as careless as all that.

Had the paper been put there for Harpur to find, put there not by Gerry, but by Stanfield or, more likely, Vine, that ace intruder? If the names were what Harpur thought, it could be one more way of incriminating Gerry and generally fucking up Ember's syndicate. Possibly Stanfield could supply the names because he, not Reid, had made contact with those two via the pub and commissioned the killing. Vine might have been in here after all and planted the paper – planted the paper for the planter of the coke. It would not have mattered if Harpur failed to discover it. An extra only. Likewise, if Gerry had found it and removed it. This kind of thoroughness was natural to Stanfield, possibly even to Keith Vine. If you were going to hit someone once, hit him twice, one for luck.

Harpur went back into the living room and picked up the

coke package. Unhesitatingly he took it to a shoe cupboard
he had noticed in one of the bedrooms. The cupboard con-
tained some very old footwear, obviously no longer used.
He shoved the parcel into an ancient desert boot and tightened the laces to make sure none of it was visible. Gerry
would not find it there, but the sniffer dogs should. Harpur
prepared to leave. Yes, 'Come out from among them'.
Impossible to ditch a lifetime just like that. How could he
be a party to putting drugs on the street after some of the
terrible cases he had seen? Christ, his daughters would be
exposed to all that very soon, perhaps were already. And
how far would thirty grand go these days?

He hurried to the rear window to check his exit was clear
and saw Reid just edging his car into the garden, between a
couple of heaps of heavy refuse. Then Gerry went back and
closed the double doors. If you could get your car off the
street in this district, you did. Or in any urban district now.
Gerry stood for a moment, his back to Harpur, and appeared
to be examining the lapels of his suit carefully. He brought
out a handkerchief and seemed to dab at a stain. Yes, spruce-
ness was his thing, even in the middle of the night. Harpur
turned. He would go up a floor, wait on the landing there,
then descend quietly once he heard Gerry enter the flat.
Before he left, though, Harpur went quickly back to the shoe
cupboard and recovered the package. The Gospel Hall was
childhood, and could not be allowed to bully him now. Paul
wrote his instruction to the Corinthians nearly two thousand
years ago. There was a new dispensation.

27

Ember closed up the club at just before 2 a.m. and sat for a while in the bar, waiting for people, and especially cars, to disperse from the yard. Then he went upstairs to his office and dressed in the dungarees.

No car owners had reported a body. Although this did not necessarily mean no one had seen Stanfield, it was better than a lot of agitation. He went outside and backed his Rover up to the water butt. Then he had a look at Stanfield's wrist and found his watch still there, so perhaps he really had stayed undiscovered. Ember risked no lights now but felt sure from his first examination that the only injuries were to the skull. He pulled a black plastic sack over Stanfield's head and tied it tightly around his chest. That should keep the blood off the Rover's boot. Stanfield was big and heavy, and it took Ember too long to load him. He dragged him over to the car and sat him against the rear fender. Then he had to take him in a sort of embrace, an arm under each of his, and lift him until the rim of the boot was in the small of Stan's back and the head in the sack began to tilt back into the boot compartment. Quickly Ember brought his arms clear and, reaching down, swung Stanfield's legs over and in.

He had put out the security lights in the yard but street lamps gave a gleam even this far. Houses bordered the car park, and Ember felt on view as he struggled, even though it was so late. Once Stan was aboard and the boot lid shut, Ember went back into the club and switched the security lights on again, or their absence might be noticed. He brought a mop and swabbed the ground where Stan had lain and the side of the water butt. Then he opened the tap in the butt and let all the water out to carry anything left to the sink. He took the mop back in and washed it. Method. Thoroughness. Care. He felt proud of the ordered way his mind functioned.

He drove at 30 m.p.h. to the foreshore. The trip should have been a delight. Wasn't he going to dump the man who had very possibly ordered Christine's death, and at the exact spot where that death had occurred? He was certainly going to dump the man who was his main business competitor. Yet the feeling that he had failed persisted. He had owed it to Christine to do Stanfield personally. Instead, all he could manage was to clear up efficiently after . . . After Gerry? After Beau? After Tranter? After Lamb? After Keith Vine? Christ, anyone but Gerry. Or Beau. These were so undignified. Yet the method of killing suggested Gerry. Or Beau. Well known neither liked guns. Of them all, he wanted to think Tranter had done it, of course. Ember would feel no jealousy. For Tranter to behave like a true husband would endorse the whole concept of marriage as an institution, and Ember certainly had some respect for that.

The lovers' cars had left by the time he reached the foreshore. He drove to where the sea wall was at its lowest and the slope mild, then brought Stan out on to the grass, still wearing the sack. This stage was easier. He went to the side of the boot and lifted Stan's upper body by the shoulders, pulling it over the boot rim. His head in the sack hung back towards the ground, like some huge berry grown too much for its stalk. Ember moved around to the rear of the car and then eased the body further out until he felt gravity begin to take it. The weight pulled Stanfield's legs and feet after the rest, and Ember clung on to Stan's jacket to slow the fall to the ground a little. Only a little, because of his bulk. The hard yet rustling noise of his head in the sack hitting the grass disturbed Ember, but brought on no failure of control. For himself, he was not interested in Stanfield's watch, even though it would probably be a good one. If he had left Christine's diamond, he could leave this. His wellington boots had gone last time, and he would not have worn them, anyway, knowing what a liability they turned out. He put on an old pair of trainers, and then pulled Stanfield up the mound by his feet and down the other side. He left the body, returned to his car and drove it to the lovers' spot. Even so late, it would be less noticeable there. He climbed back up the wall and down again to where he was hidden by its height, and approached Stan.

The night was dry with a thin moon which occasionally came out from behind fast-moving clouds. To Ember, it seemed a good kind of night for disposing of a body – mostly very dark, but with these occasional brief spells of light for bearings, and to soften the undoubted bleakness of the procedures. He could see and hear that the tide was at about halfway point, which suited him, particularly if it was on the way up. He pulled Stan along to where he had brought

Christine ashore. This was convenient. He wanted to get Stanfield into the same deep gully. There the body would be unobserved from the wall, and perhaps channelled out to sea after the tide had picked it up and then eventually ebbed. Apart from that, though, he still felt eager to get this circular effect in things, the symmetry. It spoke a message, audible at least to Ember, possibly to others. For Stanfield, her killer, to disappear down the very route she had been recovered in had rightness to it. That rightness was not in the league of rightness that would have come if Ember had killed him, but valid all the same. He wanted to think of himself as more than just an undertaker. Losing Stan's remains had to be emblematic.

He walked into the mud as far as he could, and then got down again and edged his way forward on one hand and his knees, later on his stomach, still drawing Stanfield along by the feet. There was less water than when he had retrieved Chris, so Ember had no help now from buoyancy. Rigor had not quite reached Stanfield's limbs yet and his arms were strung out loose behind his head as if searching for something to hang on to. Despite the tightness of the cord around the plastic sack, mud was forced up into it as Ember and the body progressed: the skirts of Stan's jacket had been pushed back up towards his shoulders by the movement forward, and this may have worked the encircling cord loose. Instead of clinging to the outline of Stan's face, the sack now became rounded and solid, like a great black Humpty-Dumpty head, out of proportion even to Stanfield's large body. Ember wondered what Stan's supposed ancestor, Clarkson Stanfield, marine painter, would have made of this special kind of coastal scene. 'Soon be there now, Stan,' he said. 'God, but you earned some enemies.'

Ember could hear the tide swilling gently into the gully not far ahead. He retained all his hatred for Stanfield, yet experienced a kind of tenderness, too. You had to sympathize a little with someone who had been so on top and confident, yet now had his face and lordly moustache buried in a bag of mud, and all the strength and arrogance of his body gone. Ember took a short breather, resting his head on Stanfield's shoes, and wondered whether it was unnecessarily humiliating to drag him by his feet rather than his hands. In old Westerns Indians would savagely tow a white man behind a horse like this. It was too late to swing Stan around now, though. Ember went on, tired, slower. After a few minutes he said: 'Here's where I commit you to the deep, then, Stan. And stay committed, will you? Try to make it to France again.' Stan was on his back, and before abandoning him, Ember folded his arms across his chest and pulled his jacket down neatly. He considered removing the plastic bag. You never left anything of yours for investigators no matter how apparently anonymous it might be. Science was so fly these days, and it would be absurd to get done for killing Stanfield when he had not killed him and should have, especially if it were Gerry or Beau who had killed him. God, imagine going down in place of one of those two. Ember found he could not bear to take the sack off, though. He dreaded facing that face in its present state. Stanfield was the prick of pricks, yet there had been a proud glow of liveliness about him, and Ember did not want to see how far it had been brought down. This, also, would have been emblematic. It said what would happen to everyone.

He returned to the shore, part crawling and sliding, then walking when the mud grew firmer near the shingle. He made for his car. By the time he had incinerated his dungarees, showered and changed at The Monty, it was approaching dawn. He drove home. Margaret woke up as he climbed into bed and glanced at the bedside clock. 'More trouble at the club, Ralph?'

'No, not trouble. A celebration that went on a bit, that's all.'

'Celebration? Whose?'

'A decent occasion,' he replied. 'Everything done very nicely.' Lying relaxed at her side he thought that perhaps there could be a spell of normality to life now. He tried to work out which of these women around after Christine he liked the best: Beau's Melanie, Foster's Deloraine or Vine's Becky, once she had had the child, obviously.

28

When Harpur reached home very late he could see Denise through the uncurtained sitting room windows up a ladder hanging a sheet of wallpaper alongside the fireplace. So as not to spatter her clothes or hair, she had put on a blue one-piece swimming costume and an old red bobble hat belonging to Jill. She worked swiftly, and as Harpur watched, she finished hanging this piece, came down the ladder and began to paste up another on the trestle table. He went close and tapped the glass. She looked over angrily. Perhaps she thought Vine had returned and changed his window. Recognizing Harpur, she smiled and continued to paste. He saw now that the floor of the sitting room was strewn with what he took for a moment to be flecks of white paint. Then he realized they were fragments of paper. Maybe there had been some disaster with the decoration, though he could not make out what. He let himself in and, by the time he opened the sitting room door, she was up the ladder again hanging another piece.

'Where did you learn?' he said.

'At home, of course. I brought my bathing suit specially from the flat.' She did not look around but spoke at the wall as she concentrated on smoothing out the paper.

'You're quite a sight from outside. Well, and from inside.'

'I've had some spectators. I thought you were more. A woman up a ladder gets some men going.'

'Yes.' Yes. He picked up one of the small pieces of paper and recognized a few words in his handwriting, including 'afford them this protection' and 'naturally pay me.'

She must have sensed what he was doing and said: 'I ripped up your letter.'

'Why scatter it?'

'I wanted to make a gesture, didn't I? Impact. So you change your mind.' She came down the ladder again and sat on the settee, yawning. There were some spots of paste on her left cheek and shoulder. 'I asked myself, Am I going to be party to such crazy risk-taking?'

'What did you answer?'

She waved her hand at the specks of paper. 'That. It was a stupid, posturing letter, Col, and probably worthless in any true crisis. If you were discovered, Iles would never have been able to put things right, suppose he wanted to, and no jury would have believed you were in it other than for swag. To them, and to the world, you would have looked despicable. I could not have stood that, Col – because I know how strong and straight you are. And I don't mean just *that*. Oh, I know, corner-cutting, but ultimately your straightness is the you-ness of you.'

He was carrying the coke package in another supermarket carrier bag he had found in the car. 'I also wrote a bit in the letter in case I was killed,' he replied.

She bowed her head so he could see only the crown of the bobble hat, and she thumped her bare thigh repeatedly with her fist. 'Of course there was. I'm supposed to let you walk into such danger? For Christ's sake, Col, why don't you grow up? You're going on forty. I mean, forty! You've been at something like that tonight, have you? Your damn kids – I ask where are you, and they give the formula as if I'm a stranger: "detained on official business, but probably won't be very long. Unexpected demands of the job." But really they're as worried as I am.'

'They don't know anything, Denise.'

'Of course they don't know anything. None of us knows anything. Why we're frantic.'

'*They* don't get frantic.'

'Oh, they can sense when there's special peril about. I can hear it in their voices, even when they're trotting out this rubbish.'

'You've told them nothing?'

She did not answer that, as though the question were contemptible. It was.

'Can we go into the kitchen?' he said. 'The neighbours, Denise. It's bound to look odd, a woman in a bathing suit and red hat agitated on my settee towards dawn, and all these empty shelves. People up for an early pee across the road and glancing in – it would be a talking point in the shops.'

'You're bourgeois, Col. Stuff neighbours.'

'We're of our communities, Denise, and communities have ground rules.'

'Jesus,' she replied. 'Communities have heard of DIY.' She followed him into the kitchen, though. There was no blind or curtain here, either, but the window gave on to the

269

garden, not the street, and the garden had a screen of trees: why Vine always came that way. Harpur and Denise sat at the table, and he made some tea and did a fry-up meal. He had left the carrier bag on one of the kitchen chairs, and she reached into it and brought out the package in its bright, repaired gift-wrap paper.

'Is it a present?' she asked. 'For me?' Her face cheered up. 'No.'

'Col, I thought perhaps – well, yes, perhaps a ring.'

'You didn't. A package that big? You want a ring? An engagement ring? I don't believe it.'

'Just a ring,' she said. 'Marriage with an older man would be a difficult matter. We've agreed on that.'

Harpur said: 'I'm not older. If you think of the right man, I'm younger. Jimmy Carter or Gielgud. You want an engagement ring which is not an engagement ring.'

'Yes, like that. I've always told you, I'll probably marry someone else, my own age, in a . . . in a different kind of job, not that there's anything wrong with yours, obviously.'

'Obviously.'

'But I'll always be seeing you.'

'Fucking me?' he asked. 'I'm your piece on the side.' He brought the food over.

'Right. That deserves some sort of recognition, some sort of ring, I would say,' Denise replied.

They ate and drank, and Harpur said: 'Yes, fair enough, it does. I'd be proud if you wore it. I'll get you one. But the package is not that. Spoils of war.'

'Stuff?'

'I recovered it tonight – in just the type of allegedly useless operation that made you tear up my letter.'

'But wrapped like this?'

'So people might think it was a ring,' he said.

'In a package that big? But not really very big. It can't be just grass. Wouldn't be worth your while. Coke?'

'Probably.'

'Crack?'

'Just coke. The slower, more adult burn.'

She passed a hand over the wrapping. 'What will you do with it?'

'Log it in at headquarters and have it locked up as eventual evidence.' Well, no, he would not, but he liked the notion that she thought him straight, and that she said so in a nearly convinced tone. This was such an improvement on Megan. It was worth working on with lies. 'But, obviously, I won't be putting it in yet. As you know from the vandalized letter, I'm acting alone. How would I have half a kilo of coke?'

Denise chewed away on some bacon for a while. 'I don't really get it, Col. You bring the stuff, but not the dealer?'

'In good time.'

'But this much coke – it must be worth tens of thousands. Isn't that enough to nail him with? And isn't he going to be alerted when he misses it?'

'I—'

'Often, I don't believe you, Col. I do think deep down you're straight, but very deep down sometimes.'

'I'm running a quite complex scheme. I mustn't act hastily.'

She drank and gazed at him in that intelligent questioning way of hers across the tea. Undergraduates were trained to probe. It was a pain. Harpur opened the package and emptied some coke from a sachet on to a clean plate. 'Nobody's going to know how much I recovered. We could have a snort.' He refused to be called bourgeois by some kid.

She put the cup down with a bang. 'Are you demented? There's no curtain.'

'Fretting about the neighbours, are we?'

He brought a clean knife and kneaded the powder. Then he tore a couple of squares of newsprint from the *Daily Mail*, tipped equal portions of the coke on to them and made two rolls. He handed one to Denise and carefully gave each of his nostrils a helping from the other. She looked appalled and scared, and this delighted him. It was an encounter he had won, and he liked her horror of drugs. After a couple of moments she put her head back and sniffed a couple of good fills from the roll.

It did take longer to get things going than crack, but Harpur knew it would come, and anticipation was half the enjoyment. No, about a hundredth, but nice all the same. He had read somewhere that a coke fix was like 10,000 orgasms, but happily this did not prevent you trying to assist it to 10,001 or even 10,002 during the high. He sat gazing at nothing, and something. Whenever he was drug-enhanced, Harpur experienced a very specific, very brilliant, very narrow euphoria, invariably religious. At these times, he believed in the salvation of the world, and accepted absolutely and joyously that because he was in that redeemed world he, too, was saved. Perhaps all drug takers had this experience, and heaven would be full of junkies. At these times, he achieved the sort of blessed state that Lane so endlessly and hopelessly sought.

When on a fine high from fine stuff, like this tonight, Harpur often found himself eavesdropping on the Trinity as they decided what to do about the Fall. He would listen as they came up with that sparkling solution, the Atonement. He thrilled to the gameness with which this was accepted by the Second Person. Everything would be all right for everyone. Watching God, Harpur knew he had never witnessed better chairmanship of a meeting, certainly not by Lane. Yet the discussion among these Three was not merely competent. It had heart. Each of them wore what might be a club tie, amber background, with paschal lamb motif. This would be a reasonable club to get into, and Harpur had the feeling that they *did* mean to extend membership and would be ready to look at new entrants such as himself and Denise, if it was mixed. Adam turned up at one stage, wearing a kind of sarong. He was apologetic to some extent, and yet with a stupid it's-done-so-forget-it aura, too. There was no crowing over him during the interview, just constructive warmth. Altogether, what came out was an astonishingly loving plan. Harpur would invariably hear worldwide applause and see celebration rockets in colours he could not put a name to, but which told the wondrous tale just the same. 'Do you see the lights?' he asked Denise.

'What? Lights? Oh, yes, yes,' she said.

'He's such a thinker, God.'

'He's always been known for that,' she replied. 'I wonder about this coke and ... well, Undercover must be your second name, though obviously not one to go on your job papers. Tell them the initial stands for—'

'Unsung.'

'But not by me,' Denise said.

*

Well-established daylight and the sound of tapping awoke him. He was in bed. Denise lay in his arms. She still wore the bobble hat, but not the bathing suit. 'God,' he muttered.

'He's such a thinker,' Denise replied.

'God, Denise, I think I hear Keith Vine.'

'In the day?'

The bedroom door was pushed open, and Harpur saw Hazel and Jill there, with tea. Jill seemed about to tap the door again, although it was no longer shut. 'We heard voices, so thought it would be OK to come in now,' Hazel said. 'We've tried before.'

'But Blottosville,' Jill said.

'It's midday,' Hazel said.

'Why aren't you in school?' Harpur asked.

'Saturday,' Jill replied.

'Of course it is,' he said.

Hazel placed a cup of tea on the floor each side of the bed. 'We had a bit of a row about it, but eventually decided to throw that stuff on the kitchen table down the toilet,' she said. 'It's no good to you, Dad. We've had lessons about it. You must have heard.'

'Or to Denise, though younger and fitter,' Jill said.

'It made her hang one of those pieces of wallpaper upside down,' Hazel said, 'but not wishing to sound ungrateful for her help.'

'That was before she had any,' Harpur replied.

'And then like a snow storm all over the sitting room floor,' Jill said.

'You didn't fit them together for a good read, did you?' Harpur asked. 'Did you?'

'They're down the toilet, too,' Jill replied.

29

Lane said: 'And Stanfield, gone?'

'How it appears, sir,' Iles replied. 'Dropped off the map.'

The chief allowed some tiny symptoms of joy to touch his pallor. It was as if he feared to exult full out, in case the hopes were foolish. But one or two veins reddened with pleasure and excitement. 'Ah, perhaps my – that is, *our* – domain can return now to its old wholesomeness and peace, strong in its own identity and sound popular culture.'

Iles said: 'Whenever I hear the words "popular culture" I reach for my Rilke.'

The chief part relapsed. 'Of course, Stanfield might return, might return and resume. This is not some business trip?'

'Colin says no, sir,' Iles replied. 'His information, from the customary secret and sacred source, states this was a considered exit, isn't that so, Harpur?'

'The rumour is he simply baled out, without explanation.'

'Rumour?' Lane cried. 'Do we have to base our—?'

'You know Col's rumours, sir. More solid than the tablets of stone. Stanfield probably loaded his pockets with the company gains and went, while there was time. Valparaiso? Tahiti? Antigua?'

'But why?' Lane asked. 'Not to look a gift horse in the mouth, but why?'

'This gift horse is Col. No, don't look him in the mouth.

It's a drab view, but all right to throw him a bit of sugar. You see, in line with your strong wishes, sir, he's managed to pressurize these syndicates so much that even someone as hard as Stanfield feared he might be pounced on.'

Lane smiled, and those veins flashed again: 'Fine work.'

'Thank you, sir,' Harpur replied.

'But perhaps you regret missing him?' Lane said.

'I'll settle for his disappearance, sir,' Harpur replied.

'Yes,' Lane said. 'His syndicate can hardly survive his withdrawal, can it? He would have been very much the kingpin, as I understand it.'

'You have this instinctive grasp, sir,' Iles replied.

They were in Harpur's room at headquarters again, Iles pacing majestically in one of his country suits, and Lane crouched forward on the edge of Harpur's armchair. It was another of those informal meetings, designed to relax the participants, yet the chief himself never reached relaxation. Lane was in shirt sleeves, his tie loosened, and without shoes. 'I see a real beginning to the cleansing that occupies my dreams,' he declared.

'May I offer tentative congratulations, sir?' Iles replied. You say dreams. I would prefer to call them visions.'

'Someone must have them, Desmond,' Lane replied.

'Not someone, sir. It is you who do it, and inexhaustibly.'

'Oh, but we must never tire,' the chief cried, his voice brassy for a moment.

'Colin thinks it's possible Stanfield organized the killing of the woman at the foreshore, sir.'

'We've asked the Met to talk to a couple of names that

came my way,' Harpur said. 'I gather from the Yard they're famed hit artists.'

'London?' the chief gasped.

Iles said: 'What I feared, sir. They'll try to move in if we're unsubtle. Executioners, yes, but also scouts.'

'Information about London heavies?' Lane said. 'Where does this come from, for heaven's sake, Colin?'

'Apparently, these are people working out of a well-known London pub, The Sleeping Sentinel,' Harpur replied. 'Every regular a villain. You know the kind of evil place the capital specializes in.'

'One would feel soiled just to walk through the doors of a place like that,' the chief said.

'Soiled. Exactly, sir,' Harpur replied.

'But what pointed you to these people, Colin?' Lane said.

'They'll be flint when questioned, of course,' Harpur replied. 'I doubt whether any interrogation could crack them.'

*

When the chief had gone, Iles said: 'Stanfield out of the way, his syndicate falls apart, which makes Panicking ten fucking times stronger, yes?'

'Probably, sir,' Harpur said.

'Always triumph sneaks up on Ralphy Ember. So where does the tip say Stanfield's gone, Col?'

'Valparaiso? Tahiti? Antigua?'

Iles sat down in the chair just vacated by Lane, but at